# SEAGULL BAY

*Recent Titles by Janet Tanner from Severn House*

ALL THAT GLISTERS
THE DARK SIDE OF YESTERDAY
FORGOTTEN DESTINY
HOSTAGE TO LOVE
MORWENNAN HOUSE
MOTH TO A FLAME
NO HIDING PLACE
THE PENROSE TREASURE
PORTHMINSTER HALL
THE REUNION
SEAGULL BAY
SHADOWS OF THE PAST
THE TRUTH GAME
TUCKER'S INN
THE YEARS TO COME

# SEAGULL BAY

Janet Tanner

This first world edition published 2009
in Great Britain and 2010 in the USA by
SEVERN HOUSE PUBLISHERS LTD of
9–15 High Street, Sutton, Surrey, England, SM1 1DF.
Trade paperback edition published
in Great Britain and the USA 2010 by
SEVERN HOUSE PUBLISHERS LTD



British Library Cataloguing in Publication Data

Tanner, Janet.
Seagull Bay.
1. Orphans–England–Somerset–Fiction. 2. Actresses–
Fiction. 3. Nineteen sixties–Fiction.
I. Title
823.9'14-dc22

ISBN-13: 978-0-7278-6822-0 (cased)
ISBN-13: 978-1-84751-182-9 (trade paper)



*All Severn House titles are printed on acid-free paper.*

Typeset by Palimpsest Book Production Ltd.,
Grangemouth, Stirlingshire, Scotland.
Printed and bound in Great Britain by
MPG Books Ltd., Bodmin, Cornwall.

# Author's Note

*Seagull Bay*. My very first novel, and after all these years still so close to my heart.

I wrote it back in 1971, and for years it has lain hidden away in my attic, unseen but never forgotten.

I had been writing for women's magazines for five years and the idea, and the title, started out as a short story, but I soon realized that I wanted it to be much more. I lived and breathed it, and the emotion it aroused in me followed me around, an exciting aura. I scribbled away in every spare moment.

I had dreams of it being published back then, but my first editor, the legendary Lesley Saxby at Macdonald, was keen for me to write a family saga. Which I did – *The Black Mountains*, set in a Somerset mining community and spanning 1911-1919, was born. Successive novels followed in the same vein, and somehow *Seagull Bay* never saw the light of day.

I cannot tell you how wonderful it is to see my love child in print after so many years of neglect. Re-reading it brought back to me the pleasure of writing it, and those long-forgotten emotions which haunted me as I did so.

I very much hope that you will share in that magic!

Janet Tanner. March, 2009

# One

Sometimes, if I close my eyes, I can see Seagull Bay just as it was that day in 1963 when I first met Sandy Collins: the sea shaded in broad bands of azure, cobalt and aquamarine, with purplish splashes where it moved lazily around the underlying rocks, the sky, blue as periwinkles between the white herring-bone clouds, shimmering as it merged with the water on the distant horizon. The beach was a narrow rim of pale gold, never quite letting the sea touch the cliffs except at the very tips of the bay, where the boulders and rocks and tumbled pebbles stood sentinel, and scrambling down the cliff path I thought that it was like the palm of a giant's hand, a giant who had enchanted me with some magic dust so that he could hold me captive and watch me live out my life for his amusement.

I was very young then, both romantic and fanciful, forgetting the tragedies that had already scarred me by playing a game of pretence that no one else could share.

That afternoon the giant was sleeping. In spite of the high tide there was a stillness about the bay, an air of waiting. Even the gulls, which usually wheeled and cried overhead, were resting white specks that rode the gently moving waves. The tranquillity was so complete that even the soft crunch of my sandals on the loose rocks was a sacrilege.

I dropped the last few feet on to the loose shingle, rounded the boulder at the foot of my secret pathway, and stopped, the feeling of expectancy crystallizing into disappointment and indignation. For my bay – the bay I loved with a jealous, possessive love – was not empty and waiting for me alone that day. A stranger was there before me.

He didn't look up. He sat, motionless, hunched over a sketch block, a pencil poised between thin, brown fingers. And as I looked at him, at his faded T-shirt and salt-stained jeans, at the sun-bleached fair hair curling down over the nape of his neck, at his tanned arms and broad shoulders, I knew, with the odd instinct that women prefer to deny, that every detail of this moment was going to be recorded and stored within my memory until the end of time.

Then, without looking up, he spoke, and the moment passed, leaving only a feeling of indignation. For to me, in my bay, the intruder had said casually, 'Hello. Where did you spring from?'

I stared at him coldly, trying to decide whether to answer or ignore him. Then, without meaning to, I said, 'Who are you?'

He got up, flipping over whatever it was he'd been drawing and putting the book on a boulder. He smiled a slow, challenging smile that might almost have been insolent if he hadn't been several years older than me.

'Well, I'm Andrew Philip Charles Collins, but don't let that worry you. My friends call me Sandy.'

'How did you get here?' I asked. It came out sounding like an accusation.

He pointed to a beat-up looking rowing boat pulled up on to the sand at the water's edge. 'Voila! The best way to find secluded coves. And how did you get here? You didn't come in from the sea, unless you're a mermaid.'

'Do I look like a mermaid?' I asked sarcastically. Then, as he appraised me with the same insolent grin, my annoyance became tinged with embarrassment and I felt hot colour flooding my cheeks.

'Not a mermaid, no,' he said. 'For a start, you don't have a fish tail. And I imagine mermaids as pink and white, with long golden hair. You're too dark. You might get away with being a South Sea Island girl if you put on a grass skirt though.'

That was too much. The colour in my cheeks deepened. 'Who are you, anyway?' I asked haughtily. 'A holidaymaker?'

He laughed, throwing back his head with a spontaneous derision that made me even more uncomfortable. 'Do I look like a holidaymaker?' he asked, parodying my remark to him. 'No, sweetheart, I'm afraid there's no way I could afford the luxury of a holiday. I . . .' He paused, and I wasn't sure if it was for effect, or while he decided what to say. Then: 'I . . . sell hot dogs.'

It was the final straw. Speechless I stared at him, hating him for his arrogance and for being here, polluting the place that meant so much to me, my secret place, my haven. I gathered what was left of my composure and said frostily, 'Well, I should be very much obliged if you wouldn't come to this particular bay again. I'm sure you could take your boat further up the coast.'

Then, without waiting for his reply, I began to scramble back up the cliff path, and every step of the way I felt his eyes following me. I was hot, bothered, steaming with annoyance; everything about him had got under my skin. Especially as I knew that all the points there were to be gained from the brief encounter had gone to him.

It was as I walked back to Sturvendor across the moors where the gorse grew in thick golden clumps and the heather thatched the rough turf with purple, that I realized how odd it was that I should feel so possessive of Seagull Bay – I, who had been a stranger here myself three short years ago.

Odd, and yet maybe not so odd. For I had found it just when I most needed a secret hiding place where I could be alone with my grief, my memories, my hopes and fears, and my bewilderment at the way my sheltered life had shattered into a million pieces around me; a place where there was no one to look at me with pity, or try too hard to be kind to me.

I was grateful for the kindness people showed me, of course, but sometimes I felt so suffocated by it that I wanted only to escape, to be able to cry without anyone knowing, and to remember my home in Canada and the mother and father I would never see again.

I was just fourteen years old when my parents were killed, and already I had to close my eyes to picture them clearly: my tall, good-looking father and my mother with her pretty, carefully made-up face, and hair that always managed to look as if she'd come straight from the beauty parlour. Other things I remembered so clearly that to even half-think about them could be a physical pain – my mother's perfume, woody, bitter-sweet; the way my father would rumple my hair when he came home from a business trip, laughing when I protested, calling me his 'little girl'. Once they had been part of a life I'd taken as much for granted as drawing breath. Now they were gone, lost completely and forever when a light aircraft crashed on a clear blue morning in spring.

*It shouldn't have been a beautiful morning*, I thought. They should have died in autumn when the world was dying with them, not at the beginning of the year when life is fresh and young and green. And there should have been some way of knowing as I came down to breakfast that morning that never again would it be like this. Then I could have stopped and watched them: Mummy in her gay housecoat, squeezing fresh oranges in the liquidizer, Daddy sorting papers into his briefcase. I could have savoured every tiny detail and tucked it away for all time in my storehouse of precious memories.

But I didn't know. To me it was just another morning when Daddy was going away on one of his business trips, and the only difference was that this time Mummy was going with him. So I didn't do or say or think anything special. I just poured myself a glass of orange juice and put a piece of bread in the toaster and, because I knew they were rushing and I was probably in the way, I stood by the window whilst I nibbled it, looking down across the broad drive and the familiar flower beds and lawns without really noticing them at all.

'You will be all right, Dawn, won't you?' Mummy fussed. A school friend was coming home to spend the night with me, but she still looked worried.

'Of course I'll be all right,' I said, and Daddy, looking up from his papers, winked at me.

'She's a big girl now, aren't you, kitten?' I grinned at him, my mouth too full of toast to answer, and he went on, 'Anyway, we'll call you tonight, and we'll be back tomorrow evening. Just don't get up to too much mischief, OK?'

Then he went back to sorting his things, and Mummy disappeared to finish her packing, and I got myself ready for school.

*If only I'd known*, I thought afterwards. I'd have hugged them, and told them I loved them, said all the million and one things that get forgotten in the humdrum day-to-day business of living. If only I'd known . . . But I hadn't, and perhaps it was just as well, because to have known would, after all, have been unbearable agony.

So I called them 'goodbye' cheerfully and normally and it never occurred to me for one moment that I'd never see them again. Flying was normal to us, a part of life. And no one thinks of death on a clear blue spring morning.

After the accident no one quite knew what to do with me. Mummy and Daddy had friends, of course, and they all flooded me with a sympathy that I found strangely embarrassing. But understandably, none of them were sympathetic enough to want to take on a fourteen-year-old orphan permanently. Daddy's family was scattered the length and breadth of the American continent and most of them had the same kind of busy, business-fuelled life that he had had. But into the gap stepped Aunt Frances, the sister Mummy had left behind in England sixteen years before. Her cable arrived the day before the funeral. She couldn't come to Canada herself, but I was to be put on the next plane to Heathrow. She and Tony, her schoolmaster husband, would meet me and take me home to Sturvendor, the Somerset seaside town I'd heard so much about but seen only once, when I was ten years old.

From now on, it was to be my home.

It was raining the day I arrived in Sturvendor. The clouds hung heavy and grey over the cliffs, blurring into the sea until you were no longer sure which was which, and the rain lashed mercilessly at Uncle Tony's immaculate but ancient Morris. The overworked windscreen wipers laboured helplessly and water, seeping through somewhere over one of the rear windows, fell in monotonous drips on to my knee.

I sat and watched the town pass the window, seeing and yet not seeing, and I wondered if I ought to tell someone about the drip. But I couldn't summon the energy to make the effort to speak, and, anyway, it seemed likely Aunt Fran had already noticed it. She was sitting in the front, next to Uncle Tony, but she had swivelled round with one arm along the back of the seat so that she was looking at me, and she was chattering with the sort of forced brightness most people used with me since Mummy and Daddy had been killed.

She was rather pretty, I decided detachedly, and she looked a bit the way Mummy used to look in the mornings before she put on her make-up. The rain had made her hair curl instead of going lank, and although her mouth was smiling, her big, brown eyes had an anxious look to them. I thought maybe I would like Aunt Fran.

I remembered once overhearing Daddy talking about her. 'She's a jewel. Tony doesn't know when he's well off . . .'

And Mummy, with a quick, furtive look in my direction, had said, 'For heaven's sake, Greg. Not now . . .'

The words had stuck in my mind, lending an aura of mystery to our distant relations, and occasionally I'd wondered what Daddy had meant. Well, maybe now I'd find out, I thought, and my eyes slid along to the back of Uncle Tony's head. His hair was longer than most men wore it in those days, growing thickly down over the collar of his polo-necked jersey, and I thought he didn't look much like my idea of the headmaster of Sturvendor Junior School. I'd expected him to be stern and a bit faded, with chalk marks on his coat. Instead he looked more like a sportsman of some kind: big and chunky and more used to open air than the classroom.

'I wish Serena could have come with us to meet you,' Aunt Fran was saying, 'but we don't like her missing school unless it's absolutely necessary.' She paused, then, as if anxious to fill the silence, rushed on with. 'It's funny, isn't it? You're both the same age – well, only five months between you, anyway, your birthday in March and Serena's at the end of August—'

'It's lucky they're both girls,' Uncle Tony interrupted, and his deep voice seemed to fill the little car. 'Otherwise I don't know what we'd do with you, Dawn. You and Serena will be doubling up, you know.'

'Oh!' I said, startled, and Aunt Fran looked at me anxiously.

'You don't mind, do you? We just haven't got another room. There's only the box room, and I don't think we could get a bed in there. Not and be able to close the door . . .'

'No, I don't mind,' I said. But I did. I'd always had a room of my own. Of course, I hadn't expected anything as big and convenient as my studio room at home in Canada, but I'd thought at least in this strange and alien world there'd be somewhere I could be alone – to set out the few things I'd brought with me, and to cry, as I'd felt like doing ever since the plane landed at Heathrow.

And what about Serena? What would she think of having to share her room with a stranger? She wouldn't like it, surely.

'Serena's looking forward to having company,' Aunt Fran said, as if she'd read my mind. 'I know you two are going to be great friends.'

The knot of loneliness inside me tightened, and I wondered suddenly how I could bear it. My home, my friends, all the people I knew and loved were half a world away. I still couldn't accept that I'd never see them, or my parents, again. I had a feeling that under the aching numbness there were things too awful to be faced and I clung desperately to the things that were upsetting me here and now – normal, bearable trials like this unknown girl, Serena, secure in her own little world, and the way that everyone would expect us to be friends just because we were cousins and the same age.

*We'll probably hate each other*, I thought, and tears of panic threatened, aching behind my eyes.

'Here we are then,' Aunt Fran said. 'Home at last.'

The front of Sturvendor Junior School ran parallel with the road, one storey of grey stone with arched windows and twin doors at each end marked 'Girls' and 'Boys'. Uncle Tony turned the car into a narrow drive that ran alongside the playground and I realized that the house had been tacked on to the back corner of the school building as an afterthought. From the outside it looked quite large, and I was surprised that there were only two bedrooms big enough to use. I sat looking up at the windows with curtains of old-gold brocade and the slate roof topped with a forest of chimneys and a weathercock.

'Come on then, Dawn, we'll make a dash for it. Uncle Tony will bring your cases.' Aunt Fran was holding the door open for me and I swung myself out of the car and followed her up three grey slab steps to the front door. 'Let's get in and put the kettle on, shall we? I could do with a nice cup of tea.'

The hall was large and square, obviously meant to be impressive, but I soon discovered it had been designed at the expense of the other rooms. There was a poky lounge, a dining room that seemed to be bursting with furniture and a narrow kitchen that reminded me of a corridor. After the airy brightness of our kitchen at home, its walls hung with copper pans, spices and pot plants, it was unbelievably dark and depressing. Aunt Fran lit the gas ring under the heavy, old kettle, led me into the dining room, and gave the fire a poke before taking off her coat and turning to me.

'Sit down, Dawn. Make yourself at home.'

I sat, awkward and ill at ease, my hands gripping the wooden arms of the fireside chair.

Serena will show you your room when she gets in from school. I think I'll leave it to her.' Aunt Fran set out cups and saucers on the table, where no amount of polishing could hide the scratches and scorch marks. 'Such a nuisance, really, you having to share. We had the extra room before they made it into a bathroom. Now, just when we need it . . . Still, we couldn't do without the bathroom now, could we?'

There was a photograph on the sideboard, a little girl with fair, curly hair and a dimply face. Serena, I supposed, at about six or seven. Had she changed much, I wondered. I looked around for a more recent photograph, but I could see only blurred holiday snapshots and a school portrait where Serena looked very young. Nothing to tell me what the girl I was to share a room with was like now.

Uncle Tony came in shaking the rain out of his hair and holding his hands out to the fire. 'Who'd think it was April? It's cold enough for Christmas!'

'Have you put the car away, Tony?' Aunt Fran asked. 'I was thinking you could meet Serena at the bus stop. She'll get soaked otherwise.'

Serena, I learned, was a pupil at Sturvendor Grammar School on the other side of town, and it was likely I'd be joining her there. Uncle Tony hadn't wasted much time, and I guessed he'd expect me to be an academic credit to the family, as Serena was sure to be. I hoped he wouldn't be disappointed. I knew myself to be a very average pupil in everything except English Literature, where I'd always shone. And, of course, drama. But I didn't think Uncle Tony would count drama.

The front door slammed and Aunt Fran went pink. 'You're too late, Tony. Serena's here now.'

It's odd, isn't it, how often first impressions are the right ones? Often, in the weeks to come, I was to hate Serena – hate her for belonging where I didn't belong, for trying to comfort me when I just wanted to be left alone, for her well-meaning fussing and her occasional stabs of sharp, hurtful honesty. But that afternoon, in Aunt Fran's cramped little dining room, I saw a schoolgirl in a dripping mackintosh whose huge, hazel eyes were as wary as I knew my own must be, and felt, for the first time since Mummy and Daddy were killed, that maybe, after all, I wasn't quite alone.

Years afterwards, Serena was to tell me she'd felt the same way about me. 'I hated the thought of you coming. I thought you'd be terribly Americanized and want to change everything. I didn't want to share my room with you, and I was scared stiff of having to try to be nice to you every minute of the day. But you weren't a bit the way I expected. I mean, you looked scared too . . .'

'Serena, dear, this is Dawn,' Aunt Fran said.

I smiled awkwardly. 'Hello.'

She smiled back, and I thought that really she hadn't changed at all from the photograph on the sideboard. 'Hello.'

Into the awkward silence that followed Aunt Fran said, with forced brightness, 'Come along then. Let's have a nice cup of tea and get to know one another, shall we?'

I don't remember much of my first weeks at Sturvendor. I was still too numb to realize the full meaning of what had happened, and I moved in a kind of black dream from one day to the next, behaving mechanically, doing the things that were expected of me, and fighting the choking bouts of loneliness and homesickness as if they were enemies I could keep at bay forever by sheer force of will.

Dimly, I was aware that everyone was making a special effort to make me feel at home. Aunt Fran fussed and chattered, refusing to leave me alone for a single second and making disapproving faces at anyone who mentioned anything connected even remotely with Canada or my parents. Serena cleared out piles of her own treasures to make room in her cramped cupboards for the things I'd brought with me, and did her best to protect me from the natural curiosity I attracted when I joined her at the Grammar School. Even Uncle Tony, who, I discovered, was much too busy with school activities and with coaching the local junior football team to spend much time at home, made an effort to show me the beautiful countryside that surrounded Sturvendor: the majestic rolling moorland, the secret wooded valleys, the streams that swelled to rivers on their way to the sea.

But all the while nothing was real to me but the ache of loneliness, the sense of waiting, and the feeling that this was just an interlude in my life and that soon I'd wake up back home in Canada and it would be Sturvendor and England that were the far-off dream world.

As the days grew longer and the weather warmer, the town began to come to life. One by one the beach shops and arcades opened and the holidaymakers poured in, spending their money and leaving their litter.

Serena confided to me that she hated them. 'It's a beautiful coast,' she told me, 'and they ruin it with broken bottles and fish-and-chip wrapping. Daddy says we need the tourist trade, but I just wish they'd all go away.'

I didn't care much either way. It wasn't my town and it wasn't my beach. I had no more right there than the holidaymakers.

It wasn't until the end of the summer that the anaesthesia of shock began to wear off for me, and I realized I would never be going home. Slowly, the vague ache inside me, the feeling that tomorrow some mystical, uncertain something was going to happen, began to be replaced by bouts of black, all-consuming depression, and I realized that nothing *was* going to happen. I was going to be here in Sturvendor tomorrow and tomorrow and tomorrow.

Autumn came in early, with everlasting rain and high winds that brought the leaves down from the trees long before they should have fallen, and I felt worse than ever. It was so sad to see the summer dying this way; so pitiful that all the things that had been young and green such a short time ago looking brown and withered. It had ended too suddenly – cut down, it seemed to me, in its prime, as my parents had been. And I found myself aching for them with a pain that was physical, and longing for the glory of the red and gold Canadian autumn that always made me quite sure spring would come again if only I was patient.

Small things upset me now, and I found I cried too easily – I, who had always been so proud. I would feel my lip tremble if anyone so much as hinted a reprimand; be ridiculously disappointed when Aunt Fran served peas instead of corn with chicken.

The little house where there was never any privacy was claustrophobic; Uncle Tony's old Morris was a junk-box; Serena's friends seemed smug and self-satisfied, and emphasized my own lack of belonging. Sometimes, in an effort to release the weight of tension within me, I tried to goad Serena into a quarrel; afterwards, when I was quite sure she was asleep, I'd cry quietly into my pillow, sick with shame and self pity, yet desperately afraid she'd wake and know that I was crying.

And then, quite by accident, I found the bay.

It was in October, a still, quiet day when the rains had stopped at last, leaving the sky a pale, washed out blue above the gunmetal grey of the sea, and it was Aunt Fran's birthday.

For some weeks I'd been trying very hard to adjust to life in Sturvendor, and as part of my effort I'd been making a tray cloth for Aunt Fran.

I'd never been very good at sewing. Usually, however hard I tried, my stitches refused to come out even. But Serena, who was a superb needlewoman, had been embroidering a tablecloth as a surprise present for her mother and I'd been watching her, filled with envy at the delicate, veined work.

'I wish I could sew like you!' I told her. 'I'd love to make something really super.'

'Why don't you then?' she asked.

I laughed. 'Me? I'm the original ham-fisted clown. A five-year-old could do better.'

Serena didn't reply, but she searched in her workbox and brought out some cream-coloured loose-weave canvas and skeins of brightly coloured wool.

'You could do this. You only have to count the holes. It's called Binca. It's simple, and it looks super.'

At first I was doubtful, but under Serena's tuition I managed a trial bit and was surprised by how good it looked.

'Make a tray cloth,' Serena suggested. 'There's just about enough material.'

Fascinated, I followed the instructions on a pattern she found for me. Never before had I sewn anything that didn't make me want to cringe, and I was delighted with the bright, professional look of the bold stitches.

'You're a genius!' I told Serena, ridiculously pleased with myself.

Serena and I spent hours on our needlework. She was a perfectionist and I found it a novelty and oddly soothing. It was nice, too, to be making a present for someone, and for the first time in months I felt as if there was a purpose in my life. I worked with love, wanting to sew into every stitch my gratitude for all Aunt Fran had done for me, and trying desperately to make up for all the times I'd resented the fact that she wasn't, and never could be, my mother.

The night before her birthday I sat up until one o'clock to finish it, working by the light of the little table lamp so that no one but Serena would realize I was still awake. Then I left it spread out on the bedside table so I could see it as soon as I opened my eyes in the morning.

Aunt Fran's birthday was on a Saturday, so there was no rush for school. I packed up my tray cloth in some gift paper I'd bought in town, and Serena and I trooped down the stairs together singing 'Happy Birthday to You' and 'Twenty-one Today' at the tops of our voices.

Aunt Fran was at the sink doing some washing and her face flushed with pleasure when we thrust our parcels at her.

'Darlings, you shouldn't have! You don't get much pocket money . . .'

Serena and I looked at one another and shared a grin of secret amusement.

Aunt Fran undid mine first, and I watched, suddenly shy, as she pulled the tray cloth out of its wrappings.

'Dawn! You clever girl! Did you make this? It's just what I wanted!'

I glowed with pleasure, bursting to tell her all about how I'd discovered the joys of Binca, but she had put it on one side and begun unwrapping Serena's present, a funny, expectant look on her face. A feeling of something that might have been disappointment clawed at my stomach.

Aunt Fran opened the tissue paper and took out Serena's tablecloth. For a moment she didn't speak, and she looked as if she was going to cry. Then she said, in an awestruck tone, 'It's *beautiful*!'

'Do you like it?' Serena was rosy with pride.

'Like it! Oh, darling, it's the most beautiful thing! Far too nice to use! Oh Serena . . .!'

She hugged Serena, lost for words, and I turned away. Loneliness and hurt was spreading and growing inside me, searing wherever it touched. For I knew that however much Aunt Fran might thank me for my present, it was Serena's she was really pleased with, not just because it was a finer piece of work, but because it was Serena, her daughter, who had done it. I could understand that, and I didn't really blame her, but it hurt all the same. Because there was nobody to be especially proud of me any more.

I followed them into the living room, and while Aunt Fran showed her presents to Uncle Tony I hung back in the doorway, blinking away tears, and remembering all too clearly one of my own mother's birthdays, years ago, when I was just a little girl. I'd made a birthday card for her – crayoned a picture of a field and a river and stuck some grass and a pressed flower on to it. Inside I'd written 'with love from Dawn', and I'd worried like mad because I'd smudged the 'Dawn'. But Mummy hadn't minded. She'd kissed me and looked at me just the way Aunt Fran had looked at Serena, with eyes that were suspiciously bright, and she'd left the card propped up on the shelf long after all the others had been taken down. Then, when she could leave it there no longer, she'd put it away in her handkerchief drawer with some of her other treasures.

I wondered what had happened to that card now. It wouldn't have meant anything to whoever had cleared up Mummy's things. They'd have looked at it without much interest and thrown it away. Who but a mother would want a smudged and faded birthday card?

Serena and Aunt Fran went back into the kitchen, and Uncle Tony got up from the pile of exercise books he'd been marking and went with them. I hovered in the doorway, fighting back the tears that were aching in my throat and wondering if they'd notice I was behaving oddly. I didn't want them to notice. I didn't want to spoil Aunt Fran's birthday by bursting into tears. Which is exactly what was going to happen if anyone said a single word to me.

I looked at them, grouped there together, seeing them through a hot mist. They were a family, complete in themselves. I was an outsider. For all the pretence, I didn't belong at all. If I made myself scarce, they probably wouldn't even notice. The tears in my throat hardened into a knot that almost choked me and I turned away, desperate to escape.

My anorak was hanging on a peg in the hall in a jumble with Uncle Tony's duffle coat and Serena's gaberdine mackintosh. I pulled it on and went out. After the rain the air was cold and misty. I walked up the hill towards the edge of the moors with no clear idea where I was going. It was unimportant; nothing mattered except that I should get away from the family group to which I could never quite belong, away from the house where the shared happiness only emphasized my own aloneness. I walked slowly and steadily, my hands in my pockets, my head bent so that no one would see the tears that kept filling my eyes. Presently I realized that here, on the moors, there was no one to see, and I let them run unchecked down my face.

On and on I walked, weeping freely for the first time since I had come to Sturvendor, making myself think of all the things I'd tried so hard not to think of and reliving the life that could never be recaptured. When I'd exhausted the past, and my sobs had begun to subside, I made myself think of the future, the empty, lonely, terrifying years yet to come, and a fresh wave of grief broke over me.

At last, weak from crying, I stopped walking and sat down on the turf, heedless of the damp. And it was then that I saw the path.

It was almost hidden by boulders, but when I rubbed the tears out of my eyes I saw that it wound down the face of the cliff. Curiously I lowered myself on to it and began to climb down. In places it was almost obscured by great clumps of dead thrift, and sometimes it seemed to disappear altogether so that there was nothing but a narrow ledge of shale, but some inner compulsion drove me on, and, balancing myself on jagged outcrops of rock, I managed to keep going until I reached some semblance of a path once more.

I hadn't dared to look down, and when my feet crunched on to shingle I was almost taken by surprise. I stepped out from behind a boulder and found I was in a tiny bay, surrounded entirely by cliffs and sea.

Momentarily panic stabbed at me. Supposing I couldn't get back up the cliff the way I had come? Although the tide was quite low, it still broke furiously over the jutting boulders at both tips of the bay and it was obvious that apart from the cliff path the only way of escape would be by boat or helicopter.

A curious sense of peace crept through me then. What did it matter, anyway? What did anything matter? I leaned back against the rough cliff face watching the seagulls whirling and swooping over the leaden sea, and there was something almost hypnotic about the ceaseless movement that added to my calm.

*This place should be called Seagull Bay*, I thought, and the wind, whispering among the rocks, seemed to echo the name. *Seagull Bay. Seagull Bay.*

I don't know how long I stayed there, but when at last I climbed the cliff again, scrambling over the edge on hands and knees and pausing by the boulder to catch my breath, I felt as if a weight had been lifted from my heart. I know now it was the release of tears that had worked the seeming miracle. But then I thought it was the magic of the bay. And I knew that for me it would always be my special place, my hideaway, my refuge.

As I walked back across the moors I saw Serena coming to meet me.

'Dawn, we were worried about you! Where on earth have you been?' she asked.

I hesitated, wondering whether to tell her. But I didn't. 'I just walked,' I said. 'I wanted to be on my own. I'm all right now, and I'm sorry if I worried you.'

I linked arms with her and, as we started back to Sturvendor, it never occurred to me that it would be three whole years before I shared the secret of my bay with anyone.

# Two

After I found Seagull Bay nothing was ever quite so bad again. In an alien world it was a special place, *my* place, and I could be alone there: to come to terms with the grief I had tried so hard to suppress, and to find myself again. I went there as often as I could. Even in winter, when the path was rock hard and slippery with frost, I'd manage to scramble down, and it never occurred to me to be afraid, though I knew that if I slipped it might be days before anyone found me.

Under the sheltering cliffs I watched the squalls of winter give way to sweeter, but often treacherous spring, and I grew to love every nook and cranny, every sea-washed rock and tuft of thrift with a jealous, possessive love. And as the sun grew stronger and warmed the stone I felt as if I, too, was beginning to live again.

At first this made me feel guilty; acceptance seemed a betrayal of everything I'd lost, and I fought it, forcing myself to think of the things that hurt most. But gradually the brooding moors and the stark cliffs and the sea, with its ever-changing moods, became more real to me than the pines and the mountains of Canada that could still, at times, fill me with an unbearable, bitter-sweet longing. Gradually, I learned to be at ease with Aunt Fran and Uncle Tony instead of feeling they were kind strangers, whilst my parents became shadows – dear, almost too perfect in memory, but shadows all the same.

In the bay, sitting on the boulders with my knees drawn up to my chin, I thought about them all, and always the solitude of the place brought me peace. I never told anyone about it. To share it, I felt, would be to break the magic spell. But I did occasionally feel guilty about keeping it secret from Serena.

I hadn't made friends easily at Sturvendor Grammar School. Relationships had been cemented long before I arrived there, and although in the early days, when I was something of a curiosity, I could probably have become part of one group or another, I'd been too raw, and too abstracted, to want to bother. For a while they'd borne with me, feeling sorry for me because their parents had said they should, but at fourteen sympathy doesn't last long, and soon their greatest interest in me was to find out what it was like to be orphaned. That had sent me further into myself, and branded me as an oddity. But Serena and I had grown very close, feeling our way from our first instinctive liking for one another, through the dark days when I'd resented everything and everyone, to an understanding and warmth.

Serena was, I discovered, as sweet-natured as she looked. She had Aunt Fran's kind heart, Uncle Tony's quick wits and a stubborn streak that sometimes led to a clash of will between us. And in spite of her gentleness, or perhaps because of it, she could be fiercely protective of everything, and everyone, she cared about.

Oddly, or so it seemed to me, one of the people she cared about was Chris Carter. He was a square, rather serious boy with sandy hair and freckles, whose fervent ambition was to become a doctor, and who was undoubtedly the type described by the adult world in general as 'nice' and 'reliable'. Personally, I doubted whether he was clever enough to be a doctor. His class marks were never much above average. And I could never see how he came to qualify for the superlative adjectives Serena used when talking about him. But Serena was besotted with him.

The second winter I was in Sturvendor, he asked her to go out with him, and she was so thrilled I hadn't the heart to tell her he'd asked *me* out some while before and I'd refused. He took her to the cinema and that night she kept me awake for hours whilst she went on and on about him – how good looking he was, how clever, how considerate. Uncle Tony lectured her on not allowing boyfriends to interfere with her studying, and Aunt Fran fussed over her like a mother hen, insisting Chris called for her and brought her home, but I think they both expected the romance to blow over in a week or two.

It didn't. There were ups and downs, of course, imagined slights or betrayals, when Serena went about looking as if the sun had set on her world, but always, after a day or so, things were patched up and Serena glowed with happiness. They became an accepted couple at school, and, as they grew closer, I found myself shut out. Serena no longer wanted to tell me about her romance. It was private, something she hugged to herself.

At first, in spite of being glad for her, I minded bitterly. Serena's friendship had been my bridge over troubled waters. And I envied her, too, because I'd never met a boy who could make me feel that way, and I couldn't imagine that I ever would.

But before long I'd forgotten my envy. For I had a love of my own – a love that must have been smouldering deep inside me for years, but which burst on me with the suddenness of a shooting star, and grew to a passion I knew would be with me to the end of my days.

The theatre.

When I'd first auditioned for the part of Portia in the school production of *The Merchant of Venice*, I hadn't thought I stood a chance. I was perfectly certain my accent would go against me, and it wasn't until we clustered around the cast list on the notice board and I saw my name beside the leading role that I realized how much I'd wanted it.

At rehearsals I worked hard, revelling in the feeling that at last I was doing something I really wanted to do, and at home I walked around in a daze, reciting lines, living the part. On the night of the show I was terrified, standing in the wings, knees weak, throat dry, but the moment I walked on to the stage and felt the audience, a living, murmuring beast in the blackness beyond the blinding lights, my nerves dropped away and a soaring power flowed into me. This was doing what I'd always been meant to do! This was being alive! As I took the final curtain I was exultant, every vestige of loneliness and bereavement stripped away, knowing only the thrill of having been part of some strange, age-old magic. And that night I lay awake until the small hours, tensed and tingling still, reliving every moment over and over again.

For days I lived in a dream world whilst I was bombarded by praise from teachers, parents, even the local press. I walked around on a high. Then, gradually, as the drug drained from me, I felt a sense of loss as real and profound as any other. And I knew without any doubt what I wanted to do with my life.

I wanted to be an actress.

For two years I lived for my dream. Sometimes I talked about it to Serena, but always in a light, non-committal way because I didn't want her to guess just how much it meant to me. Like Seagull Bay, like everything else I cared most about, I needed to hug it to myself because I was afraid that in the light of day it would lose its power to comfort and excite me.

Serena knew, of course, that I loved the theatre. She knew I saved all my pocket money to buy tickets for shows, and that I'd been upset when the teacher who'd directed us in *The Merchant* left to take up a new post and was replaced by a studious bespectacled lady who wasn't remotely interested in putting on school productions. But she didn't know that I'd learned every major Shakespearean speech by heart, and she didn't know that I played the lead roles, as often as I could, to an audience of gulls in my bay.

Sometimes when my voice echoed back at me from the cliffs that formed a natural amphitheatre I'd pause mid line, looking around with a guilty stab of self-consciousness, afraid someone had heard or seen me. But the bay was always as deserted as the first day I'd found it, and when I finished my speech it was the roar of the sea on the rocks that provided me with thunderous applause.

I'd bow then, a sweeping, theatrical bow, and I'd scoop up a handful of sand, letting it trickle through my fingers. And, like a famous actress blowing kisses to her public, I'd whisper, 'I love you, Seagull Bay. You're mine. All mine!'

Each summer an old-fashioned repertory company came to Sturvendor. It was run by an aging, but still impressive Actor/Manager whose name was Hunter Hylton, and it played in the Gaiety, a ramshackle old theatre on the seafront. Uncle Tony told me it had been coming for as many years as he could remember, and he didn't think it could possibly last much longer.

'It'll be a variety theatre next year,' he prophesied. 'Or even, heaven help us, a bingo hall. Television has spoiled people. Who wants to see second-rate actors in second-rate plays nowadays? No one.'

I didn't agree with him. Maybe sometimes the set looked as if it might fall down, maybe some of the cast forgot their lines, and things went wrong. But the magic was there all the same: the aura of a mysterious world beyond the footlights, the smell of greasepaint wafting from behind the velvet drapes when the safety curtain was lifted, the excitement and expectation in the pit of one's stomach when the opening bars of 'The Queen' filled the theatre, the house lights going out, the spots and floods coming on. As for the players, they were gods and goddesses to me, stars in the making who worked for a pittance to gain experience, and hoary old pros, still displaying the dignity a life on the stage had taught them to assume, and somehow, to me, managing to be more romantic than sad, real-life, modern Don Quixotes.

From my weekly visits, and from studying the photographs on the billboard beside the main door, I came to know them all so well that they might have been personal friends – the young Adonis, the haughty red-haired girl, even the Hyltons themselves – Hunter, with hair slicked back from a smoothly handsome face, Evelyn, his energetic and once-glamorous wife with her savage red lips and over-bleached hair and Rosencrantz, the fat, white poodle who appeared in every play where an animal role could be squeezed in.

Sometimes I stood outside the stage door hoping I'd see one of them going in or out and wondering if I'd have the courage to ask for their autograph if I did. Somehow I doubted it. For one thing, autograph hunting would put me at an immediate disadvantage, and I wanted to be their equal. For another, the very fact that I yearned to be one of them put up a greater barrier than indifference ever could.

At the end of the season, when the shutters went up and the posters began to fade and shred under the onslaught of the wind and the salty rain, I felt as if a part of me had left with the Hunter Hylton Repertory Company. I stood beside the empty display case from which the confident, glamorous faces had smiled at me all summer and the loneliness and sadness was almost as real as when I had first come to Sturvendor.

*Where did they go?* I wondered. To other work? Or to the ignominy of dole queues and a strange variety of jobs to fill in the empty weeks that they liked to call 'resting'. And, most important of all, would they ever come back, or would the Gaiety become a bingo hall as Uncle Tony had predicted? If it did, I didn't think I could bear it.

But they came back. The company had changed, but the

Hyltons were still there, and memorizing the new faces on the billboard I wondered if my own face would one day be there, my head tilted so that my hair fell, as the leading lady's did, over one bare shoulder, the caption reading 'Dawn Stephens'. I looked at the board and saw it all in my mind's eye, just as it might be one day if only I could hold on to my dream and find the courage to bring it into the open and do something about it.

One night when school was over I left Serena to walk home with Chris and wandered on my customary pilgrimage through the town. Although it was still only May, the streets had begun to come alive, the Bed and Breakfast signs going up in the windows of the solid, respectable semi-detached house, the pavement gay with racks of paperback books and postcards, sun oil and straw hats, that spilled out from the small shops.

As I turned the corner on to the seafront the salt wind caught me, tossing my hair back from my face and blowing my skirt tight against my legs. I passed the penny-arcade, with its raucous jukebox and perpetually clanking pinball machines and one-arm bandits, glanced idly at the stream of children queuing for ice creams at the white-painted beach café. But I didn't stop until I reached the Gaiety.

There, as always, my feet slowed to a halt and I studied the posters announcing the week's performances. The show always changed on a Wednesday so that holidaymakers could see two different plays in one week, and this week they were doing the comedy *Sailor Beware* and Agatha Christie's *The Hollow*. I'd seen both plays before, they came up every year, sometimes more than once, but if I could scrape together the price of a ticket, I'd see them again.

Suddenly, the main door of the theatre flew open and a young man in jersey and jeans came out. He glanced at me and I looked away, half embarrassed. Then, as he crossed the road, I turned to watch him go, trying to put a name to him and wishing I'd had the courage to speak. It could have been Kevin Allerby, I thought, glancing back at the photographs. Without the bright lights and the make-up it was hard to tell. Or perhaps it had been a stage hand . . .

Beside me, the door banged, making me jump. The young man

couldn't have fastened it properly. For a moment I watched it rattling under the onslaught of the salt wind, but no one came from inside to close it and, half-scared, I put my hand against it and pushed gently. It opened.

The foyer was hardly worthy of the name. It was little more than a short tunnel cluttered with photographs and old handbills, and lightened by a serving hatch that was laughingly called the box office. When I'd seen it at night, brightly lit, it had a certain glamour, and often Hunter Hylton himself, resplendent in a brightly-patterned silk dressing gown and full stage make-up, could be glimpsed inside. This afternoon, however, it was almost totally dark and there was a desolate feel to it. I went across the strip of threadbare carpet and paused again, my hand on the cold, brass handle of the swing doors that led into the theatre itself. For perhaps a minute I stood there, nerving myself to open the door, and wondering what I would find on the other side. But the whole building was silent and inch by inch I pushed the door open.

It was dim inside the theatre, and a smell of dust and stale cigarette smoke made my nose twitch. The curtains that looked like lush, rippling velvet under the glow of the spotlights hung dark, dull and undeniably dirty. Yet as I stood in the half-light, my hand resting on the hard, tired back of an uncomfortable seat, I felt excitement spreading through every vein, spiralling up into a tight ball in my throat until everything else was forgotten in a rush of heady delight so strong I felt faint. In my imagination I heard the first bars of strident music as the electric organ broke into 'Beside the Seaside', smelled the first intoxicating whiffs of greasepaint as the curtains stirred. I was oblivious to everything but that this tatty, tumbledown hall was the theatre, real and live, grotty yet romantic, and I wanted to be a part of it.

'Looking for somebody?' The young man had come in behind me without my noticing and my dream disintegrated in a rush of guilty panic.

'No . . . I'm just going . . . It's all right . . .'

I half expected him to challenge me, but he didn't. He just shrugged and went down the aisle between the seats, disappearing through a curtained door at the side of the stage. The spell was broken for me, and I hurried back across the foyer. The catch had dropped on the front door; I turned it and went out, blinking in the bright afternoon sun. Behind me, the door slammed on my dream world, and once again I was back to reality.

In the schoolhouse, tea wasn't yet ready.

'It'll be an hour or more yet,' Aunt Fran said. 'Time for you do some homework if you want to.'

I should, I knew, but I couldn't face it. Not yet. My stolen minutes in the theatre had excited me, brought me tinglingly alive, and more than ever I needed to be alone.

In our room, Serena was huddled over her books, her small face solemn and owlish from too much reading. She was working hard so as to be able to see Chris for an hour or so later on, I guessed. I didn't say anything to interrupt her train of thought. I just changed into jeans and a shirt and went out again, raising my hand to her in a silent gesture of acknowledgement. Then I left the house and walked across the moors towards Seagull Bay.

As I went, I was already turning over in my mind the momentous thought that had occurred to me in the theatre.

Though I'd known for a long while now that I wanted to act, it had been a secret dream that belonged to a far-off future, a dream too precious to bring into the searing light of day. But sooner or later I was going to have to decide on a career; sooner or later I was going to have to find out whether or not I had the courage of my convictions – and whether I had the talent to break into the profession I yearned for. It was one thing to be fêted as Portia in a school play, quite another to actually make a living from acting. A nerve was jumping in my throat just contemplating the reality of putting myself on the line in that way. Was I good enough? Would I make a complete and utter fool of myself? What would Aunt Fran and Uncle Tony say? How would I go about it? The myriad questions were chasing one another round and round inside my head.

I reached the cliff path and started down, knowing that in the solitude of the bay I'd be able to think more clearly. But today there was a feeling of waiting stillness in the air that unsettled me instead of soothing me. And as I emerged from behind the boulder and saw the fair-haired stranger sitting there, sketch block on his knees, in my secret bay, I somehow already knew that nothing was ever going to be quite the same again.

# Three

It was two weeks before I saw him again, though there was not a single moment when he didn't haunt me. Lying awake in the room I shared with Serena I stared into the darkness and saw his cool, insolent smile and the arrogant lift of his shoulders, and burned with dislike for him. Each time I scrambled down the cliff path I half-expected to find him on the beach, and when I did not I was surprised by the stab of perverse disappointment that ached beneath my pretended relief. I'd been looking forward to the chance to get even with him, I told myself, to be able to say something sharp and witty that would upset his infuriating self-confidence. There was no other explanation for the sense of anticlimax.

I looked out for him in the town, too, edgy with expectancy as I walked along the streets where a hot dog vendor might park his barrow. But I never saw him.

I asked Serena if she'd seen him plying his trade, and she wrinkled her nose in disgust.

'Hot dogs? No, I haven't seen anyone selling hot dogs. I haven't even smelled them, and it's not the sort of smell you can miss very easily. He was pulling your leg, Dawn.'

'Maybe,' I said. Something about the young man had suggested he treated the whole of life as a joke. 'Maybe he was a holiday-maker after all, and now he's gone home.'

'There you are. Mystery solved,' Serena said, and drifted back into the distant dreaminess that seemed to envelop her these days. I knew there was no point in pursuing the conversation any further. Her interest in Chris was all-consuming.

In a way I envied her. It must be so good to be so happy, so secure, and to know exactly where one was going in life. For though they saw one another as often as they could, even their romance was tailored towards their future.

'Chris has to work hard if he's going to be a doctor,' Serena would say, her face shining with pride, and it was then that I didn't envy her at all, for I had the uncomfortable feeling that everything revolved around Chris, and Serena was a satellite to his sun. All her plans and ambitions were centred around him; there was nothing that was just for her. I didn't like to think of Serena disappearing into his orbit.

I never felt entirely at ease with him, either. There was something about the way he looked at me that made me uncomfortable, something strange and intense that was at odds with his otherwise easy-going personality, and I could never quite forget that once he'd asked me out. It had probably been just a passing fancy, I told myself, and long forgotten. He was in love with Serena now. But all the same, I took care never to be alone with him.

Aunt Fran and Uncle Tony seemed to like Chris though. When he was at the schoolhouse it was accepted that he should stay for tea or supper, and he was invited along on Sunday afternoon trips in the spanking new Austin that had at last replaced Uncle Tony's old Morris. He had his feet well and truly under the table, as my father would have said.

One afternoon, when Serena and Chris had gone for a game of tennis, I came home from school to find Aunt Fran buttering newly baked scones in the kitchen.

'This is a treat,' I said, stealing a scone and biting into it.

Aunt Fran looked up, her face pink and flushed from the heat of the oven.

'We've got a visitor. Your uncle met a young man, an artist, who's living in the town for the summer and thought he looked as if he could do with a square meal. As if he'd given me time to get anything substantial ready! Scones is the best I could rustle up at short notice . . . don't eat them all, Dawn!'

'They're delicious!' I wasn't altogether surprised that Uncle Tony had brought home a lame dog; it wasn't the first time he'd done something of the sort. And if it meant fresh-baked scones, I wasn't going to complain.

'Take these into the dining room, will you, dear?' Aunt Fran pushed the plate in my direction – a dangerous move! 'And tell your uncle the tea will be brewed in just a minute.'

I picked up the plate of scones, resisting the urge to scoff another, and headed for the dining room, pushing open the door with my toe. Then I stopped short, frozen by surprise and disbelief. For lounging on the sofa, and smiling the same disconcerting smile that had haunted me for two whole weeks, was the stranger from Seagull Bay.

'Well, hello!' he said, and just as it had before, his complete self-assurance both irritated and fascinated me.

I was too aware, suddenly, of my checked-cotton school dress, too aware of my scrubbed face and my hair, tied up in the way we were supposed to wear it so that it didn't hang over our collars. Taken by surprise by this stranger, first in my bay and now in my home, I felt threatened in a way I couldn't begin to understand, and as a defence I said accusingly, 'But you're a hot dog seller! You're not an artist!'

He grinned, not in the least put out. 'I don't tell everyone what I do – well, not to begin with, anyway.'

With an uncomfortable jolt I remembered the sketch pad. An artist! Of course! Why hadn't I thought of it before? They weren't unheard of in Sturvendor, and he was exactly the type: irreverent, free-spirited.

'I do sell hot dogs too,' he went on. 'When I need the money.'

'Do you two know each other?' Uncle Tony asked, looking from one of us to the other with a faintly puzzled expression.

'No,' I said, and simultaneously Sandy said, 'We have met, but you never did get around to telling me your name.'

'This is Dawn,' Uncle Tony said. 'My niece, Dawn Stephens.'

I smiled awkwardly, too conscious of two pairs of eyes on me, and put the scones down on the already overloaded tea table.

'I'll go up and change,' I said unnecessarily, and for once the distance across the little dining room felt like a marathon course.

I closed the door behind me, my heart hammering into my lungs so that each breath was a choking pain, and I gave myself a mental shake. Why should I let this boy get to me? He was just an offbeat bum with a peculiar sense of humour and he thought far too much of himself. He was probably used to people, particularly women, being fascinated by him and his bohemian lifestyle, and he got his fun from needling them.

I'd ignore him. He wouldn't like that. I'd be coolly polite, and whatever he said, or however he looked at me, I wouldn't allow myself to be ruffled.

My determination lasted exactly ten minutes. Sitting opposite Sandy at the table that Aunt Fran had covered with a lace-edged cloth to hide the burn marks, I knew that any disinterest I might be showing towards Sandy was nothing more than a defensive front. To ignore him was impossible.

To begin with, he was quite different from anyone I'd ever known. In spite of the shirt he'd worn in deference to the occasion, in spite of his hair, combed neatly now instead of wind blown, there was something about him that told me that here was a man who was as untamed as any of the seagulls that whirled over my bay. He would come and go as he pleased, do as he liked according to his codes and no one else's. Yet he was well spoken, with just the trace of a Midlands accent, he was obviously intelligent and he was surprisingly courteous to both Aunt Fran and Serena.

There was an undeniable masculinity about him, too, that I found disturbing – the sort of easy, confident strength that comes not from bulging muscles but from taut, young sinews. His shoulders were narrow but strong, his wrists under the rolled-back cuffs of his shirt were slim, sun-browned and flecked with tiny golden hairs. As I watched him I felt the beginnings of fascination stir inside me, so that against my will, against all the warnings flashed at me by the cool, challenging eyes, I found myself wanting to know more about this stranger who had, undeniably, looked so right in the wild desolation of Seagull Bay and who looked so wrong here, sitting behind a lace-covered table and drinking tea from Aunt Fran's best china.

I didn't have to wait long for my curiosity to be satisfied. Aunt Fran, besides being a chatterbox, had a genuine interest in everyone who crossed her path, and she was clearly determined to learn all she could about her unusual guest.

'We've never met an artist before, have we girls?' she said, refilling his cup and smiling at him. 'We're just so thrilled, and we want to know all about it.'

Serena, who had arrived home from her game of tennis, looked a little embarrassed, and I felt an unwilling stab of pity for Sandy. I knew what it was like to be questioned and cross-questioned; it had happened to me often enough in the days when I was a Canadian curiosity. But Sandy seemed unfazed. He shrugged, his mouth full of scone.

'It's not as romantic as it sounds.'

'Of course it is!' Aunt Fran insisted. 'Tony tells me that you live in that bungalow down on the beach – the one they used to let to holidaymakers, only it isn't in a fit state any more. That sounds terribly romantic to me.'

Serena and I exchanged glances. We knew the place she meant, and to call it a bungalow was to pay it an undeserved compliment. Situated in a curve of cliff at the far end of Sturvendor Bay, the chalet had taken the full force of the wind from the sea for too many winters, and it had become dilapidated to the point where the owner, eccentric, old Miss Chertsey from the big house on the hill, had no longer been able to rent it out for the summer season. It looked frankly grotty, from the outside, at least, and we couldn't imagine it was any more enticing inside.

A moment later our suspicious were confirmed.

'The worst thing about it is the leak in the roof,' Sandy said earnestly, though his eyes were twinkling. 'It's right over my bed.'

Aunt Fran's eyes widened in horror. 'Oh my goodness, you mustn't sleep in a damp bed! You'll get pneumonia!'

'It's all right,' Sandy said cheerfully. 'I moved the bed. And I've got a bucket to catch the drips. What really annoys me though is the noise when it rains. What with the rattle on the tin roof and the plop-plop in the bucket, it's a West Country version of the Chinese water torture.'

'What does your mother think about this?' Aunt Fran asked solicitously. 'She must worry about you, surely?'

Sandy's eyes narrowed and I glimpsed the slumbering tiger. Then he smiled easily and it was as if the moment had never been. 'She's given up worrying about me. I'm the proverbial black sheep.'

'I'm sure that's not true!' Aunt Fran protested.

''Fraid so. Dad's got an ironmongery business and he wanted me to go into it, carry on the family name, you know. The name over the door says 'Collins and Sons' – he had that done years ago in anticipation. But he'll probably give in to the inevitable one day and change it to the singular.'

'You've got a brother then?'

'Yes. Raymond. He's the one who's always towed the line. Me – I just wanted to paint.'

'Your parents must be very proud of you,' Aunt Fran said.

Sandy laughed. 'Proud? No, they think I'm lazy.'

Into the awkward silence, Aunt Fran said, 'Have some fruit cake,' and Serena asked:

'Did you go to art school?'

Sandy accepted the cake, and shook his head in answer to Serena's question. 'No, I didn't go to art school.'

'Why not?' she pressed him.

'Because I didn't want to be turned out like a hundred others. I don't want to be a commercial artist and I think the whole thing would be a bloody waste of time. Sorry . . .' He grinned apologetically at Aunt Fran. 'I'll say that again. It would be a waste of time. I look at it like this. I want to paint things the way I see them. Down here I've got the time and the opportunity to teach myself. I'm surrounded by beautiful scenery. I've got a roof over my head at a knock-down rate, a hot dog stall that brings me in a bit of cash and I can sell the odd sketch to tourists. What would I want with art school?'

I was beginning to enjoy myself, gaining confidence minute by minute. I met his eyes with what I hoped was a fair imitation of his own mocking stare. 'But haven't you any ambitions?' I asked.

He returned the stare, and to my horror I felt my cheeks beginning to burn.

'Oh yes, I've got ambitions,' he said. 'I want to be the greatest artist the world has ever seen. But I don't suppose I will be, and if not, well, what the hell? I'm living the way I want to, and life's too short to live any other way, isn't it?'

During the next few weeks Sandy became a regular visitor to the schoolhouse, dropping in for one of Aunt Fran's 'square meals' and staying afterwards to talk to Uncle Tony about everything from art to world affairs. Gradually, he came to look less out of place in the comfortable, cluttered kitchen and Aunt Fran and Serena seemed to like him. But between us the atmosphere was always the same – singing with life, as flammable as a barrel of gunpowder waiting for the spark. When he was there I found him both annoying and fascinating; when he'd gone I thought about him all the time and the thinking was a fever in my blood, so that for a while even my dreams of the theatre were pushed into shadow. The narrow, suntanned face was the last thing I saw before I fell asleep at night and in the morning my waking thoughts were of him.

I didn't want to think of him, and the fact that I couldn't help it added to my resentment. But whenever I saw him coming up the drive to the house, every fibre of my being began to sing like taut telephone wires, and I found myself wondering what would happen if we were ever alone together, and worrying a little as to how I would fare in any one-to-one encounter.

Supposing, for instance, he should ask me out? With Sandy it would be impossible to know whether or not he was just teasing; setting me up for a fall. Too often I had the feeling he was laughing at me, and the last thing I wanted was to do or say anything that would make me look foolish.

But we never were alone together, and then, quite suddenly, Sandy stopped coming to the house.

At first I thought he must be busy with some new project, then, as days passed, I began to wonder what had happened to him. Serena, too, was puzzled, and one morning she asked her father when we were going to see Sandy again.

'I don't know. He's found somebody else to feed him, I expect,' Uncle Tony said, very blasé, very non-committal, but for a moment I was quite sure there was something he was not saying. Then he began asking Serena about the history project she'd been working on, and Sandy was forgotten.

By everyone but me. Inside me, a feeling of emptiness was growing from a tiny hollow to a gaping void, and I felt I was drowning in it.

I'd resented Sandy, actively disliked him, even. But the thought that I might never see him again was more than I could bear.

For days I lived in restless world where Sandy occupied most of my thoughts. I wondered if I should go into town in the hope of seeing him, yet somehow couldn't bring myself to do that. However casual I might manage to make such a meeting appear, *I'd* know it was engineered, and I had an uncomfortable feeling that Sandy would know it too. That was almost as bad as never seeing him again.

I was on the edge of my nerves. Each morning I nursed the fond hope that today I would run into him somewhere, each evening I felt curiously let down, as if something that should have happened hadn't, or that it had happened, and I'd missed it.

One warm Sunday afternoon in May I went alone to Seagull Bay. I'd left Aunt Fran unashamedly playing gooseberry on Serena and Chris, who were sitting on the old swing seat in the garden, and I'd managed to avoid allowing her to talk me into joining them.

'You don't want to go to the beach this afternoon, Dawn,' she'd said. 'It'll be crowded with all the weekend trippers. The sun will have brought them out . . .'

'You make them sound like freckles,' I said, thinking how odd it was that, in all these years, Aunt Fran had never found out about my secret hideaway, Seagull Bay.

'I'll see you later.'

I swung the bag with my swimming things in over my shoulder and started up the hill towards the moors. The sun beat down as I walked, but I was oblivious to it. The feeling of restless anticipation was suddenly very strong in me, and as I scrambled down the cliff path it was making me almost breathless. From there the bay looked as deserted as usual. Then I landed on the shingle, rounded the boulder and saw him.

He was sitting in the same nook as before, sketch pad on his knees, eating an apple.

'Well, hello, Miss Stephens. I was hoping you might drop by.'

'Hello,' I managed. My knees felt weak; I couldn't think of a single thing to say that wouldn't betray the way my heart was pounding in my chest. Then: 'I was going to have a swim,' I said.

'Well, don't let me stop you.'

'I can't. I'm not changed,' I said foolishly. 'I usually change here.'

He looked at me very seriously for a moment, then laughed. 'No problem. You'll be quite safe behind that boulder. And I promise not to peek.'

Because there wasn't any way to get out of it without appearing silly, I crossed to the boulder and changed into my bikini. My heart was still beating a tattoo, and I was trembling with pent-up excitement. I piled up my clothes neatly, carefully concealing my bra and pants inside my T-shirt, and put them on a rock. Then, without so much as a glance in Sandy's direction, I went straight down to the sea.

I swam for a while, and then floated on my back for a while, looking up at the cornflower blue of the sky while the waves rocked me gently back and forth, and I thought how wonderful it would be to lie here in the arms of the ocean forever. But all the time I was conscious of Sandy watching me from the beach and when at last I waded out, shivering a little and shaking the water from my hair, he called to me.

'Did you know you look terrific in a bikini?'

'I thought you weren't going to look.'

'I meant I wouldn't look at your unmentionables. Don't tell me that bikini was designed to wear in a bathing tent. Come on over here and talk to me.'

I went, half unwilling, feeling in a strange way that time was standing still and Sandy and I were unreal. I sat on a rock and dried my face. Sandy was looking at me with his direct gaze and something sweet and sharp twisted inside me.

'Has anyone ever told you, Dawn Stephens, that you're bloody beautiful? I think I might paint you as a mermaid, after all. The Lorelei, maybe. Wicked and dark. Why should mermaids always be fair?'

He put out his hand and pulled me down on to the sand beside him. Instantly, I was achingly aware, and ripples flowed through my body from the place on my wrist where he had touched me, as if there had been electricity in his fingers. He looked at me for a moment, his magnetic eyes burning into mine, and I was sure, quite sure, that he was going to kiss me. But he didn't. He just went on looking at me as if he could see right inside me, into my heart, into my soul.

And I knew with the suddenness of a thunderbolt that I was in love with Sandy. Deeply, crazily, wildly, and forever, in love.

'I want to see you again, Dawn,' he said.

A shiver of pure happiness, sharp-edged with excitement, prickled up my spine and over my skin. 'OK,' I said nonchalantly. 'When?'

'I'm having bacon and eggs tonight for supper. Why don't you come and cook them for me?'

I laughed nervously. It wasn't exactly a conventional offer for a first date. 'I don't think Aunt Fran would approve of that.'

'Maybe not. All right. I'll meet you by the tea stall on the promenade. About seven?'

'All right.' My pulse was racing, excitement bubbling in me like the sweet wine we'd had with the mince pies last Christmas, and I could feel myself flushing all over beneath the intensity of his gaze.

'I'd better get dressed,' I said, very aware that I was wearing nothing but my bikini.

'Yes,' he said. 'I think you'd better.'

I disappeared behind the boulder, fumbled on my clothes over my still-damp skin. When I emerged, rubbing my hair with my towel, Sandy, and his rowing-boat, had gone.

As I walked down the hill into town that evening my heart was still racing, and a funny little pulse of nervous excitement kept jumping in my throat. I was very afraid Sandy wouldn't be there, that he had just been playing with me, or that he would have found something better to do on a fine May evening. If he didn't turn up, I'd die of disappointment, I thought. Shame too. It would be so humiliating to have to go home and admit that I'd been stood up. But he was there, sitting on the sea wall, his jean-clad legs stretched out in front of him. When he saw me, he got up and walked towards me along the promenade.

'You came then,' he said.

'Did you think I wouldn't?'

He shrugged. 'I thought maybe your uncle . . .'

I looked at him curiously. Uncle Tony *had* been a bit odd when I'd said I was meeting Sandy. Aunt Fran had been fine about it, looking almost pleased, though she'd warned me to be careful, but Uncle Tony . . . there had been something in his reaction that I hadn't understood at all.

'I don't know that that's a good idea, Dawn,' he'd said brusquely.

'She'll be fine with Sandy,' Aunt Fran had protested.

'He's a drifter. Not to be trusted.'

'Oh, for heaven's sake, Tony! It's not as if we don't know him. He's been here often enough.'

*And doesn't come any more . . .* Briefly, I wondered why not.

'Take no notice of your uncle, Dawn. Go and have a lovely time. Just . . . be careful.'

Uncle Tony had turned away, angry at being overruled, I'd thought. Now, Sandy's almost-correct suggestion that Uncle Tony might have forbidden me to come on this date reminded me, and made me wonder all over again.

'Did you and Uncle Tony fall out?' I asked.

Sandy kicked at a pebble that had found its way on to the promenade. 'No.'

'But you were really friendly. And then . . .'

Sandy shrugged, grinning. 'Oh, I'm like that. Here today and gone tomorrow.'

Sudden sweet sadness twisted inside me. I pushed it away. 'It wasn't anything Aunt Fran said, was it?' I persisted. 'She does go on a bit, I know, but she doesn't mean anything by it. It's just her way.'

'No, it had nothing to do with her. She's very sweet, and she deserves better than your uncle.'

I looked at him sharply, and at the same time a chord stirred in my memory – Daddy saying, 'Tony doesn't appreciate her.' Strange that Sandy should be saying much the same thing. To me, Aunt Fran and Uncle Tony seemed a perfectly happily married couple. I couldn't understand it.

'Let's go and play a round of clock golf,' Sandy said, and the moment passed. 'In fact, if you promise to be nice to me, I might even let you win.'

We played a round of clock golf, but we laughed so much and cheated so much that neither of us knew who'd won. And as we came off the course in the gathering dusk there was an easy companionship between us that was new, and a warmth that enhanced our first electric attraction.

'I'll buy you a drink, and then I'll take you home,' Sandy said. 'I don't want to get into trouble by getting you home late on our very first date. Or I never will be able to persuade you to come and cook me eggs and bacon.'

We went to the Smugglers' Den, a little pub almost next door to the Gaiety, and as I drank a half-pint of lemonade shandy I wondered if I should tell Sandy about my ambition to be an actress. He'd understand, I knew. But the place was noisy with chattering tourists and the hoarse squawking of a parrot whose cage hung over the bar, and, as I felt Sandy's shoulder pressing against mine as we sat close together on the wooden settle I thought, with a little thrill of satisfaction, that there'd be plenty of time to tell him in the future. Years and years – maybe the rest of our lives. It was an exhilarating thought.

Sandy and I began seeing one another regularly and the world became a magic place. I loved him with every fibre of my being, and I wondered how I could ever have thought him irritating and hateful. Everything about him, it seemed to me, was wonderful. His wicked sense of humour. His devil-may-care attitude. The way he kissed me . . .

I wondered, too, how I could ever have doubted my capacity for love. Seen through the sparkling intoxication of my happiness, everyone took on new and lovable characteristics, while petty irritations dropped away. I wanted to hug the world and everyone in it, even though I was still unsure of Sandy's feelings for me.

He wanted to see me as often as I could make it, but sometimes he would ignore me as if he hardly knew I was there. He kissed me sometimes with a hungry need that awakened every nerve in my body to tingling awareness, but sometimes he parted from me with no more than a casual wave. He would say nice things about my hair, my legs, my face, but he never said he loved me.

And, in a strange way, that felt right to me. Although I ached to belong to him, completely and forever, I actually didn't really want him to belong to me. Sandy was a free spirit; that was the way he was. If he were different, he just wouldn't be Sandy. In the first joy of new love I accepted that, and enjoyed our relationship for what it was: stormy sometimes, tender sometimes, always changing, always the same.

One Sunday afternoon, Sandy took me to his chalet. We'd been down by the harbour watching the boats, and we'd bought some fresh fish from a leathery-faced skipper whom Sandy called 'Grundy'.

'Now's your chance to show me how you can cook,' he said.

'I can't cook,' I protested. 'Aunt Fran never lets me into her kitchen.'

'I'll let you into mine. And this will be a lot better than the bacon and eggs you keep promising me.'

'You mean the bacon and eggs *you* keep threatening me with!'

We walked up the beach, hand in hand. Sandy unlocked the chalet door and pushed it open. 'Home sweet home!'

From the battered exterior, and from Sandy's mocking descriptions, I hadn't expected the chalet to be up to much. But the stark reality of it shocked me all the same. I looked in horror around the one room, taking in the damp patches on the ceiling, the yellowing paper on the walls, the odd chairs and table, and the narrow, old-fashioned bed with its faded coverlet and lumpy eiderdown that had once been floral pastels. One corner of the room had been partitioned off with plasterboard, and Sandy nodded towards it.

'My kitchen. I'm afraid I have to fetch water from a tap under the sea wall, but there is a little cooker that runs off bottled gas.'

'It's a bit . . . basic, isn't it?' I said, trying not to sound as shocked as I felt.

Sandy shrugged. 'You get used to it. It's cheap, there's a dry cupboard where I can keep my painting things and it's all I need. I've lived in cloistered comfort, and it suffocated me. This is freedom, Dawn. Don't ever try to talk me out of it.'

A million thoughts chased through my mind, then I squared my shoulders, matching my mood to his. 'Let's cook this fish then. If we can! I'm starving.'

In the event, it was Sandy who did the cooking, cleaning our catch and frying it over his gas ring with impressive ease. After we'd eaten we sat with our hands linked across the rickety, old table, talking more deeply than we'd ever talked before. I told him of my love of the theatre and my dreams of becoming an actress, and he opened up about his home, and the reason he'd left.

Until that day he'd been very reticent about his parents. Now, to my astonishment, I learned that his father's ironmongery business wasn't the small, cluttered shop I'd imagined, but a store that took up most of one street in his home town, and the house he had left to live in this damp, draughty chalet was an extravagant mock-Tudor residence with a double garage, swimming pool and orchard. He told me about it as if he were ashamed rather than proud but wanted to justify the gypsy life he led.

'The old man built the business up from nothing,' he told me. 'He can't understand why I don't want to carry it on. Can't forgive me for letting him down, as he sees it. I've tried to explain to him – it's *his* business. Whatever I did, it would still be his, while he's alive, and after he's gone too. I'm not prepared to just fall into that, as my brother is. I've got to do something myself, create something that's *mine* – and the way I want to do it is through my painting. But he wouldn't see it that way. He thinks I'm ungrateful and just cussed on purpose, and perhaps I am!'

I caught the expression behind his eyes, the secret sadness, and I wound my fingers round his, wanting him to know I understood. For long minutes we sat without moving or speaking. Then Sandy said in his old, mocking voice, 'Well, now you know all about me, m'dear,' and I knew he was dismissing the moment and what it had meant.

But as he walked me back across the beach and up the hill towards the schoolhouse there was a joy in my heart and I leaned my head against his shoulder, feeling his vibrant youth and strength, his wild freedom, flow into me. And I thought with the unquenchable confidence of the very young that I'd reached my happy-ever-after.

If only I'd known how wrong I was!

# Four

The nightmare began on a Sunday. Ever since childhood I'd thought of Sunday as a good day, a quiet, peaceful, lazy day between happy, hectic Saturday and Monday when the new week began, and that Sunday in high summer gave me no warning that it was to turn out to be one of the darkest days of my life.

We'd had lunch early, lamb with fresh mint sauce made from the great clumps of mint that overran half the bottom of the garden. Afterwards, Uncle Tony and I washed up together, because Aunt Fran and Serena were going out for the afternoon with Chris and his parents. Then, when the last of the pots and pans were stacked away, I went down to the beach to look for Sandy.

I found him outside the chalet. He'd set up his easel and was hard at work on a seascape. The proprietor of the Lobster Pot Café had promised to hang some of his paintings for sale, he told me, and as the Lobster Pot served a steady stream of customers in summer there was a good chance he'd make a few sales, at least.

I stretched out on the shingle beside him. At this end of the beach too few tides had washed the pebbles to make them into sand, and I loved the feel of the warm stones under the backs of my knees, loved running them through my fingers, sorting them into piles of smooth and rough, slate grey and chalk white. There was something almost sensuous in such total laziness, and I watched Sandy through half-closed eyes, desire and pride warming me inside as the sun warmed my skin.

At last, realizing it must be nearly teatime, I made a reluctant move. Uncle Tony would be expecting me and when Aunt Fran and Serena got back from their outing they'd be pleased to find a cup of tea waiting for them. I stood for a moment looking over Sandy's shoulder at the seascape and thinking it was probably one of the best things he'd ever done. Each wave, silver capped, seemed alive, and with artistic licence Sandy was adding an old-fashioned sailing ship to the scene. It would sell, I was sure of it, but I knew better than to disturb Sandy by saying so, and, dropping a kiss on his ear, I started back across the beach.

'See you later,' he called after me, and I waved an acknowledgement.

I walked up the hill to the schoolhouse. Across the valley I heard the church bells pealing for evensong, and suddenly I felt a sharp stab of inexplicable sadness. There was something so poignantly sweet in the sound – timeless and beautiful and haunting.

I went up the path; pushed open the back door. The kitchen was deserted. I called, 'I'm back!' but there was no reply.

Momentarily, I wondered where Uncle Tony could be. It was unlike him to go out leaving the door open, and besides, when Chris had invited him and Aunt Fran out for the afternoon, he'd said he'd rather stay at home because he had so many things to do. I shrugged mentally. Perhaps he'd gone into the school for something.

I put the kettle on and buttered some scones that I found in a tin in the larder, humming to myself and thinking of Sandy. If he sold enough paintings through the exhibition at the Lobster Pot Café he'd be able to give up the hot dog stall. I knew it was a necessity for him, but I'd never really liked it. Being an artist and living in a ramshackle cabin was romantic. There was nothing romantic about hot dogs.

The kettle boiled and I made the tea, but still there was no sign of Uncle Tony. Perhaps he'd gone upstairs for a nap, I thought. It was a warm, sleepy sort of day and I knew he'd been late home last night. I'd been in bed for what had seemed like hours when I'd heard him come in, and I never went to bed very early.

I went upstairs and knocked at his bedroom door. When there was no reply I opened it quietly and looked in, but the room was empty.

It was then that the feeling of foreboding began to creep through my veins and ran a shiver of ice over my skin. It was like the odd feeling that comes sometimes in dreams: the certain knowledge that something ghastly is about to happen, the wanting to wake up before it does.

I closed the door behind me and went downstairs again. I looked into the lounge, dim behind the curtains that Aunt Fran had pulled against the strong sunlight earlier in the day, but Uncle Tony was not there, and like the rest of the house there was an empty feel about it that added to my unease.

I went out the door into the school that Uncle Tony always used. It was locked, but I peeped through the windows all the same. The classrooms were deserted, chairs stacked on desks, blackboards wiped clean. I went back around the front of the house towards the school garden, which the older boys cultivated, and noticed that the garage doors were closed.

That surprised me. Uncle Tony always left the garage open during the day and the car standing outside on the drive until he went around at night, locking up. Today the drive was as empty as the house had been. And then, from behind the closed doors of the garage, I heard the sound of the engine running, a constant drone. With the traffic changing gear as it went up the hill I hadn't noticed it at first. Now I stood, head cocked, listening as if I still half-believed it was no more than my imagination, puzzled and with the feeling of as-yet unidentifiable dread thickening in my stomach and rising into my throat.

I looked around once more, even now half-expecting Uncle Tony to round the corner. But he didn't, and the fear and the awful suspicion I was trying so hard to hide from erupted suddenly into a volcano of panic. I ran to the garage, calling Uncle Tony's name and rattling at the main doors. They were locked. I stumbled along the side to the personal door, my legs unsteady beneath me, and as I passed the window I could see, through the frosted glass, the dark shape of the car inside. For just a moment I hesitated. Then I pulled the door open.

The fumes hit me immediately, thick, nauseating, choking off breath. I pressed my handkerchief across my face and squeezed past the car to unlock the main doors. For a terrifying moment I thought they were going to stick as they sometimes did. I shook at them wildly, and they gave. I took a gulp or two of blessedly fresh air and went back into the garage.

I could see Uncle Tony half-lying across the two front seats. As I opened the car door he slumped towards me, his head lolling like a rag doll's. I took hold of his shoulders, heaving with all my might, so that he was raised to a sitting position in the passenger seat. Then I slid in beside him.

As I took my weight off his shoulders he slumped sideways once more, this time falling on to me. I opened my mouth to scream but the fumes, filling my throat, stifled it and instead I began to cough. My foot found the clutch, and, thanking God that Uncle Tony had given me a few driving lessons, I banged the gear lever into reverse. The car jerked violently as I pressed down hard on the accelerator and shot backwards with a kangaroo leap, grazing one of the garage doors as it jarred past. I switched off the engine and hung my head through the open window for a moment, gasping and choking, my eyes streaming tears. Then I opened the door and wriggled free of the crushing weight of Uncle Tony's body.

I couldn't move him, I knew. I could only pray that with the doors and windows open the fresh air would revive him. But I think I already knew it was far too late for that. I ran into the house and dialled 999.

'Emergency. Which service do you require?' The girl's cool voice reached me through the buzzing in my ears.

'Ambulance. And police. Oh, hurry! Please, hurry!'

When I'd given all the necessary details, I banged the receiver into its rest and knelt on the cool hall floor, staring with still stinging eyes at Uncle Tony's overcoat hanging on its peg, his sunglasses and cigarette lighter on the hall table. And suddenly the fumes and the panic were fusing inside me into one nauseous wave. I rushed upstairs to the bathroom and was violently, horribly sick.

I was still washing my face when I heard the wail of the ambulance siren. I guessed the sound was carrying across the valley and it would be a few more minutes before it got here. I went into the dining room to wait, and it was then that I saw the piece of paper folded and propped up against the vase of flowers on the table.

I snatched it up, knowing instinctively that it was a note Uncle Tony had left. It wasn't meant for me, I knew, but I was past letting such a trifle worry me. Uncle Tony must have known I would be the one to find him. He owed me some kind of explanation, at least.

*'Dearest Fran,'* Uncle Tony had written. *'Forgive me for what*

*I am going to do but please understand it is the best, the only way. I've hurt you so much, I know, and I never meant to. Now, the best I can do is spare you more hurt and end the torture for us both. I can't live like this any longer.*

*I know you find it hard to understand, Fran, but none of us can help what we are. If I could make it different, I would. But I can't.*

*Look after Serena, and yourself too. I love you both so much, and I so deeply regret the shame and disgrace I have brought on you. I am so, so sorry. Goodbye, my dear . . .'*

I stared at the words, saw them blur on the page. They were riddles to me, riddles without answers. Something had tortured Uncle Tony to the point where he had felt the only way to escape was to take his own life. But what? What?

The ambulance siren wailed outside the window and I went to open the door. Close behind it was a police car driven by a young policeman and in the passenger seat was a ruddy-cheeked sergeant. They leapt out on to the drive, leaving the vehicles where they had screeched to a stop, blue lights still flashing.

Suddenly, I wanted to laugh. It was so funny, like something from a bad old film. The laughter gurgled in my throat and then exploded into hysterical peals. The policemen stared at me, stern authoritative faces above the blue collars of their uniform shirts, and still I laughed, like a dummy in one of the machines on the pier when someone has put a penny in, rocking from side to side and laughing mirthlessly, the laughter of despair.

And then the laughter was turning to sobs and the panic was back, making my throat ache and my eyes burn all over again. I allowed the policeman to take me into the kitchen and pour me a cup of the tea I'd made before the world had turned upside down, but I couldn't drink it. I was too afraid of being sick again.

As the world came back into focus I felt vaguely foolish, like a child who has misbehaved in front of visitors. The policeman who had given me the tea was still hovering and the sergeant was standing by the window, the sheet of paper on which the note was written in his hand.

I spoke to the sergeant. 'That note is private. It's meant for my aunt.'

He smiled a cynical little smile. 'I'm afraid nothing is private in a case like this. It's evidence.'

That jarred on me. I wanted to argue, but I knew there was no point. 'Is he . . . dead?'

I thought I saw a flicker of compassion in the sergeant's eyes. 'They'll try resuscitation, of course. But I don't think they'll be able to do anything for him.'

'You mean he's dead,' I said flatly.

Death was real to me. My parents had died. Yet somehow I hadn't expected it to happen again. Not so soon.

'When did you last see your father alive?' the sergeant asked gently.

'My uncle. He's not my father. He's my uncle. I've been out all afternoon. I haven't seen him since lunchtime.'

'Is your aunt out?'

'Yes. And Serena. She's their daughter. They've gone for a run with her boyfriend's parents.'

'Any idea where?'

'Down the coast, I should think. Devon, maybe. I don't really know.'

The police car driver pulled out a packet of cigarettes and offered it to me. 'Smoke, love?'

I shook my head, wishing for the first time in my life that I did. It steadied the nerves, I'd heard. The policeman put the packet back into his pocket and went to the window. I wondered what was happening outside but I couldn't bring myself to look.

'He seemed all right at lunchtime, your uncle?' the sergeant asked, and I could tell that beneath the kindness was a stubborn determination to get at the truth.

'I think so. I didn't really notice . . .'

How awful. To share a home with someone who was so unhappy they couldn't bear to live any more and not even notice.

'It's too early yet to say for sure, but at the moment it looks like suicide, doesn't it?' the sergeant said, stating the obvious, somewhat. 'Any idea why he should do a thing like that?'

I shook my head.

'Any idea what he meant by this note, then?'

Again, I shook my head.

'Ah, well, I dare say we'll find out,' the sergeant said. 'Now, could you just tell us how you came to find him? I know it's not pleasant for you, but we have to know.'

'Of course.'

I told them what had happened and when I'd finished I pressed my knuckles into my eyes because I wanted to shut out the nightmarish images. But it didn't work. They were still there, imprinted on my retinas.

'Now listen, love,' the sergeant said, 'we shall need a statement from you. Maybe it would be better for you to get it over and done with now, but if you feel it's too much for you, you can come down to the station in the morning. Which would you rather do?'

I said, 'I'll do it now.'

'OK.' He nodded towards the younger policeman. 'PC Manners will write it all down for you, and when you're satisfied it's a correct record of exactly what happened, all you have to do is sign it. All right, love?'

We were about three-quarters of the way through the statement when I heard a commotion in the hall and I began to tremble all over again as I realized Aunt Fran and Serena had come home. For a moment I sat tensely with my hands pressing against the hard rim of the table, dreading the moment when I had to confront them, and come face to face with their grief and shock. Somehow it only made my own seem heavier. Then, as I heard Aunt Fran's shrill 'What is it? What's happened?' and the rumble of the sergeant's voice replying, I used my hands as a lever and pushed myself up.

'Later,' I said to the policeman. 'I'll finish later. I have to tell them . . .'

The policeman followed me to the doorway, catching me by the arm and stopping me.

'You put the kettle on, love,' he said. 'That's the best thing you can do to help. Come on, I'll give you a hand.'

'No – I have to . . .'

The hall seemed to be overflowing with people. The police sergeant, Aunt Fran, Serena, Chris, his mother and father. Chris was supporting Aunt Fran, who looked as if her legs were giving way beneath her.

'Is there any brandy?' the young policeman asked.

'In the sideboard . . .' I'd forgotten about the brandy. It only came out for Christmas and emergencies.

The next ten or fifteen minutes is a complete blur in my memory. Only one thing stands out clearly because it was so incongruous. Chris, touching my arm. 'Are you all right, Dawn?' He was looking at me with what seemed like excessive concern. Anxious for me when he should be thinking only of Serena.

'I'm fine, Chris,' I said shortly. 'Look after Serena. She's the one who needs you.'

Much later I was in the kitchen, alone with Serena and Chris, and I thought that nothing I'd lived through so far, not even my own parents' death, had been this harrowing. Then I had been stunned, disorientated, disbelieving, but I had had only myself to think of. Now I was surrounded by a tide of raw grief.

Throughout the unpleasant practicalities Serena had been dry-eyed and white-faced, looking at everyone with a strange out-of-focus gaze, and Aunt Fran had wept hysterically. The doctor had been and had put her to bed with a sedative, and now that the police, too, had gone, the house was ominously quiet.

'Oh Serena, I am so, so sorry,' I said, knowing it was inadequate. 'I just can't believe it. I shall miss him so. He was always so good to me.'

Serena nodded, her eyes still dazed and distant. 'He was good, wasn't he? I don't understand why he should . . .' Tears welled in her eyes. 'I don't understand any of it!'

Chris put his arm around her. 'Why don't you take one of the tablets the doctor left and try to get some rest?'

Serena shook her head. 'I don't want to. Not yet. I want to know why . . .' It was a wail of anguish.

'You don't. It doesn't matter.' Chris's voice was firm, and it suddenly occurred to me to wonder if Chris knew what it was that Sandy had known, and whether that, whatever it was, had anything to do with Uncle Tony's death.

*Sandy*. As I thought his name, I was overcome with longing for him. I needed him desperately, with every fibre of my being. Serena had Chris. He'd stay with her as long as she wanted him to. And I needed Sandy so badly . . .

'Would you mind very much if I went to see Sandy?' I said. 'He doesn't know yet what's happened.'

Again an expression I couldn't read flickered across Chris's face, but I had the distinct impression he didn't want me to go.

But Serena said, 'Oh Dawn, of course. I'll be all right. Chris will stay with me until you get back. Maybe he'll stay the night. He could sleep on the sofa, couldn't you, Chris? Oh, would you stay? Please?'

Chris turned his back on me. ''Course I will.'

I got my coat and went out. It was beginning to get dark and there was one star beneath a tiny crescent moon far out over the sea. The night air was sweet and faintly salt and everything was so peaceful that it was hard to believe today had happened at all. But there was a dull ache in my head and a bursting in my chest to prove that it had.

I prayed Sandy would be at the cabin. He'd probably have gone on painting until the light began to change, then he'd have packed up his things and cooked himself a supper of sorts. He'd probably wondered why I hadn't come back, but if he'd thought I wasn't coming . . . desolation spread through me as I imagined finding the chalet dark and empty.

As I walked across the beach I saw a glow of light at the window and relief made me tremble. I began to walk faster, then to run, while the shifting, sliding pebbles tried to slow me down. By the time I reached the chalet my breath was coming in quick, painful bursts. The door was ajar, and I pushed it open.

'Dawn!' Sandy half-rose from the bed, where he'd been sitting, pleasure and surprise written all over his face. Then, as he realized something was wrong, his expression changed to concern. 'Dawn – what is it?'

The horrors of the day overwhelmed me suddenly. I went into his arms, shaking from head to foot, clutching at his sweater with convulsive fingers as if it was the only thing that could save me.

'Oh Sandy!' I sobbed his name over and over again.

He held me, asking no questions until my shuddering began to subside, stroking my hair away from my face and crooning to me as softly as if I were a child. 'Hush, my love. Hush, Dawn. It's all right.'

When I could speak again I told him what had happened. As he listened I felt the muscles in his arms tense. But he said nothing until I'd finished. Then he sat me down on the bed, wrapped me in the rough blanket because I was still shivering, and fetched a small bottle of whisky and two chipped cups from a cupboard.

'I've been keeping this for a special occasion, but you could do with it now.'

He poured some whisky into each of the cups and held one to my lips. I drank obediently, coughing at first, then feeling the liquid run a path of warmth down my throat and into my veins.

'Perhaps you'd better have some water with it,' Sandy said. He brought an enamel jug and tipped some water into my cup. 'They think he killed himself, then?' he said.

I nodded, and he put the jug down too hard on the table so that water slopped over on to the tattered oilcloth.

'The bloody fool.'

'Why would he do something like that?' I asked.

He shrugged. 'How should I know?'

'You have a good idea though,' I said. 'I can tell by your face.'

He shrugged again, not answering.

I said, 'Tell me, Sandy. I have to know.'

He hesitated for a long moment, looking straight into my eyes with a thoughtful expression. Then he sat down beside me on the bed and took my hand. 'Did you know your uncle was homosexual?'

I stared at him. The whisky was making me muzzy and the blanket felt heavy and hot around my shoulders. 'No. Uncle Tony? No, you've got that wrong. He's married. To Aunt Fran. He's Serena's father.'

'And he was homosexual. Well, bisexual, anyway,' Sandy said quietly, and the very lack of emotion in his voice was convincing, however hard it was to believe what he was saying.

'How do you know?' I pressed him. He didn't answer, but he looked away and I sensed him retreat into himself a little. 'How could you possibly know?'

He sighed, and I could see him picking his words. 'Why do you think I stopped coming to the house?' he said at last. 'He tried it on with me if you must know.'

Again, the waves of muzziness. I felt sick. 'You mean . . .?'

He must have felt me recoil a little, and he said swiftly, 'I said he *tried* it. I pretty soon made it clear he'd picked the wrong one when he chose me. Ridiculous how naive you can be though.

I really thought he was interested in promoting my work, helping me get by while I got established, and then . . .' He snorted. 'That's what hurt, I suppose. That – and being taken for a bloke who might prostitute himself for the price of a meal.'

'Sandy!' I said, shocked.

'Sorry, I shouldn't have said that. Besides, I suppose I should be charitable. The poor bloke's dead, and all because of something he couldn't help.'

The words Uncle Tony had written came back to me, their meaning all too clear. *'None of us can help what we are . . .'*

'God, but he must have been unhappy,' Sandy said. 'Married to your aunt, a father, a pillar of the community . . . and all the time . . .'

I twisted the cup, empty now, between my hands, thinking of the other young men Uncle Tony had brought to the house, of his football team, and the days and nights spent away from home.

'I suppose he was scared to hell it was going to come out one of these days,' Sandy said. 'What a stink *that* would have been! They'd have had him out of that school before he knew what had hit him. I don't suppose he ever even thought of interfering with any of the kids, but it wouldn't do much good telling their parents that.'

No, I thought, it wouldn't. The parents, angry and shocked, would forget all the good Uncle Tony had done. In a small town like Sturvendor the news would spread like a bush fire and we would all have been caught in the holocaust. This was 1963, but when it came to something like that, it might have been the dark ages. Uncle Tony had known that, and he'd taken what had seemed to him to be the only way out.

'Will it come out?' I asked. 'Is everyone going to know why he did it?'

'I don't know,' Sandy said.

We sat in silence, holding hands as if our physical contact could keep the world at bay.

'How alone he must have felt!' I said at last.

Sandy said, 'We're all alone in the end, Dawn. With people all around, there's nobody else inside that skin of yours.'

I knew what he meant. At birth, at death, throughout all the really profound events, we are all completely and utterly alone. I shivered.

'Dawn, don't.' Sandy pulled my face down into his shoulder. 'Don't take any notice of me. I was just being morbid.'

'But it's true. You were right.' I hesitated. 'I don't want to be alone.'

'You're not alone. I'm here. And if I can't get inside your skin, I can hold you so close that you'll forget we're two people. Just stay still, Dawn, and know I love you.'

For so long I'd dreamed of hearing him say he loved me, yet now it seemed so inevitable that I accepted it without any of the wild elation I'd envisioned I'd feel. But there was a warmth in me that wasn't due entirely to the whisky, and as we lay in each other's arms I felt a oneness with Sandy that I'd never believed possible. I wanted to say 'please make love to me', but there was no need. We both knew it was going to happen anyway, and we wanted it to. We were going to make love not because we were overcome with passion, or because we were afraid, but because the time was right and it was meant to be.

Afterwards, I lay in his arms feeling safer and more cherished than ever before and thinking that if only I could stay here with him forever there was nothing else I could possibly want from life.

'I love you, Sandy,' I whispered into the salt skin of his shoulder, and knew that of all the moments in my life, this was the one I wanted to preserve in memory forever, pure and intact.

Today I'd gone through hell and, at the end of it, I'd found a little bit of heaven. Today I'd been sharply reminded that death can come at any moment, to any one of us, and I'd decided to live my life to the full while there was still time. Today had been terrible and wonderful and now I was so weary that everything seemed dimmed by the need to sleep.

I longed to curl up here on Sandy's bed with the rough, old blanket covering me and his heart beating next to mine, but I knew I must not. To stay out would be to cause Serena and Aunt Fran more worry and distress, so I moved clumsily.

'I'd better be going,'

He stirred lazily. 'I'll come with you.'

We walked up the hill hand-in-hand and at the gate he kissed me.

'Be brave, Dawn,' he said softly.

I looked at the house, the house that had made me so welcome when I had been the one in distress, and the weight came back on to my heart again. Somehow I had to find it in myself to be strong for Serena and Aunt Fran as they had been strong for me. But it was a daunting thought.

'Please love me forever,' I whispered to Sandy.

But the wind had already blown the touch of his lips from mine as I walked away from him up the path.

# Five

The funeral had been meant to be a quiet, family affair, but for someone in Uncle Tony's position that wasn't possible. As I followed Aunt Fran and Serena into the dim, flower-decked church I was astonished at just how many people had come to pay their last respects. The pews were filled with friends and representatives of every organization in town, and banked against the ridge of newly-dug red earth was a mound of wreaths and sprays.

I stood, dry-eyed but distant, looking at the simple oak coffin and wondering how many of these people knew the truth about Uncle Tony's death. They knew it was suicide, of course. There was no way that could be kept secret. But as for the reason behind it . . .?

Aunt Fran had not given the slightest hint that she might suspect, or even know. Outwardly, she remained vague and bewildered, taking refuge in tears when anyone tried to ask her what Uncle Tony had meant by his note. But after the interment, as I went to take her arm to help her back across the rough turf to the path, I was surprised to see a look of pure hatred on her pale, puffy face, and following her gaze I saw a young man standing alone. He was slim, with longish waving hair and dark glasses, and instantly I connected him with the wreath that had arrived at the house this morning bearing only a black-edged card with a single word on it: *Bruno*. This young man, I thought, with a flash of anger, probably knew better than anyone why Uncle Tony had taken his life. I turned back, wanting to protect Aunt Fran from the anguish his presence must be causing her, but her eyes had become vacant and tearful again, and I knew that to keep up the pretence of believing in the happiness of her long marriage was the best way to help her now.

'Wouldn't you think he'd have had the common decency to stay away?' I said to Sandy afterwards. But Sandy looked at me with his coolly challenging gaze and said that Bruno, whoever he was, had had as much right to be at the funeral as anyone else, and probably a good deal more right than those who had simply come to gape.

'You're just trying to be unpleasant,' I told him. 'Poor Aunt Fran has enough to cope with without Uncle Tony's boyfriends turning up.'

'She must have expected it though.' His eyes narrowed. 'It must have been a hell of a strain for her, all these years, pretending to be happily married when all the time . . . And she must have been as scared as he was that it would come out one day. At least now it's over. Once she's got over the shock it might actually be a weight off her shoulders.'

I shook my head. I'd seen Aunt Fran's grief at first hand. I'd had to try to comfort her. Whatever Uncle Tony's predilections she had loved him and been prepared to live an impossible life just as long as they were still together.

'It's all so bloody unfair!' I burst out, angry suddenly.

'Life is unfair,' Sandy said. 'There's not a lot you can do about it.' He paused. 'The only good thing is that Serena doesn't know the truth about her father. She doesn't, does she?'

I shook my head. 'I don't think so. In fact, I'm as sure as I can be. She keeps going on about what a happy family they were, and she just can't understand why her father should have done such a thing. I don't think it would ever cross her mind, even if it was staring her in the face, that he might be . . .' I couldn't bring myself to say the word.

'No. She is a bit unworldly,' Sandy said.

'Unworldly?' I echoed.

'Perhaps that's the wrong word. "Pure" would be a better one. Or "innocent".'

I looked at him sharply. For once he was being absolutely serious. It occurred to me that Sandy never mocked Serena the way he mocked the rest of the world, and I wondered why.

'What are they going to do?' he asked, breaking into my thoughts.

'Do?'

'About somewhere to live.'

'I don't know. They haven't so much as mentioned it.'

In their grief, it hadn't seemed to occur to Serena or Aunt Fran that they were going to have to leave the schoolhouse. It had been their home for so long that they had apparently forgotten that it went with the job, and would soon be needed for the new headmaster. But I hadn't forgotten, and as I had lain awake, wondering about it and worrying, a solution had occurred to me. Now, tentatively, I mentioned it to Sandy. Tentatively, because it meant revealing something I'd kept secret from him.

'I did wonder if I could help out. Get some of my money released so that they can buy a little house . . .' Sandy looked at me sharply and I felt the colour flooding into my cheeks. 'The balance of my parents' estate was put into a trust fund for me,' I explained. 'I'm not supposed to get it until I'm twenty-one, but under the circumstances . . .'

Sandy raised a mocking eyebrow. 'So you're a secret heiress, Dawn?'

'Oh, I wouldn't put it quite like that . . .' I broke off, not wanting to tell him just how well off Daddy and Mummy had been. How we'd had all the material things I knew instinctively he'd hate. 'I don't know how much there is; I never asked and nobody told me. All it was necessary for me to know was that so much was to be paid to Aunt Fran every month for my keep. Mostly, I sort of forget all about it, but if there's some way I can get at it, I'd really like to help Aunt Fran out. She's been so good to me.'

'Not only an heiress, but a philanthropist to boot!' Sandy sneered.

'Shut up!' I turned away, and his fingers curled around my wrist, pulling me back to face him.

'Sorry, Dawn. Take no notice of me. You know what I'm like.'

'Too true I do!'

'For what it's worth, I think it's a great idea. Go for it, sweetheart.'

I lifted my chin. 'Oh, I assure you, I'm going to.'

The next afternoon, wearing my best primrose-yellow suit in an attempt to give me confidence, I called at the offices of Kirby, Hawsett and Dunn, the solicitors in town who were the administrators of my trust fund.

*Why should solicitors' offices seem so awe inspiring?* I wondered, trying hard not to allow myself to be intimidated by the row of brass plates on the wall outside, the highly polished hall and the general air of genteel efficiency. Even the receptionist, sitting behind a desk and flicking pegs on a switchboard, was so superior and well-groomed that she made me feel intimidated and foolish, though she was probably not more than a year or so older than I was.

'Can I help you?' Her voice, like her appearance, was faintly artificial.

I explained what I wanted and her disdain became more obvious.

'You don't have an appointment? Well, if you'd like to take a seat in the waiting room I'll see what I can do. But without an appointment . . . I can't promise anything, I'm afraid.'

She emerged from behind the counter, on which a large Xerox copying machine took up a great deal of space, and led me across the hall to a small room furnished with overstuffed chairs and a small leather-tooled table on which copies of *Country Life* and *Tatler* magazines were piled. I sat nervously on the edge of one of the chairs, trying to decide what I would say to Mr Kirby, Mr Hawsett or Mr Dunn, if one of them should deign to see me.

Ten minutes later the plummy-voiced receptionist was back. 'If you'd come this way, Mr Pidgeon will spare you a few minutes.'

'Mr Pidgeon?' I asked, puzzled.

'Yes. Mr Barrymore Pidgeon. This way.'

Aunt Fran always maintained she did not trust solicitors, and as I was shown into Mr Barrymore Pidgeon's office I began to understand her lack of confidence. He was quite young, with lank brown hair and a rosy, choirboy face, and he was wearing a shirt, the collar of which clearly lacked the stiffeners it required, so that the corners curled upwards at strange angles. He got up as I entered the room, extending his hand, and something about him reminded me of an overeager puppy. The arch young receptionist could terrorize him any time she chose, I guessed.

'Miss Stephens. Delighted to meet you. Now, what can I do for you?' His tone was breezy but slightly nervous and he was fiddling restlessly with a file, tied with pink tape, that lay on the desk in front of him. The details of my trust fund, I guessed.

'I'm wondering if I can access any of my inheritance,' I said directly. 'I'd like to be able to use some of it to help Aunt Fran buy somewhere to live.'

Mr Pidgeon smiled nervously and shook his head.

'That's not going to be possible, I'm afraid.'

'You mean I can't get at the money until I'm twenty-one?' I said, dismayed.

'Or marry. Yes, that would be the case. But I don't think you quite understand the position. There isn't any money.'

I stared at Mr Pidgeon in utter incomprehension. 'What do you mean, no money?'

The young solicitor fiddled again with the pink legal tape around my file. 'I'm afraid your parents' assets amounted to very little,' he said apologetically. 'They were very heavily in debt. There was a little money left over after all the creditors had been paid, but under the terms of the will a certain sum was paid monthly to your aunt and uncle to help with the expenses incurred in providing a home for you, as you no doubt were aware. I'm afraid that ran out a year or so back.'

'You mean they've been paid nothing for my keep for the last year?' I said, shocked and horrified.

Mr Pidgeon smiled his irritating little smile. 'You should have been told, in my opinion. But I expect your aunt and uncle wanted to spare you the embarrassment of knowing you were dependent on them.'

My stomach fell away. I sat stunned.

'Of course, if you would like to see the accounts, you are more than welcome to do so. But you will find everything is in order. I'm very sorry, Miss Stephens.'

Somehow I got to my feet and shook his moist hand once more. Somehow I walked down the staircase and past the plummy-voiced receptionist and out into the street. But I was in a complete daze. No money. There was no money to help buy Aunt Fran a house. No money to see me through drama school. There hadn't been any money for more than a year, and Uncle Tony had hidden from me the fact that I was living on his charity. Which he could ill afford.

When he'd persuaded me to stay on at school he'd known he would have to continue keeping me. Struggling to do his best for his own family, he'd still been prepared to support and do what he thought best for me, a niece who was really none of his responsibility. Gratitude – and shame – overwhelmed me that I had unwittingly been a burden on him, and I wished with all my heart that I could throw my arms around him and thank him.

But I couldn't. He was gone. The only thing I could do now was to ensure I was no longer a burden to Aunt Fran, and perhaps contribute a bit towards the budget that would send Serena to teacher training college, as Uncle Tony had wanted.

I would get a job.

But what? I wandered aimlessly through the town, glancing into shop windows and seeing nothing. The only thing I had ever wanted to do was to become an actress, but that was out of the question now. So what was left? An office? I had no secretarial skills. A shop? The shoe factory on the outskirts of town? Something rebelled inside me at the thought.

Leaving the town, I walked down the long, tree-lined street that led to the seafront. It was a pleasant afternoon, calm as early September often is, with a rich blue sky making the sea look warm and inviting. I glanced up towards the moors. Already they were ablaze with colour, purple heather and golden gorse like splashes of paint on an artist's palette, and soon the red brown of the autumn ferns would add yet another shade to the spectrum. Then, if the weather held, it would be even more beautiful than it was now, the kind of beauty that makes you hurt deep inside.

There were fewer holidaymakers on the beach now, but those who were there were making the most of it. Sunbathers were able to spread themselves out; children, allowed to roam further from their parents without fear of getting lost in a sea of bodies, were shrieking and laughing at the water's edge, carrying bucketfuls of water and sludgy sand to make sandcastles, collecting shells and pebbles and bottle tops.

Unexpectedly, I thought of Serena. 'They are so busy, aren't they?' she'd said once as we watched the children on the beach. 'Playing is a very serious business, isn't it?'

I'd never thought of it that way. To me, children were just children, and if I ever thought wistfully of long summer days that seemed never to end, it was harking back to my own childhood in Canada and the friends who had been lost along with everything else that belonged to that other part of my life.

'I love children,' Serena had said. 'I think I want about six. I can't imagine anything nicer than having a large family, can you? And it would be so exciting and rewarding, watching them grow. Taking care of them. Making sure they were safe and happy.'

'What about the bad things in life?' I'd said. 'You can't keep them in a glass case forever.'

I'd said it, I think, just to differ, because there were times when Serena irritated me, and for some reason that had been one. But now, watching those children at play, I wondered, with a chill of fear, if I might have been closer to the truth than I knew. They were so happy, so wrapped up in their safe little worlds, so blissfully unaware that anything terrible could ever happen to them. Yet there must be troubles and disappointments and even tragedies written into the stars of every one of them. In my present mood I could see none of the good things, the pleasures and the successes, the love passed from generation to generation, the closeness between a man and a woman, and I prayed to the god of the skies and the sea that fate would be kind to those children.

I found Sandy halfway along the seafront, leaning on the hot dog barrow. In deference to his customers he had put a jersey on over his salt-stained jeans, and his bare brown feet were pushed into plimsolls. He might have looked like a tramp, but he didn't. He looked strong and sexy and free.

He tipped an imaginary forelock to me. 'Good afternoon, madam. And what can I do for you? A tasty hot dog, with or without onion?'

I wrinkled my nose at the steamy pans. 'No, thank you. It's not the right time of day for hot dogs.'

Sandy sighed. 'That's what everyone seems to be thinking right now. Business is atrocious. And what are you doing dressed up like that?'

I told him where I'd been, and what I'd discovered. I was hoping for sympathy, but I should have known better.

'Why worry?' Sandy asked airily. 'What's money? My old man's rolling in it, but it doesn't make him happy. Much better to live like I do. If I don't sell any hot dogs or paintings I either starve today, or eat my own hot dogs and starve tomorrow. It makes life so much simpler, doesn't it?'

For the first time I was thoroughly irritated by Sandy's happy-go-lucky philosophy instead of admiring it.

'If it suits you, fine,' I said sharply. 'Maybe you've got no use for money right now, but I have. I wanted to help Aunt Fran, and I can't. I wanted to go to drama school, and now that's out of the question. I shall have to get some grotty job—'

'Why do you need to go to drama school?' Sandy challenged. 'I didn't go to art college, and I'm not doing so badly. If you can act . . . Can you act, Dawn? Or is it just some whim?'

'I think I can.'

'Thinking's not good enough. You have to know it – here.' He spread a sun-browned hand across the front of his jersey. 'And you have to want to do it like you never wanted anything else. So – you tell me. Can you act?'

I looked at him, standing there by his silly hot dog barrow, living proof that if you want something enough you have to go out and get it. He had self-belief. He knew he could paint, and he'd been determined to do it, his way. What other people thought didn't matter to him.

'Yes,' I said defiantly. 'I can act. And I've never really wanted to do anything else.'

Sandy put an arm round my shoulders, giving me a little squeeze. 'That's my girl.'

'The thing is,' I said after a moment, 'I really don't know where to start.'

He grinned at me. 'Let's go home and talk. I'm not going to sell any more of these bloody things even if I stay here all night.'

He slammed the cover over the steaming pans and we walked down the promenade. We must have made an odd couple – the scruffy hot dog seller and the girl all dressed up in a neat yellow suit and high-heeled shoes.

Just before we reached the chalet, Sandy, who had been silent and thoughtful, said, 'Go and see the repertory people. They're the ones to talk to.'

A nerve jumped in my throat. 'You think so?'

'Definitely. Go and see them tomorrow.'

Sandy unlocked the door and I followed him into the chalet.

Somehow, over the summer, the chalet had ceased to appal me. I'd grown used to it, I supposed, so that I no longer noticed the peeling walls and the damp patch on the ceiling.

Sandy kicked off his plimsolls and threw himself down on the bed, propping his arms behind his head, and stared into space. He seemed to have gone into a strange, morose mood.

'What's the matter with you?' I asked.

He didn't answer me directly. He just sighed and went on staring into space. Then, almost out of the blue, he said, 'They stifled me, you know. My father's success stifled me. I told you once before, he built the business up from nothing, but he'd known really hard times when he was a lad, and he wanted things to be different for me and Ray. That we'd want for nothing.'

'Ray. Your brother.'

'Yep. My good-boy brother with his nice wife, couple of kids, two cars . . . the conventional one. He drives me nuts. The way he lives would drive me nuts. Everything handed to him on a plate. His whole life mapped out . . . I just couldn't take it. But they're OK really. Good people. We just don't see eye to eye.' He squinted at me. 'I'll take you home one day and you can meet them all. I think you'd like them, and they'd certainly like you. You're pretty conventional, just like them.'

'Oh, really?' I said, stung.

'Yes, really. You like your luxuries, don't you? Good food and soft beds and nice clothes? That sort of thing means more to you than freedom and just doing what you want to do. That's why I can't help wondering if you can make a go of this acting lark. I'm just not sure you could take living like a gypsy in grotty digs, getting paid a pittance of a wage, never knowing whether you'd have a job this time next week . . . I think that what you really want, Dawn, is security and comfort, and the chance to dress up and look good and impress.'

'That's not true!' I said hotly, though a small voice inside was telling me that there *was* some truth in it. 'You make me sound very shallow.'

Sandy seemed to consider. 'Not *shallow*, exactly. It's just the way you are. You like to pretend to yourself that you're a free spirit like me, but you're not. I don't give a monkey's cuss about what people think of me. You do. As long as I've got a clean pair of jeans and a shirt that's more or less whole, I couldn't give a shit what I wear. You . . . well, take that prissy suit you're wearing. Don't tell me that's *comfortable*.'

Hurt flamed in my cheeks. I didn't know what had got into Sandy, but I didn't like it. 'I have to dress up sometimes,' I said defensively. 'There are occasions . . . Anyway, I thought I looked nice in it.'

Sandy's eyes narrowed. 'You'd look nicer without it.' His fingers fastened round my wrist, and he pulled me down on to the bed.

'Stop it, Sandy. It'll get all creased.'

He laughed. 'Just listen to you! *"It'll get all creased . . ."* Case proved, if you ask me.'

His hands were all over my lovely yellow suit – greasy hands that smelled of fried onion and sausage fat.

'Stop it, I said!' I began to struggle, trying to get up, but Sandy held me fast, pinning me down and kissing me. He'd always been very gentle with me before, but not this time. His mouth was hard on mine, his teeth raking my lips, his hands tearing at the buttons of my suit jacket and pushing up the skirt. There was a raw aggression in him that I'd never encountered before, and though it frightened me a little, it also excited me. For a few moments longer I fought him, then the heat of his passion was melting me, turning my limbs into molten liquid and sending painfully sweet arrows shooting through the deepest parts of me.

'You're mine, Dawn Stephens,' he grated roughly against my cheek. And then he was in me and I was clinging to him as if he were a life raft and I was drowning in a turbulent sea and nothing, nothing in the world, mattered except that he should make love to me.

Afterwards, we lay still, side by side on the rough blanket, the full length of our bodies just touching, our legs entwined, and I felt languorous and sated and blissfully happy. At last Sandy stirred, raising himself on one elbow.

'I didn't hurt you, did I?'

I shook my head. 'No. Well, only a bit . . .'

'That's OK then.'

Another silence. Then, as reality began to creep in, an uncomfortable little thought pricked at me.

'Sandy . . . What if . . .? You don't think . . . I might get pregnant?' For a long moment he said nothing, and the unease I was suddenly feeling grew. 'Sandy . . .?' I could hear the small tremble in my voice.

He grinned then, kissed both my eyes and my nose, and touched his lips lightly to mine. 'I suppose that would mean I'd have to marry you.'

Marry! Sandy and marriage weren't two words you'd ever expect to occur in the same breath. The silken cord of excitement tightened again inside me, and a warmth began to spread from my heart until I was glowing with it.

'But . . . wouldn't you mind?'

'I don't know. Maybe. Maybe not. It might be quite nice to have you and a baby too. Playing at mothers and fathers. Maybe I'd even take enough of the old man's booty to set up home for you.'

'Oh Sandy . . .' This was beyond my wildest dreams. I just couldn't believe it was really happening, that Sandy was saying these things.

I was right not to believe. He shifted then, swinging his legs down from the bed, going away from me.

'It's not going to happen though.'

'It might . . .'

'Well, if it does, you'll just have to get in touch with me and we'll sort something out.'

'What do you mean – get in touch with you?'

'Well, I won't be here, will I?' I'm going up to London for the winter. A couple of my pals have a flat in Earls Court and I'm going to bed down there.'

'But . . .'

'I can't stay here, can I?' Sandy said reasonably. 'I'd freeze in this chalet in winter, and I'd starve too, with no trippers to buy my paintings or my hot dogs. I'll probably come back next summer though. Unless I go to Greece . . .'

My happiness shattered into a thousand brittle pieces. A moment ago I'd thought I held the whole world, everything I'd ever wanted, in the palm of my hand. Then with a few brusque words Sandy had blown it all apart. And I could guess the reason. He wanted me to know beyond doubt that he was a free agent, that he belonged to no one, least of all me, and he could close the door in my face whenever he felt like it. Pain and hurt hollowed me out, so that I felt like a tree struck by lightning and left to rot, an empty, blackened shell.

'Well, I hope you enjoy it,' I said bitterly. I got up and dressed, keeping my back to him so that he would not see the tears shining in my eyes. I didn't want him to know how much he had hurt me. All that was left to me now was my pride.

'Do you have to rush away?' Sandy asked, unbelievably insensitive to my feelings.

'Yes,' I said. 'See you.'

'Oh, right. See you,' Sandy said. I thought he sounded vaguely surprised, as if he really didn't know what he'd done.

I walked out of the cabin and down the beach in a daze of misery. And then, for the first time, I found myself thinking of Sandy's family. Were they hurt by his arrogant refusal to be restricted by any kind of relationship, as I was? It was different, of course, and yet the same. He had a father who had wanted only to give his son all the things he himself had never had, and a mother who was sure to worry and wonder about him. But he had rejected them, shored himself up on an island of self-sufficiency that was not only his refuge but his pride. To him it would be a point of honour to take nothing from them, to stay away from family gatherings, to show no weakness in any shape or form. And they probably hurt, just as I was hurting now, those unknown people who had given life to the man I loved.

I took a pebble from the sea wall and hurled it as far as I could, watching it bounce down the steep bank to the sea, then roll and lie still, its energy spent.

In that moment I almost hated Sandy, hated him because there was no way I could break through the wall he erected around himself, no way I could hurt him the way he hurt others. And the pain and the fury and the disappointment inside me suddenly boiled over into a determination that fired me up.

'I'll show him!' I grated, and the wind from the sea took my words and tossed them back at me. 'I'll show him I don't need him any more than he needs me. I'll make my own way. And I'm starting right now!'

# Six

Next morning I got dressed in pedal pushers and a little strappy top that I thought looked actressy without being over the top and went down to the Gaiety Theatre. The main doors were locked. I should, of course, have known they would be, but as I'd walked through them unchallenged once before, I'd somehow expected to be able to do the same again. Now, standing forlornly on the pavement, I felt as deflated as a pricked balloon at a children's party.

I gazed at the photographs on the hoarding by the door as I had done so many times before, and this time, instead of inspiring me, I found the beautiful, confident faces daunting. *What right did I have to think I was good enough to step into their magic world?* they seemed to be asking.

Nervousness almost got the better of me. The company would be rehearsing, for sure. Maybe it would be better if I came back this evening, after the show, and tried to speak to Hunter Hylton then. But I wasn't sure I'd be able to summon up the courage if I hesitated, and in any case, would he be any more pleased to see me when he'd just finished a tiring show than he would be now? Better to take the bull by the horns and get it over with.

My heart in my mouth, I turned my back on the disdainful faces staring at me from the hoarding and walked around the corner of the dilapidated building to the green-painted stage door. Then, taking a deep breath, I turned the handle, opened the door, and went inside.

I found myself in a dark, narrow passage that smelled of dust and stale greasepaint. From somewhere inside the theatre I could hear the sound of raised voices – a girl's, shrill and almost hysterical, and a deep resonant voice, shaking with anger, that I recognized as belonging to Hunter Hylton. At first I assumed the new play was in rehearsal, then, as I stood in the semi-darkness, wary about interrupting them, I heard the clatter of footsteps on concrete coming closer, and a girl materialized from the gloom, half-running, her arm doubled across her face. I tried to sidestep, but she cannoned into me and we both reeled back into the door, pushing it open. In the rush of grey light I saw the tears on her face, then the door slammed after her and she'd gone.

It was no rehearsal that I'd overheard, then, but a real, blazing row. Again I quailed. Hunter Hylton in the sort of mood that could reduce one of his company to tears was hardly likely to be amenable to me.

'Bloody fool of a girl!' His booming voice was close suddenly, as if only a thin sheet of plasterboard was separating me from him. 'What makes her think she'll ever be an actress?'

I went rigid, thinking for a moment that Hunter Hylton was talking about me. Stupid, really, but I was so overcome with nervousness, and the line seemed horribly apt. Then I heard a woman's voice.

'Don't work yourself into a rage, darling. You know how bad it is for you.'

'I have a show to put on tonight, woman! A show! For my public! I am surrounded by incompetent, hysterical, stage-struck fools! Do you know what that girl did? She played a brass band sound effect when it should have been the ghostly wailing of the lost child. She ruined the scene. She ruined the play! I don't care if I never see her again . . .'

'It's a rehearsal, darling. It didn't happen in front of your public. Please God it won't. But if we don't get on with rehearsal there won't be a show at all. Come on now, darling, calm down, please . . .'

From somewhere in the general direction of the stage I heard the sound of someone hammering, and it seemed to echo the thud of my own heart. I could hardly believe the luck that had brought me here at this moment, when there might, just might, be a vacancy. I took a deep breath and walked around the partition that separated me from the Hyltons.

'Could you spare me a moment, Mr Hylton?'

Close to he was shorter than he looked on stage, but his chest, under the garishly striped shirt, was like a barrel. Grubby fawn slacks hung low beneath a formidable paunch, and when I raised my eyes to his face I saw plump, flushed cheeks, a cowlick of hair falling over his forehead, and eyes smaller and meaner than they looked when they were rimmed around with eyeliner.

His mouth tightened; eyebrows shot up into the lick of hair. 'Darling! Who the hell are you?'

'I'm Dawn Stephens,' I said. 'And I'd like you to give me a job.'

He stood back, looking me up and down in an exaggerated way that might have been business in a scene. I waited, my chin up, returning his stare with an assurance I was far from feeling. At last, when his pause had lasted just long enough for impact, he said, 'A job, darling? What kind of a job?'

'I want to act,' I said.

The eyebrows went up again. He spread his hands expansively. 'You want to act. And what makes you think you can?'

'I know I can.'

'Have you had any training?'

'Not formal. But I've always heard repertory is the best training you can get.'

'You mean you've never set foot on the boards, but you expect me to give you a job.' He patted his pockets, then turned to his wife, who was standing just behind him, watching me through narrowed eyes. 'Where are my bloody cigarettes, darling?'

'You smoked them,' she said implacably.

'Haven't *you* got any, for God's sake?'

'You smoked them too.'

He flicked the lick of hair off his forehead with an impatient gesture and waved his hand at me, dismissing me. 'I'm sorry, darling, I haven't a vacancy for a student.'

'What about the girl who just left? You just sacked her, didn't you? I could take her place.'

For the first time Hunter Hylton seemed to have let slip his direction of the scene. The muscles in his plump cheeks flexed and slackened and he jerked convulsively at the lick of hair. Into the silence Evelyn Hylton said, 'If it's any of your business, she has not been sacked.'

'That's not the way it sounded to me,' I argued, scared but determined not to show it. After all, I had nothing to lose.

'She'll be back,' Evelyn said. 'You're wasting your time, Miss Stephens.'

Another spasm of rage darkened Hunter Hylton's face and he brought his bunched fist down hard on to his plump thigh.

'Damned if she will! I've had quite enough of her hysterics and her incompetence.' He glared at his wife and I sensed the undercurrents of some private duel. 'You say you can act,' he said to me. 'Will you audition for me?'

I lifted my chin, though my knees were trembling.

'Of course.'

'Go out and get me some goddam cigarettes then, and I'll talk to you again.' Like everything else, it was a performance, and this was his exit line. He turned and swept away, pausing only to call over his shoulder, 'Senior Service'.

I was in such a tizzy it wasn't until I reached the kiosk on the corner that I realized he hadn't given me any money. For a panicky moment, as I searched in my bag for my purse, I thought I must have left it at home. Then I found it, tucked into a corner, bought a twenty packet of cigarettes and walked back along the seafront. My heart was thudding a tattoo and my fingers gripped the packet of Senior Service so tightly that I was in danger of squashing them.

I'd got my chance. But could I pull it off? I'd do my big Portia speech, I decided, but this was a very different proposition to starring in the school play. The praise and acclaim I'd received from teachers and parents would mean nothing now. In a few minutes I was going to have to walk on to the stage of a real theatre and perform in front of people who did it for a living. My stomach churned and waves of weakness sucked through me. The temptation to chicken out almost got the better of me. If I simply went home that would be the end of it. I'd never know for sure that I wasn't good enough and never could be. But I kept on walking, breathing deeply to try to calm my screaming nerves.

If I gave up now, I knew I would never forgive myself.

In the theatre rehearsals had begun again. I followed the echoing voices along the dim corridor and as I climbed three dented wooden steps I was surprised to find myself looking through the folds of musty black tabs on to the stage. It was hardly larger than our stage at school, I thought, vaguely disappointed.

For a few moments I stood watching the actors. Hunter Hylton was doing his best to direct at the same time as playing a leading role, whilst behind him two stage hands were erecting some flats into a traditional box set. No one seemed to notice me. Then Hunter Hylton made a dramatic exit, almost colliding with me.

'Ah, there you are my angel!' He strode back on stage and called to his cast, 'Take a break everyone. We'll leave it there for the moment.'

He came back to me, holding out his hand and flicking his middle finger against his thumb. I handed him the packet of Senior Service and he tore it open. A match flared and he inhaled.

'Right then. Do your stuff. I'll go out front to watch you.'

'Now?' I said weakly.

'Well, give me time to hop down into the house!' The nicotine seemed to have restored his good humour. Chuckles of appreciation came from the watching company. A couple of them were standing in the wings, but two or three followed Hunter into the stalls. They wanted to see just how awful I would be, I thought in terror, and once again my nerve almost failed me. I was quite sure that my voice would either come out as a squeak or fade completely into one of the nervous gulps that were spasming in my throat, and I couldn't remember the first line of my speech, let alone the rest of it.

Yet somehow I walked with pretended assurance to the centre front of the stage and stood there with the lights in my eyes as if this were something I did every day.

'Ready!' Hunter Hylton's voice boomed from somewhere in the inky blackness and I took a deep breath.

'The quality of mercy is not strained . . .'

As the first lines left my lips I got the measure of the theatre and the sound of my voice reaching the far wall and bouncing back to me lifted my confidence. Nerves gave a fine point to my words and I so lost myself in being Portia that when I finished I half-expected the play to go on around me until I remembered where I was.

'Something else?' Hunter Hylton called from the stalls. 'Can you give me something else? Comedy, perhaps?'

The nerves returned all of a rush. I hadn't expected to be asked to do anything else, and I'd given Portia my all. I didn't think I knew any comedy. Always it was the drama and the tragedy that appealed to me. Then inspiration struck and in my head I heard my own voice, with a thick North Country accent, intoning, *And a great big lion ate Albert . . . And he in his Sunday suit too . . .* I'd learned that monologue one Christmas to amuse the family. These professionals would probably think I was completely mad, but it was the only thing I could think of. I took a deep breath, stuck out one hip and, leaning heavily on it, began.

When I finished there was silence for what seemed like a lifetime, then somebody laughed, and Hunter Hylton called, 'Come down here, my sweetheart.'

My knees were trembling and weak from reaction, but somebody gave me a hand and I scrambled down over the footlights. Hunter was lighting another cigarette from the butt of the first.

'So,' he drawled, 'you think you can act?'

I didn't answer. I couldn't bluff any longer and besides my throat was too dry to speak. He stubbed out the spent cigarette and looked at me steadily. 'Well, I think you can act too.'

I stared back at him. Suddenly, I wanted to cry. I had to open my eyes very wide and bite down hard on my lip to stop the tears.

'Now look, my angel, we finish our season here in three weeks' time. It's not worth my while taking you on now. But if next spring, say February or March at the latest, you still want to do this, write to me at this address.' He jammed his cigarette into his mouth, narrowing his eyes against the smoke, and pulled a grubby business card from his wallet.

'But . . . I thought there was a job now . . .' I said helplessly.

He flicked at his hair impatiently and I knew that whatever clash of wills he and Evelyn had had over the girl who'd run out, Hunter had been the loser.

'Tempers sometimes flare in this business, sweetheart,' he said carelessly. 'And at this end of the season even Maura's limited experience is better than none. Now, let me tell you terms on which I'll take you. You'll be classed as a student. The pay will be lousy and you'll be expected to do everything a junior ASM would do, and a lot more besides. ASM – Assistant Stage Manager – you're familiar with the term?'

'Um . . . Yes . . .'

'Fit yourself up with as big a wardrobe as you can in case I want you to do some acting. Remember you could be playing anything from a maid to a debutante and you can't go on week after week wearing the same old thing. We have a regular local audience as well as the holidaymakers. You did realize you have to provide your own wardrobe, didn't you? I'm afraid our budget doesn't extend to dressing the cast.'

'Of course,' I said faintly, though I hadn't realized it at all. When I'd played Portia at school the needlework teacher had kitted me out with an absolutely splendid costume.

Hunter reached out and patted my arm. 'It won't be easy, sweetheart, but I promise one thing. I will make a pro of you.' Seemingly satisfied with his exit line, he turned his back on me and began rounding up the scattered cast for rehearsal.

Outside the theatre I found I was still shaking with nervousness and excitement. I stood for a moment with both hands pressed against my mouth as the momentousness of what had just happened washed over me in waves.

Hunter Hylton had said I could act. From an old professional like him it was the greatest accolade I could have wished for. And he was going to give me a job next year. It didn't matter that I was going to be a student; it didn't matter that I'd have to do all kinds of jobs for a pittance. I was going to work in the theatre, and I could scarcely believe it.

Impatience tugged at me and I wished desperately that I could begin right away. But there would have been no way I could afford to buy the sort of wardrobe Hunter wanted me to equip myself with. And, in any case, I would have felt dreadfully guilty if I'd put the unknown Maura out of a job. I had just been very, very lucky to have turned up at the theatre when I had, when Hunter had been looking for a safety valve for his temper tantrum. At any other time he probably would have sent me away without even auditioning me.

In a daze of excitement I walked down towards the beach. It was almost lunchtime, and by the miniature golf course I could see Sandy doing a good trade with his hot dog barrow. Momentarily, a jagged pain knifed through my heart as I remembered the way he'd treated me yesterday, but I wasn't going to let anything spoil my moment of triumph. It could be, I thought, that he'd been simply goading me when he'd talked about going to Greece. And I was too happy to even consider the possibility that things might not work out between us. We had something very special; that was what counted. I skipped up to him.

'I did it, Sandy,' I said, oblivious of the queue of customers and unable to keep silent a moment longer. 'He auditioned me, and he'll take me on next season!'

Sandy grinned at me, squeezing tomato sauce along a sausage. It was as if our spat of yesterday had never been.

'Great! Well done! I'll pack up here in a minute, and we'll go and celebrate.'

I waited whilst a never-ending stream of customers filed past the barrow, and the exhilaration was bursting out of me and surrounding me with warmth. When the last hungry little boy had trailed away from the barrow, biting into his bun and squirting tomato sauce down his chin, Sandy and I went to the Anchor Inn and sat either side of a table made out of a beer barrel in the public bar. Then, over half-pints of scrumpy, I told Sandy every detail of my triumph.

'Glamour on glamour!' he said when I'd finished. 'Chris will never be able to keep his eyes off you now.'

'*What?*' I looked at him over the rim of my glass. 'What are you talking about?'

Sandy shrugged. 'Surely you know the way that poor fellow feels about you? He's potty about you.'

'Rubbish!' I said firmly. 'You are joking, I take it?'

'No, I'm not, actually,' Sandy said. 'Sometimes I think he only goes out with Serena so that he can see more of you.'

'Don't be so silly!' I said, dismissing the idea. 'He thinks the world of Serena.'

Sandy didn't reply. Then, quite suddenly, he asked, 'So what are you going to do between now and next spring?'

For one heady, crazy moment I thought he might be going to suggest I went to London with him. But he didn't.

'I don't know,' I said, and the bubbles of happiness were turning flat on my tongue, like champagne left uncorked for too long. 'But it doesn't really matter now, does it?'

* * *

It didn't matter. Viewed as simply a way of earning a living between autumn and spring, all the jobs that had seemed such depressing prospects before suddenly seemed quite acceptable.

After much thought I decided to apply to the shoe factory for a job. The piece-workers there were, I knew, rather well paid, and for the moment having some cash was of primary importance. With a fat wage packet I could give Aunt Fran a fair allowance and still save for the wardrobe Hunter Hylton had said I'd need. I had the sense, too, to realize a little in the bank would not come amiss; the profession I was entering was a precarious one.

I had expected Aunt Fran to be totally opposed to the idea but to my surprise she seemed to accept it. Her first overwhelming grief over Uncle Tony's death seemed to be settling into apathy and although she murmured the sort of stock phrases she seemed to feel were expected of her, there was little heart in them.

'Just so long as it doesn't mean you'll be wanting to leave school too, Serena,' she said vaguely. 'Your father would be very upset if he thought you were going to end up . . .' Her voice tailed away and she looked at me uncertainly, biting her lip.

I was still too pleased with my achievement to be hurt by the insinuation. I'd always known, after all, that however hard she might try to treat us the same, Aunt Fran really didn't mind what I did as long as Serena was all right. Although I knew that was only natural, there had been times when coming a poor second had left me feeling lonely and raw. Now it simply filled me with a glorious sense of freedom. Sandy had had to break ties and traditions to gain his independence. My ties had been severed long ago by the tragedy of my parents' deaths. I could do exactly as I wanted without hurting anyone.

By the time the Hunter Hylton Repertory Company left and the doors of the Gaiety were boarded up for another year, I had begun work at the shoe factory. It was a boring job, and already I hated it, but every day I pushed myself harder and harder against the clock, knowing that the more shoes I stitched the more money I would earn to help me attain my dream.

Although it was October, summer seemed unwilling to concede defeat. From the bench where I worked I could look out on to the factory garden with its neatly laid out lawns edged with clouds of still-brilliant rose bushes, and the warm wind carried their fragrance through the open window to mingle with the smells of leather and machine oil. In spite of my impatience for spring to come, poignancy, bitter-sweet, twisted in me as I looked out at the russet trees and the deep blue of the sky, and with all my being I willed the sun to go on shining, the roses to continue to bloom. While the weather held, Sandy stayed on. But with the first cold blast of winter and the first lowering of leaden skies with no crack of blue to give him hope, he would pack his belongings into his canvas holdall and thumb a lift to London. When he did, a part of me would go with him, and a part would die, like the roses and the gorse, until spring wakened them again.

I lived those last weeks with him knowing a little of how a person must feel faced with the terminal illness of a loved one, knowing that time is short and there is still so much to do. Every possible joy is squeezed out of every fleeting minute, but the awareness only lends wings to the hours, and as they slip by, never to be recaptured, a panic begins somewhere deep inside. At night I lay awake listening to Serena's even breathing and reliving every minute I had spent with Sandy, processing it for my memory, storing it intact for the long winter days ahead when I knew I would begin to doubt whether summer – and Sandy – had ever really been at all.

At last the respite the weather had lent us came to an end. With no money left to pay another week's rent or buy food, Sandy decided it was time to leave for London. Desperately hoping to buy a little extra time with him I offered him my savings, but he refused.

'You need every penny, Dawn, for your future,' he said. 'And, in any case, I pay my own way. My father couldn't understand that, and I don't expect you to. But when I take money from someone I'm obligated to them, and I don't want to be obligated to anyone.'

'I understand,' I said, and I did. But understanding didn't take the sting from the rejection.

Sandy left on a Sunday morning. I sat on the bed in the chalet and watched him pack his things, and the desolation was a lump in my throat, choking off breath. Then, when he took the key from its rusty nail behind the door for the last time and said,

'Well, that's it, love,' I threw myself at him, clinging to him as if I could somehow stop him from going.

He kissed me. 'It won't be so long,' he said. But I could sense that already he was looking forwards, wondering what was in store for him in London, impatient to be gone. And I thought, *Oh Sandy, have I lost you forever?* and I wasn't sure whether the salt on his cheek was from the sea breeze or my tears.

I went with him to the main road, wanting to hold on to his hand, but discouraged by the easy swing of his arm, and feeling that already he had put me behind him. I waited with him until a car responded to his signalling and stopped, and then I watched with leaden hopelessness as he ran up the road to where it had pulled in, calling 'Bye, love!' over his shoulder and giving me the most casual of waves.

The car pulled away, disappearing around the bend. But still I stood, gazing up the empty road, unable to believe Sandy had really gone. He'd come back in a minute, surely, swinging his bag, grinning at me and telling me that he couldn't go without me.

In imagination I heard his voice so clearly that I almost held out my arms to him, and it was only when I brushed the tears from my eyes and saw that the road was as deserted as before that the stark reality came home to me.

'Stop it, you silly bitch!' I chastised myself. But my throat was aching with tears and the words came out on a strangled sob.

Two weeks later Aunt Fran heard of a house to let. The owners, a retired couple, were going to South Africa for six months to visit their daughter. They would be pleased to let Aunt Fran have it for a nominal rent, simply to know that someone they could trust would be looking after it whilst they away, keeping it aired and making sure vandals didn't throw stones through the windows.

As usual, Aunt Fran dithered, but Serena, surprisingly and comfortably in charge, made the decision for her.

'It will give you the chance to look for something more permanent without having to make up your mind in a rush,' she said. 'It's just what we need.'

So we set about the formidable task of breaking up the home that Aunt Fran and Uncle Tony had shared from the very early days of their marriage. Again, Aunt Fran withdrew into apathy, leaving most of the work to Serena and me, and between us we sorted the furniture, selling some and putting some in storage, and leaving the bits and pieces that would be useful to the new headmaster, a youngish man who had decided to get married as soon as the house became vacant.

We left one Thursday evening in November, closing the door behind us quickly before our emotions could get the better of us, and carrying our suitcases and the last few bits of our personal belongings down the three big stone steps to where our taxi was waiting.

I looked back at the house, with its bare windows letting the last of the evening light into its hollow rooms, and knew with certainty that another chapter of my life was ending.

# Seven

Winter passed on leaden feet – a hard, biting winter when the snow hung for weeks on the fields and gardens in dirty, frozen ridges and the sky and sea merged into leaden grey.

For a while when we moved into the new house it seemed that Aunt Fran might emerge from her apathy. It was a large, pre-war semi-detached on one of the myriad of small avenues that led to the seafront, and in its half-furnished state it had a coldness about it that contrasted sharply with the small, overcrowded rooms of the schoolhouse. This had seemed to act as a catalyst on Aunt Fran who was, above all, a homemaker, and for some weeks she roused herself, changing the bleached linen cushion covers and bedspreads for her own bright chintzes and chivvying Serena and me into helping her rearrange the furniture. Then, quite suddenly, her effort spent, she lapsed back into the odd, off-key limbo that was so disconcerting to see.

'What she needs is a job,' Serena said anxiously. 'It would take her out of herself, and goodness knows we could do with the money.'

But all Aunt Fran wanted to do was return to infant teaching – what she had done before she married Uncle Tony – and since she refused to leave Sturvendor the chances of finding a vacant post were slim.

Sandy wrote to me once or twice, brief, hardly legible accounts of life in London, and I wondered what he was hiding with the meaningless phrases. Although I longed for his letters, instead of bringing him closer to me they seemed somehow only to deepen my loneliness, and I couldn't help comparing him with Chris, who came to see Serena almost every day. Seeing them together was more hurtful to me than I could have believed possible, and when they were at the house I tried to keep out of their way.

With the miles separating us, I could see all too clearly how tenuous my relationship with Sandy really was, and at times I tried very hard to put him out of my mind. I even went out once or twice with local boys who asked me. But it did no good, and only left me more certain there could never be anyone but Sandy for me. For better or for worse, I loved him, and I could only exist in the hope that he might be missing me just half as much as I missed him.

Christmas came and went, a wretched time when we all pretended a jollity we were far from feeling. I'd written to ask Sandy to stay, thinking that not only would it mean I'd see him again, but also that if he were here it would detract a little from the awful family vacuum Uncle Tony's death was bound to create at the festive season. But he'd replied that he'd promised his parents to spend the holiday with them, and although I knew they saw little enough of him, the knowledge that he'd turned down my invitation in their favour was an extra twist in the spiral of my misery.

Spring, thankfully, came early. The skies were blue and open even before the first new buds had formed on the trees, and their stark, bare arms reached for the sun with a majesty that was both noble and touching. The sea was brittle blue and the silver-capped waves shimmered and danced in tribute to the passing of the blustering storms of winter that had made them grey and yellow monsters.

With every sign of spring my heart lifted, and the day I found a drift of purple crocuses under the plane tree in the garden I wanted to skip and sing because it was the only way to let out all the unexpected joy that was trapped inside me.

In February I wrote to Hunter Hylton and waited for his reply in an agony of suspense. When the badly-typed Manila envelope fell through the letter box I was almost too nervous to open it. Then, as I read the contents, my nervousness was transformed into heady excitement, and I didn't know whether to laugh or cry. Unbelievably, Hunter Hylton hadn't forgotten me. This season, when the repertory opened in Sturvendor, I would be joining the company.

For the next weeks I hardly had time to spare Sandy a thought. I handed in my notice at the factory. I bought clothes I thought would be useful to me. I counted off the days in my diary like a school child waiting for the end of term.

And then one afternoon, coming home from work, I pushed open the door of the house that was at last beginning to seem like home and heard a voice I instantly recognized, yet could hardly believe was real, coming from the kitchen.

'Sandy!' For a moment I stood wrapped in wonder, then, with a rush of trembling eagerness, I half-ran down the hall.

He was sitting at the kitchen table, a mug of tea between his hands, looking somehow oddly shy. He was thinner than I remembered him, and his tan had gone, leaving his skin pale and washed out. But when he smiled at me, his face creasing into its familiar lines, my heart thudded, and for the moment I wanted nothing but to simply stand there and look at him, relishing the taste of a dream suddenly become reality.

'Hello, Dawn,' he said casually.

'Hello.' My own voice was unsteady, but it didn't matter. Nothing mattered but that he was here.

'Isn't this a lovely surprise?' Aunt Fran was saying. Her face was flushed with pleasure and she looked like her old self again.

For a moment I couldn't speak and Aunt Fran went on, 'You know Dawn is going to work in the theatre, I suppose, Sandy? What do you think about it?'

'I think she's going to be a star,' Sandy said, and behind the flippancy his eyes were appraising me, devouring me, burning with the same fire that was licking through my own body.

I wanted to go to him then. I wanted to put my arms around him and feel his body, hard and lean, against mine. Desire was a physical ache in me, and I knew the feeling was mutual. But Aunt Fran, regardless as ever of our need to be alone, went on fussing and chattering and we had to content ourselves with making love with our eyes.

'Are you here for the whole summer? Where are you staying, Sandy?'

'Same place. My chalet.' He was still watching my every move. 'I thought the winter might have finished it off, but it's still standing.'

I'd thought winter might finish it off too. It had been one of the things that had tormented me when the frost had driven hard cracks into the earth, and more often than I'd cared to admit I'd walked to the end of the beach, tapping experimentally on the flimsy walls and peering through the grimy windows.

'I'm sure it can't be good for you there,' Aunt Fran said. 'You'll—'

'Get pneumonia,' Sandy finished for her. 'I know, you've told me that before. Don't worry, I won't. And if I have to die, I'd like it to be here anyway. There's nowhere on God's earth quite like Sturvendor.'

I looked sharply at Aunt Fran, but the reference to death had gone unnoticed.

'What have you been doing with yourself all winter?' I asked. His eyes crinkled wickedly, and I laughed. 'Just the censored bits, if you don't mind.'

Odd how I could joke about my deepest fears now he was here with me and our love was an almost tangible thing again.

'Painting,' he said. 'I had some things accepted for minor exhibitions, and I sold some too. And I got a couple of magazine commissions. I don't think I shall need to bother with hot dogs this year.'

'What are magazine commissions?' Aunt Fran asked.

'Illustrations. Very commercial. But they pay well.' He grinned at me. 'It's funny the way you can't really do without money, however hard you may try.'

'Welcome to the world, Sandy,' Aunt Fran said.

We finished tea and I offered to help Aunt Fran with washing the dishes – Serena had gone direct from school to Chris's house, and wouldn't be home until much later.

Aunt Fran smiled her old, bright smile. 'I can do these. Take Sandy into the lounge. Go on – no arguments.'

We left her humming as she ran water into the yellow plastic bowl in the sink.

The lounge was dim in the failing light. There was no fire, just a pile of crumpled red paper to disguise the bare grate. A lounge fire was a luxury we couldn't afford now. I indicated the sofa but Sandy ignored me. He caught at my arm without speaking, turning me to him. For a long, timeless moment we looked at one another, and it was as if we were not two people, but one. Then he pulled me close and all the aching frustrations of the past months were drowned in one soaring, dizzying wave of love.

I tried to say 'Sandy', but I couldn't speak. Then his lips were on mine, one hand tangling my hair, the other cupping my breast, and there was no need for words. We clung together, our bodies straining for contact, our need too great for caution.

As if from a long way off I heard the clatter of plates as Aunt Fran washed up in the kitchen, but it might have been another world.

'Tonight?' Sandy said. 'You'll come back with me tonight?' His voice was ragged.

I tried to nod, my face buried in the cleft between his chin and shoulder. 'Yes,' I whispered.

And I knew in that moment that whatever Sandy did, however much he hurt me, as long as there was breath in my body I'd forgive him and love him still.

The Hunter Hylton Repertory Company arrived the first week in April, and the dream I'd lived for so long became reality. Not that I was doing much acting – that, I soon discovered, was limited to very small parts, which I had to somehow manage to do in between being the company's general dogsbody. But I didn't mind. I'd happily have swept floors just to be part of it. And sometimes I did – the stage, anyway, such as the time when a cushion burst, spreading feathers everywhere like a snowstorm.

Usually, I was Assistant Stage Manager, chasing around in my oldest pair of jeans and making sure the assortment of props were where they were supposed to be. Newspapers and artificial flowers that had to be changed between acts to give the illusion of the passage of time, candlesticks, stuffed birds – all were my responsibility. I lived in terror that the matches wouldn't be on the table when the leading man wanted to light a cigarette. I worried whether I would ring the telephone when I was supposed to, whether a door handle would come off in someone's hand, if we would all choke on the saltpetre fumes that provided the smoke for an imaginary stable fire, if the set was going to fall down. And I loved it all.

I found the small parts fantastically rewarding. It was a revelation to discover there was far more fun in playing an adenoidal Cockney maid for two and a half pages than doing three whole acts as the glamorous, predictable, boring lead. And the easy relationships within the company pleased me, as did the feeling that at last I was doing something I really wanted to do.

I made friends with a girl called Julie Sawyer. She was some years older than me, in her middle twenties, and quite experienced. She usually played leads and looked fantastic on-stage, but off it she was scruffy and slap-happy, wearing old sweaters and mules and a scarf tied turban fashion over her hair.

Julie was very blasé about the stage.

'I'd get out tomorrow if I could,' she told me, 'but there's nothing else I can do, except go on the streets, and I don't think I fancy that.'

I thought she was joking, but she assured me she was quite serious.

'When I was your age, I thought the world was my oyster,' she said, pulling on her cigarette. 'I was headed straight for stardom, or so I thought. Going to be the new Marilyn Monroe or something. The stage used to turn me on – you know, the lights and the music and the feel of an audience out there watching you. And the curtain calls when you smile into the spotlight that's blinding you, and your name on the programme and your photograph outside the theatre . . . Oh, I loved it all, and I suppose in a way I still do, but . . .'

'But what?'

'But now I've seen the other side too. I've seen girls who sleep around in the hope of getting to the top and end up degraded and hurt and still absolutely nowhere because they simply weren't good enough, but the guy who was accepting their favours had too much sense to tell them that. I've been out of work for so long I've been dead sure I'd never work again. Now, instead of enjoying the season I'm doing, I'm thinking in the back of my mind: *But what about the autumn? What will I do then?* I don't suppose you feel that way yet, kid. But you will.'

I had no answer for her. I hadn't thought of it that way. For me each day was a glorious new beginning, and at the end of the season there was a whole new page in the book of my life on which nothing, as yet, had been written. I refused to believe that page was going to be blotted with disillusion.

And yet behind Julie's blasé front I thought I could glimpse the girl she had once been: a pretty, dimpled, golden girl who thought she might be the next Marilyn Monroe. That was the sort of dream people laughed at if you said it out loud, and yet deep inside, if they were honest, they probably had a dream that was just as crazy. There must be hundreds of would-be Jim Clarks and Lulus under all sorts of unlikely skins up and down the country. There must be a little dream of Rod Laver or Maureen Connolly in every kid who is good with a tennis racquet, and if the young rural district councillor admitted the truth, his dream would probably be of Westminster and Downing Street.

But for some of them the dream became reality. So why not me? Even if I never became a star, I could be successful and happy in my career. There was no reason for me to become one of the bitter and jaded.

'Go to drama school,' Julie advised. 'It doesn't mean you'll automatically be a success, but it does help.'

'I couldn't afford it,' I said.

Julie stubbed out her cigarette and pushed the packet into her jacket pocket. 'Try for a scholarship. There are all sorts of ways. Don't fall into the trap of being like me. It's bad for the soul to be bitter and twisted. You know what I wish? I wish I was a farmer's wife, with cows to milk and hens to feed and half a dozen strapping sons to look after me in my old age.'

I laughed. Imagining Julie as a farmer's wife was just too funny. But at that time I hadn't yet come to realize the tragedy of the girl, and the way she would make jokes about the things that really mattered to her, so much that to be serious about them was more than she could bear.

When I told her about Sandy she shrugged and raised her eyebrows. 'Men! They're all the same, damn them. They'll take what they want from you and leave you the minute something younger, or prettier, comes along. The trick is to get in first, take what you want, and then leave them for something richer. You know that song, "Diamonds are a Girl's Best Friend"? Well, it's true. Whatever else goes tawdry and loses its value, a diamond is always there, bright and hard and beautiful.' She lit a cigarette. 'Not that I've got any, of course.'

'Julie,' I said, 'I believe you're outrageous on purpose. You don't mean a single word of it. If you did, you wouldn't want to be a farmer's wife.'

'That's only so that I can bury my diamonds in the pig pen,' Julie said.

'You'd like Sandy,' I said. 'He's a bit outrageous too.'

Julie's expression became serious and there was something in her eyes I couldn't read. 'Be careful, Dawn. You're so bloody vulnerable. I can see myself at your age when I look at you. And now look at me! An almost has-been who'll never do anything but act for a few crummy holidaymakers who just want somewhere to go to get out of the rain. My private life is a mess too. Did you know I was married once?'

'No, I didn't know,' I said. 'What happened?'

She shrugged, the old Julie beginning to reappear. 'Oh, the old, old story. He was on the boards too, and vain as they come. He needed other woman to bolster his ego. At first I minded like hell, and then I stopped minding and found someone else. End of story.'

'And the someone else?' I asked her.

'Went the same way. I tell you, darling, they all do. Now, come and have a bacon butty with me and forget it.'

I went with her, but I couldn't forget it. It made a sad hole inside me to think that somebody like Julie, who had once been young and eager like me, should be so torn-up inside, so terribly cynical. And I prayed that Sandy and I wouldn't turn out like that. If we did, I didn't think I'd want to go on living.

I first noticed the change in Serena towards the end of May. Since I'd been with the Hunter Hylton Repertory Company I hadn't seen much of her. Our hours at home hardly coincided at all, and by the time I came in at night, dropping with tiredness, Serena was usually already asleep, the pile of books she'd been studying for her coming exams piled beside her bed.

That night then, I was surprised to find her sitting on the stool in front of the dressing table. When I opened the door she was brushing her hair, but I had the feeling she'd only snatched up the brush when she heard me coming up the stairs.

'Hi Dawn.' Her voice was too quiet, and yet too bright. 'Good show?'

'Not bad. No disasters, anyway. Are you coming to see it tomorrow?' Serena was usually in the audience once a week.

'Probably.'

'Are you feeling all right?' I asked, thinking she looked unusually pale.

For a moment she didn't answer, then: 'Yes, I'm tired, that's all.'

'Come to bed then. You'll never pass your exams if you work yourself to a frazzle.'

She muttered something, too low for me to hear, got up and started getting undressed. But I couldn't help noticing that she seemed to be deliberately keeping her back towards me, which I thought was odd. Serena and I were long past being coy about seeing one another naked. And when she got into bed she pulled the covers up to her chin and lay staring into space while I got undressed myself.

'You've got to stop worrying about your exams,' I said. 'I know you're desperate to do well for your parents' sake, but—'

'Oh, for goodness sake, Dawn, stop going on about my stupid exams!' Serena exploded, and she sounded perilously close to tears.

I looked at her narrowly. 'It's not Chris, is it? You two haven't fallen out?'

'No,' Serena said. Just that. For a long moment I had the feeling she was on the verge of saying something else, telling me what it was that was upsetting her, but she didn't. She just switched off the light and pretended to be asleep. But for a long time I could hear her snuffling softly in the darkness.

Something was clearly very wrong, but I didn't want to press her until she was ready to tell me about it.

It was another two days before I found out.

I was sitting tucked into a cleft in the cliff face in Seagull Bay, a dog-eared script of *Ladies in Retirement* propped up against my knees whilst I struggled to memorize the part of Lucy, the cheeky little maid, which I'd been cast for, when a shadow fell across the book. I looked up, startled, to see Chris standing there. He looked, I thought, very serious.

'I thought I'd find you here, Dawn. I wanted to talk to you . . .'

'To me?' My mind was still half on Lucy. 'What about?'

He sat down beside me, found a small pebble, and tossed it towards the sea.

'I don't quite know where to begin.'

I put my book down then, the part forgotten, and turned to look at him. 'Is it about Serena?' I asked, thinking of the bedtime tears and how quiet she'd been the last few days.

'Not exactly.' He paused, and there was an awkwardness between us that was almost tangible. Then, to my absolute surprise, he said, 'You know the way I feel about you, don't you, Dawn?'

'What?' I said stupidly.

'You must know.' His words came rapidly now, as if having begun he couldn't stop. 'I've been crazy about you ever since you came here. Even when we were kids.'

'Chris . . .' I protested helplessly, wanting desperately to stop him before he said something we'd both regret but not knowing how.

'Look, Dawn, I know you don't feel the same way,' Chris stumbled on. 'I know it's Sandy with you. But I keep on hoping that one day you'll realize he's – well, not worth it. Maybe then there'll be a chance for me.' He laughed, a small snort of self-derision. 'I know it's a pipe dream, but you have to tell me, one way or the other, if I've got any chance at all.'

I stared at him in horror, thinking that Sandy had been right all along. I'd thought he was joking when he'd talked about Chris's feelings for me, but he hadn't been. Suddenly, so many little things made sense – the way I sometimes caught Chris looking at me, the awkward way he made me feel – and yet, even now, I could hardly believe it.

'But what about Serena?' I said, angry that he was betraying her by having this conversation.

'I didn't come to talk about Serena,' Chris said stubbornly. 'I came to talk about us.'

'There is no us.'

'You mean there's no hope for me,' he said flatly.

'None. If I've given you the impression there was, I'm sorry.'

'No, you haven't,' he said. His face was bleak, and suddenly, mysteriously, he looked much older. 'It was just that I had to be sure now, before . . .'

'Before what?' I asked.

There was a long silence when the only sounds were the sea, pounding against the rocks at the tip of the bay and the soft suck of the waves on the shingle. Somewhere up over the cliff a solitary gull mewed.

'Serena and I will be getting married,' Chris said.

The roar of the tide reached a crescendo inside my head, drowning my thoughts and my senses.

'Married?' I repeated stupidly. 'But you're going to university. Serena's going to teacher training college.'

'I think that will be out for both of us,' Chris said. 'I shall have to get a job if I've got a wife and baby to keep.' I stared at him, shocked, and he shifted awkwardly on the rock. 'Serena's pregnant.'

'Oh my God.'

So that was what was on her mind, what she hadn't felt able to tell me. I suddenly found myself remembering how I'd thought it was odd she had kept her back towards me when she undressed; now I understood the reason. Why, oh why, hadn't she told me? I'd known there was something wrong. I should have wormed it out of her, and then maybe she wouldn't have felt quite so bad, so alone.

And now . . . Suddenly I was so furious it made me tremble.

'You absolute pig!' I shot at Chris. My voice was low, but it seemed to reverberate from every boulder. 'I cannot believe this!'

'These things happen,' Chris said, defiantly, like a little boy caught out in a naughty act.

'I don't mean *that*,' I grated. 'Although heaven knows I would have thought you'd have had the sense to make sure she didn't get pregnant just now, when you're both working your socks off to get qualified for your careers. It's this. Coming here behind her back, asking me if I . . .' Words failed me. I pounded my script against my knees in helpless anger. 'That is the lowest thing I've ever come across. She's worried out of her mind, counting on you for support, and you . . . You come here and ask me . . .'

Chris stood up. 'I'm sorry. I shouldn't have come.'

'Too right, you shouldn't!'

He half-turned to go, then swung round once more, his face naked with pleading. 'You won't tell her?'

'I should do. I should let her know just what you're really like.'

'But you won't. Please, Dawn . . . I'll make sure she's all right, I promise. Like I said, I'll marry her, look after her and the baby. I've already told her that.'

'Then why . . .?'

'I just had to know,' he said, sounding horribly upset. 'The thing I couldn't have stood would have been to discover too late that you . . . I had to know for sure that there was no chance for us . . .'

I couldn't quite work out the logic in that. 'Well, now you do. And you'd better make very sure you don't do anything to hurt Serena, or you'll have me to answer to.'

'Goodbye, Dawn,' Chris said and there was something so final in the way he said it that it frightened me. Surely he didn't mean to walk out of our lives? He'd said he'd stand by Serena, but what had he meant by that cold, toneless 'goodbye'?

It was only later that I understood.

When I got back to the house Chris and Serena were there together, and Aunt Fran was so flushed and agitated that I knew they'd broken the news to her that she was going to be a grandmother. Over Serena's head, Chris's eyes met mine – cold, hard, distant, disowning everything that had passed between us. And I knew what his goodbye had meant.

He had been shutting me out of his life, closing a door on a hopeless love that he'd carried deep inside him, unknown to any of us, for as long as he'd known me. Thinking of the way I felt about Sandy, I felt a moment's true compassion for Chris.

# Eight

Serena and Chris were married very quietly on a Wednesday afternoon in July, just a week after they left Sturvendor Grammar School. Serena looked pale but pretty in a blue dress that was loose enough to conceal her thickening waist, and she was given away by Uncle Max, a cousin of Uncle Tony's.

Uncle Max was a big, powerful man with horn-rimmed spectacles and hair that was greying attractively at the temples. Because he worked for an oil company, and spent most of the year out of the country, we rarely saw him, but whenever he visited he took over the whole house by the sheer force of his personality. He was the obvious choice to lead Serena up the aisle.

I sat in the front pew with Aunt Fran and wondered how she was really feeling. From the moment Serena had told her about the baby she hadn't behaved at all as I'd expected her to. Instead of tears and recriminations, she'd launched herself into a frenzy of organization. She'd baked and iced a two-tier wedding cake, and planned and prepared a buffet reception that would have done credit to the finest hotel in town.

The afternoon before the wedding we'd gone to the church and filled it with flowers, banking them in the ledges beneath the vaulted stained-glass windows and around the stone font, and arranging a huge vase at the chancel steps. And all the while she had fussed and chattered like a clockwork doll that's wound too tight, and there'd been an air of unreality about her.

Now, though, as the organist began playing the Bridal March and Serena came up the aisle on Uncle Max's arm, I stole a look at her face, gaunt suddenly beneath her frothy hat, and realized that the bustle and energy had been her way of trying not to think of how all her hopes for Serena were ending this way, in a wedding that would set tongues wagging all over town. The arrangements had kept her too busy for too much thinking, but now there was nothing left for her to do but sit back and watch as her little girl became a wife.

Chris was waiting at the chancel steps, straight-backed and vaguely uncomfortable in a new dark suit that made him look much older than his eighteen years. He turned to smile at her, a small, warm, private smile; his hands were steady as he placed the ring on her finger and his voice never faltered as he made his vows. But I couldn't help wondering what he was feeling as he spoke the age-old words, 'And forsaking all others, keep me only unto her, as long as we both shall live.'

Chris had asked Sandy to be his best man. Sandy had gone home to fetch a suit for the occasion, and for the first time since I'd met him he looked what he was – the well-educated son of a wealthy man. The suit was well-cut and clearly very expensive, and Sandy wore it with a throwaway, easy grace. Somehow the suggestion of lithe muscle beneath the faultless tailoring made him even more aggressively masculine than usual, and the facade of convention only accentuated his unconventionality.

The vicar led Serena and Chris to the altar steps; Sandy was left alone. Now, just when I'd thought the most emotional part was over, tears pricked my eyes and I knew they were for all of us – for Chris, trapped by a moment of careless irresponsibility; for Serena, who should have been a radiant story-book bride in white satin with a veil and a huge bouquet of roses; and for myself, because I wanted to stand beside Sandy at the altar on any terms at all, and I wasn't sure I ever would.

At last the service was over and we filed out into the sunshine. A photographer Aunt Fran had booked was waiting, but I could see that Serena was close to tears and wanted only to get away.

'You look absolutely lovely,' I whispered to her.

She sank her teeth into a lip that wouldn't stop quivering. 'Did you see Mummy crying?' she asked. 'I did that to her, Dawn. She's had so much to put up with, and now I've let her down and upset her all over again.'

'Mothers always cry at weddings,' I comforted her. 'Even I was crying!'

But I knew how Serena felt. She was so sensitive to other people's feelings; she wanted everyone to be happy, hated to think that she had been the cause of any kind of upset. It was probably the generosity in her nature that had got her into this, I thought. She'd wanted to please Chris so much that it had outweighed her natural reserve. And she would almost certainly have been against taking any precautions. To plan love-making instead of leaving it as a spontaneous gesture of love would probably seem immoral to her. And so, inevitably, she had ended up pregnant, while girls far more promiscuous than her did not.

Back at the house the guests crowded into the big front room where Aunt Fran had laid out her buffet. A cork popped and Sandy began to pour drinks while I helped Aunt Fran carry around plates of sausage rolls and canapés. In a corner, Uncle Max buttonholed me.

'Who is your young man, Dawn? Can we expect wedding bells for you next?'

'I shouldn't think so,' I said lightly, ridiculously afraid Sandy might overhear. 'Would you like a sausage roll?'

He took one. 'Of course, we can expect great things from your career, from what I hear of it.'

'I hope so,' I said.

'How old are you, Dawn? Eighteen? Ye Gods, it's hard to believe you're that young. In my day girls of eighteen were giggly children. You're a woman. And even little Serena is married. I don't know . . .'

From across the room someone called, 'When will we be seeing you on television, Dawn?' and I managed to make my escape.

When it was time for me to leave for the theatre the party was still going on. Serena and Chris had left for their few days' honeymoon in Cornwall an hour before, and I'd expected the others to drift away, but they'd stayed, enjoying the family get-together, and as I came downstairs after changing into my working clothes, laughter and snatches of conversation billowed out of the front room on a cloud of tobacco smoke.

I pushed the door open a trifle hesitantly, uncomfortably conscious of my old jeans and sweater but feeling I ought not to leave without saying my goodbyes. And felt my heart come into my throat with a sickening leap as I caught sight of Sandy in the fireside corner.

He was with a girl. She had been introduced to me earlier as a cousin of Chris's, and I hadn't taken much notice of her. Now, suddenly, I was all too aware of cornflower-blue eyes in an elfin face and straight blonde hair falling in a shining curtain to her shoulders. She was smiling at Sandy, a teasing, provocative smile, and though I couldn't see his face, I knew he was smiling back.

A knife-thrust of anger, sharper than was reasonable, misted my eyes with scarlet, and I took a step into the crowded room, ready to do battle. Then I stopped short, realizing this could be a horrible mistake. At the moment Sandy was merely flirting. But if I went in with all guns blazing I could make things a hundred times worse.

With a tremendous effort of will I backed out of the room. No one had noticed me and I felt a flush of relief rising in my cheeks, as if I, not Sandy, was the guilty one. But as I walked down the path my heart was heavy in a way that was quite new to me, and I realized that it was the fear of something like this happening that had haunted me ever since Sandy had come back to Sturvendor and I'd realized that, for all the ecstasy of our first meeting, nothing had really changed for him.

He was still the old Sandy, totally uncommitted. Last year I'd loved him for it, and it hadn't mattered that I didn't own even the smallest part of him. I'd been happy just to be with him, to see him and talk to him and feel his arms around me. My love had been too fresh and new to spawn jealousy.

That had begun in the dark winter months. I'd known then in my heart of hearts that there must be other girls, but they had been shadows in faraway London, and I'd been able to pretend they didn't exist, helped by the certainty that if he came to Sturvendor again it would be partly because of me and because he'd realized we belonged together.

Well, he'd come back, and nothing had changed, except that I was a year older and less easily satisfied with nothing but dreams. Whilst Sandy . . .

A sense of hopelessness oppressed me suddenly, and, swinging my bag up on to my shoulder, I began to run, as if I could leave all my fears and doubts behind me. But the weight was still on my heart when I reached the theatre, and all night too. As I scurried about my hundred and one menial tasks I could see nothing but the blonde smiling up at Sandy and Sandy smiling back.

Aunt Fran said, 'He saw her home, you know.'

I took a quick gulp of coffee. The too-hot liquid seared my

lips and throat, but I hardly noticed. It was the tight, constricting pain in my chest I couldn't ignore. He'd seen her home. He must have known someone would tell me, but it hadn't made any difference. He'd seen her home.

'She's staying for a few days, I believe. Making a holiday of it.'

Aunt Fran was scraping toast that she'd burned into the sink, her back towards me and I was glad she couldn't see my face.

'Lucky old her!' I said. Even to my own ears the voice didn't sound like my own. It was too high, too brittle.

Aunt Fran didn't reply, and in the silence the pain in my chest began to spread. I'd been right, then, to be jealous. What I'd seen hadn't been just harmless flirting; it had been the prelude to something more.

Sandy had another girl. As yet, the enormity of it hadn't come home to me properly, and I didn't want it to, especially not here in Aunt Fran's kitchen, where my only privacy was a turned back.

I stared deliberately at the tablecloth, tracing a pattern with my eyes in an effort to ignore the void under my heart, but the bright checks blurred and merged until I could no longer see them.

'Dawn . . .' Aunt Fran had come over to the table. Now, she hovered uncertainly, the toast gripped too tightly between her fingers. 'I don't know if I did right to tell you, but I don't want you to be hurt . . .'

My chin went up. *Oh no, let's not hurt Dawn . . .* I swallowed against the lump in my throat. 'It doesn't matter either way. Sandy's a free agent. If he wants to take someone else home . . .'

It was useless. The lump in my throat was too big. It was growing by the minute, sending out fingers of pain that made every bit of my body ache. I put down my cup with a clatter. I crossed the room and ran upstairs. I wished there was time to go to Seagull Bay, but there wasn't. I was due at the theatre for rehearsal in half an hour.

*Oh God, I haven't even got time to cry!* I thought, and then, in a sudden, surprising burst of anger, *Why should I cry anyway? Why should I let the bastard upset me?*

My defiance was short lived. I sank on to the stool in front of the dressing table, my hands cupping my chin. From the mirror my face, pinched with hurt, looked back at me, and I thought, *I'm not really pretty at all. Not half as pretty as she is . . .*

The pain began again then, wave upon wave of excruciating pain that blurred my eyes and made me feel sick. I saw Sandy and the girl again, smiling teasingly at one another, only now I carried the picture forward frame by frame so that in imagination I saw him kiss her, twist her hair the way he twisted mine, fold her body under his with deft, masterful ease. In imagination I saw it all, and the agony was so great that it was all I could do not to cry out. I muffled it with my fist, biting into the flesh, and with the sharp, physical pain, sanity began to return.

Maybe that was all there was to it, I thought, just a quick kiss and cuddle in the dark. I could ruin everything by being too hasty, accusing him of something he might not have done or trying to force him to be true to me before he was ready. Freedom was the most important thing in the world to Sandy, and if I protested about him flirting with other girls he'd see it as an attack on that freedom. He would leave me as surely as he'd left the home where he'd felt restricted, not necessarily because he cared more for any of the girls he might dally with, but because he would resent me for trying to stop him.

If I wanted Sandy, I must be patient. However long it took, I must wait for him to come to me of his own accord. It would be painful, perhaps it would last for a little while, perhaps forever, but it was that or lose him. And I knew that I couldn't bear to lose him.

My resolve lasted exactly two weeks. Working late in the evenings, I found myself constantly wondering what he was doing and who he was with. Although he'd promise to meet me after the show, I couldn't help but think of the long hours of the evening when he knew I was safely out of the way. And whereas before I'd respected his need for privacy, now, when he made some excuse for not seeing me, I was ridden with doubts and jealousy.

One afternoon, inevitably, I went beyond the bounds I'd set myself.

'I may not be able to meet you tonight,' Sandy said. 'I want to go over to Dunkery Beacon and watch the sunset. I had an idea for a painting.'

An idea for a painting? Or something else entirely? Hating myself, I protested, 'But you'll be back in heaps of time!'

'If I am, I'll meet you as usual,' Sandy said. 'I'm just warning you, in case I'm not.'

Jealousy speared me with sharp barbs as I imagined Sandy with the blonde, or some other unknown girl, on Dunkery Beacon. 'Is she pretty?' I asked bitterly.

Sandy's eyes narrowed. 'Is *who* pretty, Dawn?'

Knowing I'd fallen into the trap I'd so wanted to avoid, I wished I could bite off my tongue, but it was too late to back down now. 'Don't tell me you haven't been seeing someone else. You're seeing her tonight, aren't you?'

Sandy's expression frightened me. He had suddenly gone cold and withdrawn, and I knew he wasn't going to satisfy me either way. 'If I want to go to Dunkery Beacon, Dawn, I'll go. I'll go when I want and with whom I want.'

'So you are taking someone!' I flung at him.

'I didn't say that. But it's no business of yours anyway. You don't own me.'

In that moment, I hated him. I hated him and his irresponsible ideas and his uncommitted way of life. I wanted to scream at him, words that would slice through the armour of his indifference and hurt him as he was hurting me. But I knew tears were perilously close, and I had no intention of giving Sandy the satisfaction of seeing me cry. So I managed to grate out, 'I see,' before turning my back and walking away from him.

He didn't call after me, or make any move to stop me, and as I walked, head held high, I wondered wretchedly if this was the end, and everything was over between us.

I didn't see Sandy for a week. Every day was a lifetime filled with hope and disappointment and self-hate because I couldn't stop caring, and every night when I came out of the theatre I stood for a few moments, looking up and down the street in the vain hope that he would appear. He didn't, and I went home alone to the room I'd shared with Serena and which was now mine alone.

I missed Serena. For years I'd longed for a room of my own. Since that first night in the schoolhouse when I'd seen the poky room with so little room for my things, and no privacy, I'd cherished memories of what I'd taken for granted in Canada – the luxury of somewhere where I could do exactly as I pleased without having to consider anyone else, have the space to hang my clothes and set out my toiletries, and to have the guarantee of not being interrupted when I wanted to be alone. In the weeks before the wedding I'd happily planned how I'd rearrange things to suit myself when Serena left.

But I'd forgotten that her personality was in the room along with her hairbrush, make-up and clothes, and I hadn't realized I'd grown so used to having her there that her very absence would be unsettling. Like a man who can still feel an arm or leg long after it has been amputated, I couldn't believe Serena was no longer there, and the sight of the empty rail in the wardrobe and the unnatural tidiness of her side of the dressing table started a sweet sadness in me.

At least Serena was happy, I told myself. She and Chris had moved in with Chris's parents until they could afford a house of their own, and I'd seen her only a few times. But there'd been a glow about her, as if now, in the safety of her marriage, she could allow herself to enjoy her pregnancy, and I'd felt that her rounded figure and smoothly serene face would have made a perfect model if Sandy had wanted to paint a picture of the Madonna and child.

Her parents might have wanted Serena to be a teacher; all she'd ever really wanted was a home of her own, a family and Chris. I only hoped he'd be good to her.

He'd found himself a job in the laboratory of a chemical establishment that had opened just up the coast. It was a poor substitute, I guessed, for the medical profession he'd wanted to take up, but at least, Serena told us, he'd be able to move around within the organization until he found a niche to suit him, and if he worked hard the chances of promotion were good.

'And he will work hard,' Serena said. 'That's Chris. And a family is the best incentive he could possible have, isn't it?'

I hoped she was right. Certainly, Chris seemed to have settled into married life, and the baby, when it came, would forge an extra bond between them.

And then fate played one of its cruellest tricks.

It was a Saturday afternoon, heavy and oppressive with the threat of thunder hanging in the air. I was upstairs, resting before going to the theatre, and trying to learn next week's part, when I heard someone banging at the front door. For a minute I waited to see if Aunt Fran would answer it. She was downstairs, I knew, and visitors were usually for her. But I couldn't hear any sound of movement, and before I could swing my legs off the bed the knocking had begun again, loud and insistent.

'All right, all right!' I muttered, heading for the stairs, but before I was halfway down the handle rattled and the door burst open. 'Chris!' I said, startled. 'What on earth is the matter?'

He stood in the hall, one hand still on the door knob. He was pale, but his face was shining with sweat. 'Is Serena's mum in?'

'Yes – she's about somewhere. But what's happened?' I was shaking with sudden apprehension.

'It's Serena. She's in hospital. They think she's losing the baby.'

Ridiculously, my first reaction was relief. I'd had visions of something far, far worse.

The back door slammed. Aunt Fran must have been in the garden. As she came into the hall and saw Chris there, I saw the same horrible apprehension I'd felt a few moments ago mirrored in her face.

'Chris?' she said, her voice rising on a tremor.

'It's all right, Aunt Fran,' I said. 'Serena's OK. It's the baby.'

'She's not bloody OK!' Chris burst out indignantly. 'She's having a miscarriage!'

I shot him a hard look, warning him to calm down. 'For goodness sake, come in. I'll put the kettle on.'

'What's happened?' Aunt Fran was asking anxiously.

'She's having a miscarriage,' Chris said again, but calmer now. 'I was out. I ran Mum and Dad into Taunton, and I damned well stopped a while watching the cricket. When I got back I found her. On her own. The neighbours were out, too, and of course we're not on the damned phone. Serena had heard somewhere you should keep your feet up if something like that happens, and she was doing just that, and praying I'd get back soon. I went for the doctor straight away, and he had her into hospital. But they don't hold out much hope of saving the baby.'

'Never mind making tea, Dawn.' Aunt Fran was searching frantically for her handbag. 'I'll go to the hospital with Chris now.'

'OK. If there's anything I can do . . .'

'We'll let you know,' Aunt Fran said.

When the door had closed after them, my initial relief began to pall in the dawning realization of what it would mean to Serena if she lost the baby. I pictured again her smooth, fulfilled face, the comfortable stance of her waiting body. Maybe theirs had been a shotgun wedding, but this was one baby who was very badly wanted. With it, they would be a family. Without it . . .

I hoped Aunt Fran might phone with news of Serena before I left for the theatre, but she didn't. All evening I found it impossible to concentrate on what I was doing, and it was only thanks to Julie that I avoided a catastrophe that could have cost me my job.

'I've lost the sandwiches!' I wailed, laying the table with the props for one scene. 'Oh, hell, what have I done with them? Hunter can hardly play a tea party scene without any food!'

Julie came around the corner of a flat, pushing them towards me. 'You left them in the dressing room. I just rescued them. Rosencrantz was about to tuck in.'

'Oh, hell! Thanks, Julie.'

She grinned crookedly. 'Don't know why I bothered, sweetie. If the poodle had eaten them at least we'd have had to have some fresh ones, instead of the same dried-up crusts all week. They make British Rail catering look positively five-star, don't they? And they'd probably have finished off poor old Rosencrantz.'

Everyone laughed. The poodle, fat, smelly and perpetually under our feet, was hardly the most popular member of the company. It was galling to see him fed on tinned salmon 'because of his digestion' while the rest of us were hard put to it to afford bread and cheese on our meagre salaries, and the thought of him wolfing the stale sandwiches that were made to last the entire week of the show for the sake of economy was amusing.

I was all too aware, though, of what would have happened to me if the sandwiches had disappeared just minutes before they were needed, and I forced myself to concentrate on the hundred and one small but vital tasks that kept the show running smoothly.

It wouldn't help Serena, or anyone, if I lost my job. But for once I got no pleasure out of being part of the magic world of the theatre, and when the Hyltons had taken their last lingering curtain call I rushed through my jobs and grabbed my coat.

In the narrow corridor behind the stage, Hunter stopped me. 'I wanted to tell you, my angel, that you're going to be the perfect Daphne in next week's production. I'm very pleased with you.'

Normally, the praise would have delighted me. Tonight my only concern was for Serena. 'Good,' I said, trying to slip past him.

Hunter put up an arm to bar my way. He'd put on a faded silk dressing gown, but he was still wearing full make-up. Beneath it, his face glistened with perspiration. 'Don't run away, my angel,' he said.

I gave him a startled glance. For all his flowery talk, Hunter had never made a pass at me before, but this, unmistakably, was a pass. My mind, already occupied with Serena, flicked over the possible ways of rebuffing him. I didn't want to show him the slightest encouragement but to be too blunt might be even more disastrous than losing the sandwiches.

'Hunter . . .' I began sweetly, but before I could get any further I saw his lustful leer change to guilt, and his arm dropped to his side.

'As I was saying, my angel, you're a good little actress,' he said. 'I shall have to consider you for more important roles.'

He patted my shoulder in a gesture that was almost paternal, and I glanced round to see Evelyn watching us from the top of the steps.

'That would be good,' I said. 'Goodnight, Hunter. Goodnight, Evelyn.'

Neither of them replied, and I found myself hoping desperately that Evelyn didn't think I'd been encouraging her husband. If she did, heaven only knew what form her revenge would take. But for the moment, I wasn't even going to think about it. I pushed open the stage door and went out into the darkness.

'Dawn,' said a voice behind me.

I turned, breath catching in my throat.

It was Sandy.

* * *

'Hi,' he said.

'Hi.'

For a whole week I'd been hoping he'd be waiting here for me; now it had happened. But I'd wanted to relish every moment of making up, and I couldn't. There were too many other things on my mind, and I felt that I was spinning in a kaleidoscope that distorted every part of normal living into something unfamiliar and dark with menace.

'You don't seem very pleased to see me,' he said.

'I'm worried about Serena. She was taken to hospital this afternoon. They think she's having a miscarriage.'

'I know,' Sandy said. 'I saw Chris. She's lost the baby.'

There was a soft drink can in the middle of the pavement. I kicked it as hard as I could, and it clattered against a lamp-post before rolling into the gutter. 'Damn!' I said. 'Damn, damn!'

'Calm down,' Sandy said, putting his hand on my arm. 'Serena's all right, you know.'

'Yes, I suppose so.'

I couldn't explain the anger inside me. I knew the world was full of senseless injustice; I'd known it for a long time. And there would be other babies for Serena. Only, I knew instinctively that would be of no comfort to her now, lying flat and empty in her hospital bed and knowing that the life inside her had slipped away without ever having been born. Had it been a boy or a girl? Would it have been like Chris, or like Serena? We'd never know that now. It had gone forever in a gush of blood and gore. Tears, sharp and salt, stung my eyes.

'Don't you understand?' I said to Sandy. 'It was this baby she wanted.'

We walked in silence for a while, then Sandy said, 'Will you come to the chalet, Dawn? There's something I'd like to show you.'

He helped me down over the sea wall and we walked across the shingle. As I waited for Sandy to unlock the door, the wind blowing off the sea cut through my sweater, raising goose bumps on my arms. It reminded me too sharply that the summer was slipping past, and with it the summer people, the Hunter Hylton Repertory Company and probably Sandy too. The chill bit deep into my bones, filling me with apprehension. I didn't want winter to come.

Sandy pushed the door open and lit the gas lamp with the box of matches he kept by the stove. The soft light made an oasis, leaving the corners in deep, mysterious shadow and muting the effect of the ugly bare furniture. Without speaking he walked over to his easel and pulled it into the circle of light, turning it fully towards me.

And then I saw the painting, a beautiful landscape of a sunset over Dunkery Beacon in Sandy's unmistakable style, and I knew it was the painting Sandy had brought me here to see.

'It's beautiful,' I said. 'Honestly, breathtaking.'

Sandy looked at me, and there was a hint of wickedness behind his pride. 'And not a girl in sight, you see.'

I echoed his bantering tone. 'Not even a very plain one.'

'Certainly not that,' Sandy said, and he kissed me.

I locked my arms around him, feeling his hard strength against me, knowing again that I could be happy with Sandy forever, wanting nothing but to be close to him and to love him. Under my eager mouth his skin tasted salt, and his hands, as he undressed me, were gentle and unhurried. Afterwards, he kissed my eyes, my ears and the tip of my nose, and caressed every inch of my body as if he could remember it for always in the touch of his fingers.

'Stay with me,' he whispered, and I snuggled my face into his shoulder and curved myself around his hard hip, and Sandy pulled the blanket over both of us. The last sound I heard was the distant rhythmic roar of the waves and the soft patter of rain beginning on the window. Then drowsiness overtook me and I slept.

It was almost light when I awoke, a cold, grey light creeping in between the roughly drawn curtains. The roar of the sea was much louder now, and the drag of the waves on the shingle made a constant accompaniment to the hiss of rain against the window and the occasional slap of a piece of tar-paper roofing, which must have come loose and was being worried by the wind.

I looked at my watch, but it had stopped, and I had seen too few dawns to be able to guess at the time. Beside me, Sandy was fast asleep, his hair falling across his face in a way that made him look curiously defenceless, the coarse blanket pushed aside by one bare arm.

Tenderness welled up in me and flowed into the deep bowl of sadness I was feeling for Serena. I stretched out a tentative hand to touch Sandy, wanting to find comfort and oblivion in the warmth of loving. He moved, a small, impatient jerk away from me, and I withdrew my hand and lay for a moment watching him sleep. Then I got up and dressed. If I went home now I would be saved the embarrassment of Aunt Fran knowing I had been out all night, and besides, in spite of what Sandy had said last night, I had an odd feeling that he would prefer not to find me here when he woke.

I opened the door and stepped out into the cold, grey dawn. The wind drove a flurry of rain into my face and I bent my head to tie a scarf over my hair.

'Good morning, miss.'

The sounds of the gale must have muted the footsteps on the shingle because the voice from behind me startled me so much that I actually jumped. I spun round. It was a policeman – booted, helmeted, the collar of a heavyweight mackintosh turned up to deflect drips.

'Good morning.'

'You're up and about very early.' He was looking at me curiously and I realized he was waiting for some kind of an explanation.

'I've been staying here,' I said foolishly, realizing that with no raincoat, on a windswept beach, it seemed an unlikely story.

At that moment the door of the chalet swung open and Sandy, wearing only a pair of jeans, appeared. 'What's going on?'

'Can we come in for a minute, sir?' The constable shook the water from his dripping mackintosh as if to indicate that he wanted to get out of the rain, but, as I saw his practised eye taking in every corner of the room, I knew there was another reason.

'What is it?' Sandy asked again.

'We're looking for a young man, seventeen or eighteen, thin, dark. Wearing a navy-blue donkey jacket and probably in a hurry. Have you seen anyone like that about, sir?'

'Obviously not,' Sandy said shortly. 'I've been tucked up in bed and fast asleep. Why do you ask?'

The policeman turned to me and I saw officialdom slip a bit.

'There's been a break-in in town. The sports shop. A lot of guns have been taken, and ammunition. This lad was seen running away. We don't like people trotting around with guns, so if you see anything, let us know. But I wouldn't approach him if I were you.'

Sandy laughed. 'Don't worry, mate, I won't.'

As the policeman left there was a shout from higher up the beach and a second policeman headed in our direction.

I half-closed the door and Sandy began, 'Hey, Dawn, where were you going so fast?' but I waved a hand to hush him. I wanted to hear what the two policemen were saying. It wasn't easy through an almost closed door, even one as thin as this one, especially with Sandy snorting impatiently and saying he was going back to bed, but I did manage to get the gist of it.

'They think he's got a boat now,' I said, as the voices died away. 'There's been one stolen from the harbour and a man answering the description of the suspect was seen rowing out to sea. What will they do now do you think?'

'I haven't a clue.'

'Perhaps he'll make for Devon.'

Sandy snorted again. 'He'll have a job making for anywhere in this weather. Are you coming back to bed?'

'No, I'm going home,' I said. 'See you.'

I opened the door and as the fierce wind snatched it from my grasp my thoughts went again to the man in the rowing boat. He probably wasn't an experienced sailor or he'd at least have gone for something with an outboard motor. I didn't think an experienced sailor would have considered for one moment rowing out into the bay in this wind and with the currents in this direction.

It was getting light fast now, but a thick greyness still clung to the sea and tried to stop the yellow-topped waves from racing and leaping. I shivered and pulled the already-wet sleeves of my sweater down over my wrists. If I was glad of anything at that moment it was that I was on the beach and not being tossed about by the angry sea.

And then the mist shifted a little and I saw it – a boat, looking like a child's toy as the waves lashed it, just inside the curve of the bay. There was someone in it, and even at this distance I could see he was in trouble. He'd lost his oars, I thought, and as I watched a wave caught the boat, spinning it like a top. I thought it would overturn, but when the wave broke the boat was still there, and the man, seeing me, began to wave his arms for help.

I stumbled back up the beach and into the chalet.

'Sandy – he's out there, in the bay! We've got to help him!' Sandy must have dozed off again because it took him long seconds to sit up, rubbing his eyes with the back of his hand. 'We've got to get your boat and go out to him!'

'We wouldn't last two minutes in this weather,' Sandy said. 'And if we didn't drown, he'd shoot us.'

The lifeboat maroon cracked sharply, and Sandy said, 'There you are, the lifeboat will be with him in no time at all.'

'It may be too late!' I cried, urgency making me shake. 'We're here. We've got to do something!'

'There's nothing we can do. Be reasonable, love. With my leaky old boat, you might as well swim out.'

I ran back to the window, half-afraid the man would have disappeared, but he hadn't.

'Oh, somebody has to help him!' I pressed my hands over my mouth, the horror of what I was witnessing bringing me close to tears.

And then, suddenly, the lifeboat appeared. I could hardly believe the time it had made, and yet it was here, cutting through the water towards the tiny, tossing boat. We watched the rescue, although the waves often obscured our view, and when at last the lifeboat turned back towards the shore I realized that I was shivering violently.

'I must go.' I didn't mean my voice to sound flat, but it did, and Sandy said:

'What's wrong?'

'Nothing.'

'You think I should have taken my leaky old boat out to that bloke, don't you?' Sandy said.

'No, no. It would have been stupid. I got carried away.'

It was true. I didn't really want Sandy to have risked his life. It wouldn't have helped anybody. And yet somehow the man who put common sense before heroism didn't quite fit the image I'd always had of Sandy. It left me feeling curiously deflated.

I smiled at him and kissed him lightly because I didn't want him to know what was going on in my head. 'See you tonight?'

'I expect so,' he said.

# Nine

By the end of August I was beginning to worry about what I would do at the end of the season.

'You need an agent,' Julie told me. 'If you don't have one you'll find yourself in a vicious circle – without an agent you can't get a job, and without a job you can't get an agent.'

'I got this one,' I pointed out.

Julie shrugged. 'All right, don't take any notice of me. It's your funeral.'

'So how do I go about getting an agent?' I asked, ashamed to admit I didn't really know the first thing about the business but realizing I shouldn't be too proud to take advice.

'Sometimes one comes in and watches the show,' Julie said. 'If he likes you he'll come backstage afterwards and make you an offer.'

'What sort of an offer?' I asked dubiously.

Julie pulled a face. 'Chances are it'll contain a proposition. Believe me, darling, the casting couch is alive and well. But don't be fooled into giving your all to some charlatan who promises you the earth. Whatever you do or don't do, you won't get any work between now and the pantomime season. To be honest, darling, the best advice I can give you is to marry your Sandy and give up this bloody awful life.'

I wasn't going to admit to Julie that I really didn't think that option was on offer, and for once her cynical manner really depressed me. When she talked this way it was all too easy to see how disillusion could begin, corroding ambition, destroying self-respect.

'I'll find something,' I said, my voice gritty with determination.

Julie sighed. 'When you've waited with two dozen others in a draughty rehearsal room for hours, shaking with nerves, all keyed up to do your best, and then some bum just says, "Thank you, we'll let you know," in a tone that tells you right off you'll never hear a word from him, you'll think of what I said,' she told me sadly.

At first it seemed dreadfully likely that she was going to be proved right. The vacancies for young actresses advertised in *The Stage* were few and far between – though it seemed female vocalists were always wanted – and I got nowhere with the couple of jobs I applied for. Then, to my amazement, an agent actually turned up.

He was a seedy little man with a cheap cigar stuck to his bottom lip, and I was almost physically sick when I remembered what Julie had said about the propositions he was likely to make me. But to my relief I was able to fend him off without too much trouble, and a week or so later he got in touch to let me know he'd actually got me a job with a small company who were going on tour in the autumn doing Shakespeare and the classics in schools all over the country.

I was over the moon. 'Shakespeare! Would you believe it? It makes me a real actress, doesn't it?' I said to Sandy as we celebrated with a bottle of cider and pretended it was champagne.

'What's real about acting?' Sandy asked with a lift of his eyebrow, but I was used to his little ways by now and much too happy to care.

I had expected Aunt Fran to express concern for my moral welfare when I broke the news to her, but instead she actually seemed quite relieved.

'You mean you won't be wanting to stay in Sturvendor this winter?' she asked, piling a Cornish pasty – her speciality – on to my plate.

'Well, no . . .'

'In that case . . . I'll let you into a secret, Dawn. You know I have friends in Bristol? Well, they've told me about a job in a nursery school near them. And they said that, if I wanted it, they know of a flat almost next door to them, which is vacant. I haven't mentioned it before because I didn't want to push you out, but . . .'

A flood of warmth humbled me and made my eyes prick with sudden tears. For the first time in perhaps twenty years Aunt Fran was free to go where she wanted and do as she liked, yet she had been holding back for my sake. I leaned across the table and squeezed her hand.

'Of course you must go, Aunt Fran, if that's what you want. And you mustn't worry about me. I'll be fine. But I'll never forget what you've done for me. And one day I hope I'll be able to repay you.'

She smiled at me, her eyes misty. 'You've already done that, Dawn. Many times over. And you've been like a sister to Serena – the sister I was never able to give her. She thinks the world of you, you know.'

'And I of her,' I said. 'It's a two-way thing.'

As we finished our supper I found myself watching Aunt Fran, registering all the hundred and one small things about her that I'd come to take for granted, and which would soon no longer be part of my everyday life. In a way it was sad, and yet it was a natural ending, for both of us. I was glad for her, that she was beginning to rebuild her life. She'd be a superb nursery teacher, I knew. And whether she was preparing nature tables with wild flowers and owl pellets or guiding buttons into buttonholes and small fingers into gloves, she would be filling the emptiness left behind when tragedy had torn her life apart.

One evening towards the end of the season Sandy and I walked up on to the moors. The soft blackness of the earlier nights had come down over the hills, and the firebreak paths between the bracken were lit only by the bright moon. The air was mild, though, and still smelled of summer, so that it was hard to believe that the death that is autumn and winter could be so perilously close.

We walked in Indian file down the firebreak, laughing and joking and feeling totally alive. Then, when we reached the road again and crossed it, we found ourselves on a piece of rough ground that sloped gently down towards the edge of the cliff. Far below, the sea was pounding against the rocks, sounding unnaturally loud in the utter stillness, and Sandy put his arm around me, drawing me down beside him on the damp, scratchy turf.

'How would you like a holiday?' he asked. 'A real break before you go off demonstrating to all those lucky school kids that Shakespeare can really be rather good fun?'

'A holiday would be heavenly.' The summer's rep had tired me more than I could ever have expected, and a real, away-from-it-all break was just what I needed. But there was a problem.

'I don't have any cash to spare for that sort of thing though,' I said regretfully.

Sandy picked a long stem of grass and tickled my nose with it. 'Well . . . I've sold three paintings today. Three! So I reckon I could afford to treat you. It won't be the Savoy, of course, but . . .'

'But what about saving some for the winter?' I said cautiously, when all I wanted to do was hug him and squeal with delight. But Sandy was so irresponsible, someone had to stop and think.

'Damn the winter,' he said. 'Live for today, Dawn. We could fall off our perch tomorrow.'

'I sincerely hope not!' I told him. 'I've got a whole lot of living to do before *I* do any such thing.'

'You don't have any say in it, though, do you?' Sandy had gone serious as he sometimes did. 'When you read about accidents in the paper, the people who get killed are just names to you. But each of them had got up that morning feeling just like you do now. They had plans for tomorrow and next week and next month and I'll bet not one of them thought "I'm going to die today". But they did.'

'I know all that, Sandy,' I said quietly. 'Perhaps you've forgotten that my parents . . .'

His face went contrite and embarrassed. 'Oh Dawn . . . I'm sorry . . .'

I shook my head. 'It's all right. I don't mean to be so sensitive. It's just that even now, after all this time, it hurts just as much when I really think about it. I've got over losing them, just about, but I never really stop regretting all the things I didn't do and say, and I wish like hell I'd been nicer to them.'

There was a silence and I knew instinctively Sandy was thinking of his own parents. Perhaps he was realizing they wouldn't always be there. Perhaps he was remembering something of his childhood, and the days when they had been his whole world. Whatever was in his mind, locked away behind those opaque eyes, he said, 'Perhaps we could go and see them for a weekend. And then on the way back we'll have a few days in the Cotswolds. What do you think about that?'

I nodded. 'Fine.' Anywhere would be fine if I was with Sandy, and I liked the idea of meeting his parents too.

The repertory season ended a week or so later with tears and hugs and an almighty party. I both enjoyed and hated it, alternating between sadness that this extraordinary season was coming to an end, and bubbling with excitement for the future. Hylton was even more theatrical than usual in his effusive thanks to all of us; Evelyn, with Rosencrantz in her arms, kissed us all – even me, whom she'd never liked; and Julie got horribly drunk, which I thought was a pity, since it was the way everyone would remember her.

I wondered if we'd ever all be together again. It was the end of an era.

I was ridiculously nervous at the prospect of meeting Sandy's parents. He had phoned them to say we were coming, and when I questioned him about their reaction he was, as usual, evasive.

'What did they say?'

'Oh – the usual things.'

'But were they pleased?'

'I think so.'

They would certainly be pleased to see Sandy, I thought. But I had no idea whether they would welcome an unknown girl.

We went up to the Midlands by coach. Sandy had wanted to hitch-hike, but I absolutely refused. I could hardly hitch up the M5 with my best luggage and wearing clothes that were fit for meeting Sandy's parents, and I had no intention of arriving in a pair of dusty jeans with a haversack slung over my shoulder.

Sandy laughed at me when I told him this, and said I was a middle-class snob who'd never, in a million years, find the courage to opt out of society. But he let me have my way with the irritating air of one indulging a troublesome child.

It was early evening when the coach set us down. We walked along the grass verge of the main road, where the traffic chased nose to tail, until suddenly, unbelievably, there was a gap in the hedge and a sign, half hidden by brambles, announcing: Coppins Lane. No Through Road.

Sandy turned to me. 'It's all so twee it makes you sick, doesn't it?'

'It's rather nice,' I said, thinking that if Sandy's father was able to afford this pseudo-countryside, instead of living in the noise and grime of the city we'd just left behind, good luck to him.

'It's phoney,' Sandy said. 'A pretence of rural heaven for people who don't know the difference.'

Ingle Nook, Sandy's home, was the last house in the lane. It was hidden from its nearest neighbour and from the road by a high hedge that afforded a fair degree of privacy. Sandy led me up the gravel drive that curved in an arc to the front door, and I found myself faced with a huge mock-Georgian mansion.

'Hideous, isn't it?' Sandy said cheerfully. He rang the bell and pushed the door at the same time, and I had to remind myself that this was his home. It seemed so unlikely! Sandy belonged in the tumbledown chalet, not in this genteel luxury.

The hall was square with a gleaming parquet floor. I hesitated in the doorway feeling like an intruder, and as the tuneful chimes of the bell died away, Sandy tossed his holdall on to the elegant telephone seat and called, 'Anyone at home?'

'Andrew, dear, you're here!'

There could be no mistaking that the woman who emerged from one of the white-painted doors that opened from the hall was Sandy's mother, although she wasn't in the least as I had imagined her. True, her iron-grey hair had been freshly set as I'd expected, but beneath it her face was bland and beaming, an ordinary rosy-cheeked face without a trace of artifice, and she was wearing slacks and a big over-shirt rather than the twin set and pearls I'd pictured. She was unashamedly plump, and she exuded an enthusiasm that seemed to reach out and envelop me.

'And you must be Dawn. I'm so pleased to meet you.'

She came across and hugged me, and I felt my awkwardness melting away.

'Andrew tells me you're an actress! How exciting! You must tell me all about it. And I want to hear what Andrew's been up to too. He won't tell me himself, you know. He never does.' She put her free arm out to embrace Sandy, but he gave her hand a quick squeeze and slid past her. I prickled with annoyance at him. Couldn't he be generous enough to give his mother a hug when she was clearly so pleased to see him?

To make up for him, I said, 'It's lovely to be here, Mrs Collins. Sandy's talked so much about you.'

'Is Dad at home?' Sandy asked, and, as he spoke, I saw a man coming down the stairs.

'Just changing, son. Haven't been in very long. Good to see you.' He shook Sandy's hand and smiled at me. 'And this is your Dawn.'

He wasn't a big man; in fact, he was several inches shorter than Sandy's mother, and he was lean in the same way as Sandy, but there was an energy about him that reflected a man who had built a business from one small shop, a man who had started out with no more than a million others but had used his drive and flair to carve out a standard of living they could only dream of.

'My, son, you know how to pick a pretty face, I'll give you that!'

I was both embarrassed and flattered. And I realized, with a feeling of relief, that I'd passed the first test. Sandy's parents seemed to like me. I was almost ashamed to realize just how important that had been to me.

We drifted into the dining room, where the table had been set for an evening meal, and chatted for a few minutes. Then Mrs Collins turned to Sandy.

'I've put Dawn in the room next to yours, dear. Perhaps you'd like to take her up and show her where the bathroom is while I serve.'

I followed Sandy up the broad staircase, feeling my feet sinking into the thick pile on the carpet with each step. Sandy turned the handles of doors and pushed them open as he passed.

'Bathroom. Loo. And this is your room.'

He stood back for me to pass him and I saw a cool green and white room that might have come straight out of *Homes and Gardens*. It was, I thought, the most beautiful bedroom I had ever seen. After the cramped muddles of Aunt Fran's house, and sharing a bedroom for so many years with Serena, this felt like a room I could spend my life in, letting it sooth me when I was tired, delight me with its decor when I wasn't. But Sandy, coming up behind me and putting his arms around me to cup my breasts in his hands, only said, 'If you're afraid of crumpling up the bed you can always crawl in with me.'

I twisted away from him. 'For goodness sake, Sandy! Your mother is only just at the bottom of the stairs!'

He laughed, but there was a note in the laughter that I didn't like.

'Have I got time to change?' I asked. 'I feel so sticky.'

'You look fine. Better not keep them waiting.'

In deference to that I made do with the briefest of washes, splashing cold water on to my face and dabbing cologne behind my ears, but I couldn't help noticing that the bathroom was very much designed for the use of visitors – a beautifully uncluttered room, without any of the usual tubes of toothpaste and ends of soap that make a bathroom look lived in. I guessed that Sandy's parents had an en-suite, and I basked for a moment in the feeling of luxury that gave me.

Dinner was a pleasant meal, and I wondered why on earth Sandy had given up all this to live in a shack on baked beans and bacon. His parents, too, were so nice, so concerned about him, so welcoming to me. And I felt an unexpected bond with Mrs Collins, perhaps because we both loved Sandy and had had to come to terms with his unconventional standards.

'We never expected Andrew to lead the sort of life he does,' she said to me when Sandy and his father had gone out into the garden, leaving us alone. 'It's such a tenuous existence. I expect it's silly of me, but I do worry about him. And his father doesn't understand him at all. He wanted him to go into the business, you know. All the time he was building it up, he was almost driven. He wanted to have something to hand over to his sons, to give them the sort of start in life he'd never had. But Andrew poured scorn on it. It hurt his father a lot.'

'He's doing what he wants to do,' I said. 'I don't think he could be happy doing anything else.'

'I'm sure you're right. But Ken doesn't understand that. He thinks Andrew disapproves of our values and our lifestyle. And that is a kind of rejection he finds very hard to come to terms with.'

What could I say? I wished very much that I could tell her that it wasn't so, but I couldn't bring myself to lie.

'Anyway, dear, I'm very pleased that Andrew has you.' She changed tack seamlessly, smiling at me with a warmth that seemed to come from the heart. 'Really, I mean it. We couldn't be happier.'

My cheeks grew hot as I realized that Mrs Collins had taken this visit to mean something far more than Sandy had intended.

'We're just friends,' I said, a little too quickly. 'That's all.'

I saw the disappointment flicker in her eyes briefly, then the bland smile was back.

'Of course, dear. I didn't mean to imply . . . but I can see that Andrew thinks a lot of you. Shall we go into the garden and look for them?'

The rest of the evening was pleasant and uneventful and if I felt that there were undercurrents on both sides I did my best to ignore them. Sandy's parents were clearly trying very hard to impress on him – and me – that there was nowhere in the world quite like home, and Sandy might be quite unable to resist the occasional ironic remark, but generally speaking the atmosphere was far better than I had dared to hope. After drinking the cups of hot chocolate that Mrs Collins insisted both Sandy and I should have, I went happily to the green and white room and crashed in the comfortable bed.

Next morning Sandy took me on a conducted tour of the places he'd known when he was growing up – the school he'd attended before his parents had decided to send him to boarding school; the park where he used to take Scruffy, a mongrel dog he'd once owned, and still spoke of lovingly; the river where he used to swim and fish. He showed me the block around which he and the other boys had chased each other in forbidden cycle races, and the place where he used to catch a bus to the speedway stadium. He even showed me the seat where he'd kissed his first girlfriend, and all the time he joked and laughed, reliving old experiences and long-lost emotions, until I said:

'Don't you ever wish you were back here, Sandy, amongst all the things and people you know so well?'

He stopped laughing. 'God, Dawn, you sound like my mother.'

'What's wrong with your mother?' I asked. 'She's a very nice lady.'

Sandy kicked at a stone. 'She stifles me. She wants to own me – run my life the way *she* thinks is best. She's always been the same. She makes out it's for my own good, and thinks she knows best, but she goes on and on until I have to leave or go crazy.' He caught up with the stone and kicked it a little further, talking more to himself than to me. 'Stupid, really, but I always hope deep down that it will be different. That I could come home without her climbing on my back. But that's not going to happen. It's the way she is, and she can't help it. And the way I am, I just can't stand it.'

'Oh Sandy, I'm sure she doesn't mean—'

'Take this time,' he went on. 'Because I've brought you, she thinks she can hear wedding bells. She'd love that. Organizing a wedding. And she can even see wayward Andrew settling down at last. Maybe living round here, so she can inveigle you into her clutches the way she did Ray's wife, Jennifer. Then she has some grandchildren to stifle as well. Terrifying, isn't it?'

'I think you're being a bit unfair,' I said, but Sandy laughed bitterly.

'She's won you over already, has she? Oh, well, that's Mum.'

'She thinks your father feels you've rejected him,' I said. 'He built up the business for you and Ray, and now—'

'Don't kid yourself,' Sandy said shortly. 'He didn't do it for us. He did it for himself. Maybe it makes him feel good pretending otherwise, but if he'd really cared he'd have been there when we wanted him, not out making a pile of dough.' He paused for a moment, then went on, 'Growing up in my family wasn't a whole load of fun, Dawn. And I've often wondered which came first in the vicious circle. Did my mother get possessive over us because Dad was never there, or did *he* find an excuse to occupy his time because she was always so preoccupied with Ray and me?'

I said nothing, but I felt dreadfully sad. This visit wasn't going to be any different. There would be no happy-ever-afters for Sandy and his family. The differences ran too deep.

'At least you're not like that, Dawn,' Sandy said, sloughing off the recriminations and draping his arm round my shoulders. 'You don't try to tie me down or tell me what to do. And after tomorrow I'll have you all to myself.'

Perhaps it was because he had pointed it out that I began to notice just how clingy Sandy's mother was. But by the time our visit came to an end I was beginning to understand why Sandy felt as he did. Warm, enveloping hugs and continuous enquiries after our welfare that had seemed pleasant and welcoming the day before had begun to feel like the bars of a cage, and the thinly veiled hints about weddings, homes and settling down were at first embarrassing, then irritating. As for Mr Collins, he had clearly lost the ability to connect with his son years ago, though I couldn't help pitying him as he strove to find some point of contact.

What had begun as a pleasant and promising weekend had degenerated slowly but surely into a time bomb, which I was terrified might explode before we left. But it didn't. And when we came down to the hall with our packed cases there were genuine tears in Mrs Collins' eyes.

'It's been lovely, Andrew. You're such a naughty boy not to come more often. Promise you'll come again soon. And Dawn, dear . . .' She caught me in a bear hug. 'We are so pleased to have met you. And next time I hope there will be some *good news* that you have to tell us.'

Sandy grinned mischievously. 'You mean that you're going to be a grandmother again?' he said, and, as the hot, flustered colour rose in her cheeks, my heart went out to her yet again. She loved him, but she didn't understand him at all, and she never would. Her tragedy was that the harder she tried to draw him close to her, the further she would drive him away.

I kissed her on the cheek. 'Thank you for having us. It's been lovely.'

We walked down the drive, and she was still at the door, waving and calling goodbye, when we turned into the lane. The house was hidden now from view by the high hedges, and suddenly I felt free, free, like a child who has spent all day in a stuffy classroom watching the day pass by outside without him when the dismissal bell rings. I skipped and twirled my vanity case in an arc in the air and laughed up at Sandy.

'You really are wicked! You shouldn't have said that about the baby.'

He grinned. 'Couldn't resist it. Anyway, after this week it will probably be true.'

'It had better not be!' I had to practically run up the lane to keep up with Sandy's jaunty strides.

We took the coach to Cheltenham and then we went by bus to a village Sandy knew. I'd never been to this part of the world before, and I was enchanted by the road that led up and over the Cotswolds, winding between dry stone walls and fields and woods, and surprising me every so often with thatched cottages and houses of golden stone.

'This is real country,' Sandy said. 'And Mum and Dad would have forty fits if they had to live in it.'

The bus set us down in the centre of the village and Sandy pointed out a pub-cum-hotel. 'That's where we're staying.'

I was a little disappointed that, instead of the golden stone, our pub had white pebble dash, but it looked quite old, and behind it a curve of the Cotswolds lent a majestic backdrop. We went into the bar, where several locals looked up from their pints of beer to study us, and Sandy spoke to the landlord. He came out from behind the counter, a big man with a stomach bulging out over the waistband of his trousers, and led us through to the stairs.

'I'm sure you'll be comfortable. Anything you want, just let us know.' His accent was a thick warm burr. 'There we are then.'

He threw open the bedroom door and put my case and Sandy's haversack side by side on the rug beside the double bed. I waited for him to say something about another room, then realized he wasn't going to. Across his shoulder, Sandy's amused eyes met mine, daring me to say a word.

'We don't do lunch as such, sir,' the landlord said. 'But we've snacks in the bar if you fancy a bite to eat. Ploughman's or home-made pasty or sandwiches . . .'

I waited until he'd gone before I turned on Sandy. 'Have you registered us as man and wife?'

Sandy took off his jacket and threw it down on the bed. 'Nothing so hypocritical. You know my feelings about so-called morals.'

'Sandy, you had no right!' I was furious. 'It would serve you right if I walked out of here right now.'

Sandy shrugged. 'Oh Dawn, illogical as ever. You've slept with me at the chalet, why not here?'

'That wasn't planned. This is more . . .'

'Comfortable?' Sandy suggested.

It was a wonderful holiday, a halcyon oasis in the midst of my turbulent life. We walked for miles, sometimes talking, sometimes in silence, hands touching, while the magic was there between us, a tangible thing. We lazed. We laughed. We sang Beatles songs, striving for the harmony the Liverpool quartet achieved, but never managing to be quite in tune. And alone with Sandy in the room he had taken for us, I felt more like a honeymooner than a holidaymaker.

Being with Sandy twenty-four hours a day I could take pleasure in so many little things. Lying back against the pillows I watched him shave while the morning sun slanted through the half-drawn curtains and reflected patterns of light from his razor on to his chin. I watched him dress, memorizing every movement of his lithe body and locking it away for all time in the treasure house of my memory. And as I watched with love, shivered with heightened awareness beneath his touch, and joyfully gave him my soul and my heart as well as my body, I tried to forget that for us tomorrow was never certain, never planned.

In those few stolen golden days there was a closeness between us that had never been there before, and while Sandy slept at night I lay beside him and prayed that it might be this way forever.

On the Friday evening after we'd eaten dinner, Sandy and I went into the pub lounge and carried our drinks over to our favourite place – a carved oak settle in the corner beside the great open fireplace. We'd had a tiring day, hiking across the open hills until we'd found an elevated spot with the fields and woods spread out in a thousand shades of green beneath us and the river Severn a silver thread in the distance. There we'd eaten our packed lunch, and when we'd finished Sandy had got out his sketch pad. It was the first time this week that he'd done any drawing, and, as I sat watching him deftly capturing the scene, I had suddenly been touched by the old familiar feeling of helplessness that came from knowing Sandy was slipping away from me, back into himself. I'd panicked then, but it had seemed that the more I had grasped at the day the faster it had whirled by and now, as I curled my fingers around his beneath the heavy old refectory table in the pub lounge, I was mourning the fact that tomorrow would come and there was no way that I could stop it.

Into my dreaming mood Sandy said, 'I'm pleased with that sketch I did this afternoon. I think I'll do a watercolour from it.'

I nodded and was suddenly aware of a man crossing the room towards us. He was a tall figure in a white alpaca jacket and polo-necked sweater, with hair grown long at the back to compensate for receding temples. As our eyes met he smiled vaguely, then, looking straight at Sandy, he motioned towards the chair opposite ours.

'May I?'

Sandy nodded, and the man put his drink down on our table.

'It's Sandy Collins, isn't it?' he said, half-apologetically.

Sandy's eyes narrowed. 'Yes.' His tone was guarded.

'I'm Charles Beacham. I'm an art dealer with a small gallery, and some of your work has passed through my hands. When I heard an artist was staying here I took the liberty of peeping into the register, and, of course, I recognized the name at once.'

As he spoke he proffered his hand, and I saw Sandy come alive. It was as if this week he had been sleeping, I thought, and now, with the arrival of this stranger, he had woken again to the world that was his life.

'I particularly liked your seascape,' the man was saying, and I knew instinctively he was talking about Sandy's painting of Seagull Bay.

How long ago now it seemed since I had first seen it! How warm and idyllic the days had been then, and how naive and fresh I had been! If Sandy had suggested a holiday then, such as the one we had just enjoyed, I would have been quite sure it heralded a concrete relationship between us, not marriage necessarily, but something just as stable, the end of my search for something to fill the empty place within me that had been left by my parents' death. But now I knew I was as far as ever from the rainbow's end. I'd glimpsed, briefly, the way it could be between a man and a woman. But my days with Sandy had been ended abruptly by a man in an alpaca jacket.

Feeling out of place suddenly, I drained my drink and stood up.

'Dawn?' Sandy said, but he didn't sound overly concerned that I was leaving.

'I'll see you later,' I said.

My voice was determinedly light, and it wasn't until I stepped out of the bar into the soft velvet of the night that I allowed the smile to leave my lips, and bowed my head under the weight of foreboding that had overcome me.

# Ten

I missed Sandy more that autumn than I'd ever missed him. When we parted, it was as if all our previous goodbyes and all the days I had ever known without him were heaped together into one enormous mountain, and I wondered how I could bear the weight on my heart.

The schools tour, when it began, did little to help. 'The Tempest Players' was a second-rate company with second-rate costumes and props, the digs we found ourselves in were seedy, and the rest of the actors were bitchy and miserable. Maybe last year I would have enjoyed it, just to be in the theatre, but after a hard summer's rep the gilt was off the gingerbread a little. But I tried to remain positive. Every time I climbed a narrow staircase in a grotty boarding house, where stale cabbage smells hung among the aspidistras and yellowing net curtains, every time I fell exhausted into a lumpy bed beneath a cracked picture proclaiming 'Home Sweet Home' or 'Suffer the Little Children' and every time I had to miss a meal in order to buy myself a lipstick or a jar of cold cream, I told myself I was lucky to be working at all. And I guessed that if Sandy had been there, or even within a hundred miles, I'd have viewed the whole experience very differently.

Since we'd parted at the end of our holiday I'd seen very little of him. I was upset but not surprised that he did not write, and when I tried to contact him at the flat he shared with his friends in Earls Court, I drew a blank.

'Dawn—? Oh, yes, Dawn!' his flatmate said vaguely into the telephone. 'He's in Southend this week. Can I get him to ring you or something?'

'Ask him to write,' I said, feeling as if the bottom had dropped out of my world. I had no idea what Sandy could be doing in Southend and it felt as if he'd cut himself off from me completely. I worried desperately for a week or more that I might never hear from him again; after all, with Aunt Fran in Bristol, Serena and

Chris married and living with Chris's parents, and me on tour, the old set-up had been completely blown asunder. Then, in the same post, came a note from Sandy apologizing for not having been in touch and promising to write a proper letter when he had time, and six closely-written pages from Serena. I studied Sandy's note over and over, trying to read something into the few scrawled lines, but I could not, and at last I put it away not knowing whether to be relieved to have heard at all or despondent that he had not written at greater length. As to his promise to write again, I didn't hold out much hope of that. Sandy was a great one for promises, but I doubted whether he'd find it any easier to make time to write next week or next month.

Serena's letter began optimistically. 'Dawn. I had to write. I have such fantastic good news.'

My first thought was that she was pregnant again. But, as I read on, I discovered this was not the case. Instead, she and Chris had found a home of their own: a cottage on the cliffs overlooking Seagull Bay.

'I'm so excited I don't know whether I'm coming or going,' she had written, and in her choice of phrase I could almost hear the bouncing burr of her voice. 'Do you remember that darling cottage up on the cliffs? Well, it's going to be ours – mine and Chris's. I could hardly believe it when I saw the picture on the board in the estate agent's window. I flew home and dragged Chris out, and we went straight up there. It's even more super than it looks, small but sort of olde-worlde in the nicest possible way, all pretty beams and snoopy little corners. And the view! Oh Dawn, it's out of this world! As you can imagine, I was terrified we wouldn't be able to afford it, but Chris made them an offer and they accepted it! I think they wanted a quick sale, and this is a bad time of year for people to buy cottages on cliffs. Now, of course, we have the worry of raising the deposit, but Chris's parents are being wonderful, and we'll make it, even if we have to sell everything we own!

'At the moment it's called Maes y Coed, or something in Welsh, after the place where its present owners lived or honeymooned or something, but I've decided to change the name to Sea View Cottage. I know it's corny, but I don't care. That's the way I think of it.'

There was more, much more, with Serena's happiness brimming out of the pages, and, as I read, I was glad for her. Serena deserved to be happy. I hadn't thought she would be, with Chris, although I knew she adored him. But it seemed I'd been wrong. And nothing could have pleased me more.

It was while I was on the schools tour that I decided to try for a place at drama school. Once, in the long-ago past, I'd discarded the idea because I'd thought I couldn't afford it, and although I knew I still couldn't do it unaided, I'd now learned about the financial help that was available – county grants and scholarships paid for by the TV companies. But the first step was to get a place. Eagerly, I sent out for prospectuses and studied them far into the night. Then I applied to two schools – one good and one not-so-good.

I'd thought the audition I'd done for Hunter Hylton was the most nerve-wracking I'd ever have to do, but I was wrong. Then I'd been young and brash, hardly aware of how much I still had to learn. Now, even with some professional experience behind me, it seemed an impertinence to be here within the hallowed walls, actually daring to think myself good enough for them to invest their time in me. I went away convinced I'd never make the grade and lived for a few weeks in a black pit of depression. Then to my unutterable delight came the news. I'd got my place – and at the school of my choice. All that remained between me and my ambition was the small question of money. And for a little while, feeling like one of the seagulls that soared high above my bay, I didn't even think that would be a problem. If I could get a place at a respected drama school I could get a scholarship – couldn't I?

And so there were more auditions, more waiting, and gradually the depression came creeping back. The schools tour was over, Christmas had come and gone, and I had no work and not much incentive to find any.

To relieve the boredom I did a few weeks as an extra in a film being shot on location in the wilds of Yorkshire, but the hours were awful and the money worse, and I felt totally cut off. Shivering in a thin dress on the Dales, I got a severe bout of 'flu, and when at last I struggled out of my sick bed I decided the best tonic I could possibly prescribe for myself would be a visit to Sturvendor.

I rang Serena to ask if it would be convenient.

'Oh Dawn, you know very well you can come whenever you like!' she told me.

And, gratefully, I replied, 'In that case, Serena, expect me on the next train!'

Serena's Sea View Cottage was everything she had said it was. Perched high on the cliff, it gave a panoramic view of the headland and the beach and the grey swirl of the Channel, and, as I knelt on the chintz-covered window seat, looking out, I thought that if I could live here with Sandy and raise a family I'd never give another thought to drama school.

'Well, do you like it?' Serena asked. She was beaming with rosy pride. 'There's a lot to do, of course, and Chris never seems to have the time. He's gone over on to the sales side – I told you – and it means he works dreadfully long hours. He's got such a big area to cover. I never know when to expect him home. In some ways I wish he was back in the laboratory, but I suppose if he's happy . . .'

'That's the main thing,' I agreed. 'And what about Aunt Fran? Has she settled in her new home?'

Serena smiled. 'Yes, thank goodness. She's a natural-born teacher. She should never have given it up. And it really was the right thing for her, making a clean break. She's been able to start all over afresh.'

Her face clouded momentarily, and I knew she was remembering her father. To change the subject, I began telling her about my place at drama school and the scholarship I was hoping to get.

'Oh, you'll get it, Dawn!' Serena enthused. 'I know you will. You're so good!'

I pulled a face. 'I wish I had your confidence. The theatre is jam-packed with good people, most of them a lot better than I am, and hundreds of them are out of work. There just aren't enough jobs to go round. So why should I be special enough?'

'You're too modest,' Serena said. 'And I can't wait for the day when you're famous and I can tell people oh-so-casually that you're my cousin and my best friend. Now, how about a cup of tea?'

'Good idea,' I said. Nobody could make tea like Serena.

'What are you going to do in the meantime?' she asked while the pot brewed.

'I don't know. Get a temporary job, I suppose. But I can't help feeling it's not worth it until I know about the scholarship. And Sandy should be here soon . . .'

I said it tentatively, ashamed suddenly for Serena to know how little I'd seen of him this winter and half-afraid that this summer he may decide not to come to Sturvendor. For all I knew, he could have decided to work his passage to Australia! Or the chalet could have finally blown away in a winter storm. Anything could have happened, and I wouldn't know . . .

Serena's eyes met mine and flickered away. Then she pushed her hair away from her face and said awkwardly, 'He was here a couple of weeks ago. He called in on his way to visit someone in Cornwall.'

There was a knife thrust of pain in my stomach. Sandy had gone to Cornwall to visit someone, but he hadn't taken the trouble to look me up.

'Dawn . . . I think you ought to know. There was a girl with him.'

The knife twisted deeper, searing me, taking my breath. Why did someone as sane as I was cling to a love that brought me nothing but pain? Why couldn't I accept Sandy for what he was, and what we had shared for what it was, and leave it at that? That Sandy had actually taken someone else to Serena's house was proof that he did not care if he upset and hurt me. And yet it was all part of the defiance that was Sandy. If I tackled him about it his face would become a resentful mask and he would say, 'I'll do what I like, Dawn. You don't own me!' As if he was the one who had been wronged. And I would be left with the feeling that Sandy had forced the confrontation to prove to himself, yet again, that he was right to live the way he did. Because to face the possibility that he simply didn't care about me or my feelings was more than I could bear.

'She was an awfully untidy girl,' Serena said, as if that made it all right. 'All denim and cheesecloth and masses of hair. But she didn't look clean to me. If that's the sort of girl Sandy wants to be with he's not worth bothering about, Dawn.'

I didn't answer. I couldn't. I just went on staring out of the window as if my life depended on it.

After a moment Serena said, 'You will stay with us while you're waiting for the result of your scholarship application, won't you, Dawn?'

With an effort I swallowed the knot of tears that had gathered in my throat. 'Oh Serena, I don't want to impose . . .'

'Impose, indeed! I shall be glad to have you here.'

I wondered if Chris would be glad. I rather thought he might like his wife and his fireside to himself.

'In fact, I shall be really offended if you don't, Dawn,' Serena insisted.

I couldn't argue; I didn't have the stomach for it. More than anything in the world I wanted to be in Sturvendor, my haven. 'OK. Just as long as you promise to turn me out the moment you've had enough of me,' I said.

'Oh Dawn.' Serena sighed. 'Just shut up and have another cup of tea.'

Sandy arrived a week or so later. He arrived one bright but blustery day and picked up all the threads as if the last months had never been. And I, fool that I am, let him. I didn't even question him about the winter and the girl he had taken to Cornwall; I knew all too well what his answer would be. And I had decided. Whatever it said about my tattered pride, I would rather have Sandy on his terms than not at all.

Perhaps one day things would be different and he would be ready to settle for just one woman, and perhaps that woman would be me. If not – we'd just have to go on as we were. For, however much he hurt me, the fact was I loved him. And there could never be anyone else for me.

I'd set up an arrangement to have my mail forwarded to me in Sturvendor, and as soon as the typewritten envelope dropped through the letterbox I knew it was the result of the scholarship. I picked it up and turned it over between my hands, my tummy a quaking, shaking jelly. Taking a deep breath, I ripped open the envelope. And felt myself go numb.

I hadn't got it. They 'regretted to tell me' . . . and all the rest. *Well, that's it*, I thought, coolly, rationally, but I felt sick through and through all the same. And as I stood there, holding the remnants of my dreams, I realized just how much it had mattered to me that someone should have thought I was good enough to back with money. Their confidence in me was just as important to me as the cold, hard cash to feed and clothe me.

Serena came in and I tossed the letter towards her, mock-carelessly.

'So, now you know,' I said, and there was a hard, bright edge to my voice. 'I'm not Sarah Bernhardt after all. I'm just another deluded, stage-struck idiot.'

Serena had gone pink with indignation. 'Oh Dawn, it's not fair! You're good! I know you are. They have to be blind not to see it.'

A small laugh tickled in my throat that Serena should think she knew better than the TV people, and then, suddenly, I wasn't laughing but crying. I hiccuped tears into my clenched fist and felt them scald my cheeks. A failure. That's what I was. A bloody failure. I couldn't keep my man, and now I knew I wasn't any good as an actress either . . .

'Dawn, don't!' Serena pleaded, and then: 'Dawn, Chris is here . . .'

The last words worked a miracle that no amount of comfort could have done. My tears stopped instantly. I had too much pride to let Chris see me crying.

'Hi, Chris,' I said tonelessly, without turning round.

'Chris, if Dawn wants to do another season with Hunter Hylton, it would be OK for her to stay here, wouldn't it?' Serena was saying impulsively.

'Oh Serena, no . . .' I swung round, remembered my swollen eyes, and turned hurriedly away again.

'Dawn's always welcome,' Chris said. 'She knows that.'

There was an odd note in his voice that made me uncomfortable, but I was too preoccupied to take much notice.

'Hunter may not even want me,' I said, trying to sound bright and careless.

'He'll want you,' Serena said confidently.

And for once she was right.

'Dawn, my angel, I didn't know how to get in touch with you,' Hunter gushed when I telephoned him. 'The girl I engaged to play leads has gone and got a bun in the oven. Stupid, stupid little minx! The moment I heard, I thought of you. I think you could cope with it. You came on very well last year, and learned your stagecraft fast.'

'I learned what cigarettes you smoke, you mean,' I said sarcastically.

His chesty laugh roared down the line, filling me with aching nostalgia. 'Cheeky little Dawn, as ever! How I would have missed you, my angel!'

'It's nice to know someone would,' I said wryly, and wished the comment had not been so uncomfortably close to the truth.

The summer progressed much as the year before had done, only now I was a year older and a good deal further down the road to disillusion. Sandy did not have the hot dog stall this year. He was selling quite a lot of his paintings, and doing some water colour portraits for local people too, and he reckoned it paid him to spend his time with his brushes and easel now.

'Someone else can have the steamy bangers trade,' he said loftily. 'I'm earning my living the way I want to now.'

I nodded. Maybe it was precarious. Maybe it was a poor living by some standards. But to be able to keep himself through his painting was an achievement he could rightly be proud of.

*If only my career could reach such dizzy heights!* I thought. But then Sandy didn't need to earn as much as I did. All he needed, apart from food, was a packet of razor blades, and if he couldn't afford them he could always grow a beard. But with me it was an endless round of stockings and lipstick, cotton wool and cold cream and yet more stockings, besides giving Serena money for my keep and trying to save for the capital expenditure of new clothes. In the end I gave up buying stockings, and instead bought a bottle of wet-white – a strange, brown cosmetic, which the chemist in town made up and sold me in a corked medicine bottle – until my legs got a decent tan, but even then it was hard to make the money go round.

For the first time I began to worry about the future. Somewhere along the line I seemed to have lost my sense of direction, and that in itself was a form of depression. And so I drifted on, until one day something happened to make me stop short and take stock.

It was a Sunday in July. I woke to a dull grey light that made me think it must still be early morning, but the clock beside my bed told me it was eleven, so I knew the greyness must be caused by rain clouds.

'Damn,' I said softly. I hated wet Sundays. They were such a waste of the one day of the week that I had to myself. I lay for a few moments while all the corners of my mind came awake, and then I remembered that today Serena was going to Bristol to visit Aunt Fran. She had gone alone because Chris had a lot of paperwork to catch up on, and she had asked me to get his lunch.

I drew the curtains to let in what there was of the thick grey light, slipped on my cotton housecoat over my nightdress, and padded downstairs to make myself a cup of life-saving coffee.

As I passed the dining room door I glanced in and saw Chris at the table with all his paperwork spread out in front of him. Not wanting to disturb him, I went on into the kitchen and plugged in the percolator. Then, while I waited for it to heat up, I stood by the window flicking through the Sunday supplements that had been delivered.

It was a small, unexpected sound that made me look up, and to my surprise I saw Chris standing in the doorway. He didn't make a move to come in, and he didn't say anything. He just stood there, a strange, intense expression on his face, and with a stab of discomfort I found myself wondering how long he had been there.

'For goodness sake, don't look at me like that!' I said sharply.

Chris didn't move. He stood there, his eyes devouring me, and suddenly I was remembering that day he'd come to me in the bay to ask if there was any chance for him. In all that had happened since, I had put it out of my mind, told myself it was just a momentary whim born of panic when he'd been faced with having to marry Serena; now I saw the way he was looking at me and knew that it had been much more than that. He'd wanted me. And nothing had changed since.

'Chris, stop it!' I said again.

A muscle moved at the corner of his mouth. 'You shouldn't come down dressed like that if you don't want me to look at you,' he said.

Defensively, I pulled my housecoat around me, and as I did so I was suddenly horribly conscious of just how flimsy it was. At the theatre I walked around in much less and thought nothing of it. But I was not at the theatre now.

'In that case, I'd better go and change,' I said coolly.

But Chris was blocking the doorway and he refused to move out of my way. As I tried to pass he caught at my wrist, holding me fast, and his eyes, dark with desire, never left my face.

'Let me go, Chris,' I said, quietly but firmly.

The muscle beside his mouth moved again, but he did not let me go.

'I want you, Dawn,' he said, and his voice was so low and so intense it frightened me. With an abrupt movement, I wrenched my arm free.

'For God's sake, Chris!' I snapped. 'Serena is only in Bristol. She hasn't taken off for the moon.'

'Would it make any difference if she had?' Chris asked.

'You know it wouldn't,' I said coldly. 'You've always known.'

I saw the pain dart across his face and it stunned me to know I could still hurt him so much. Then his eyes narrowed to pinpoints of something close to hatred.

'Then why do you go on tormenting me?' he rasped. 'You don't want me, but you won't let me go. You stay here, flaunting yourself, driving me crazy. And Serena won't hear a word against you. You're a bloody selfish witch, and I just wish you'd get out of our lives.'

For a moment I stared at him, stunned by the vehemence of his attack. Then the truth of what he had said began to sting me with sharp barbs. I had taken advantage of Serena's friendship without stopping to think what I was doing to her just by being here. And, by imposing on Chris's hospitality, I was unintentionally torturing him day by day. Somehow I drew myself tall.

'I'm sorry, Chris,' I said. 'I never meant to hurt anyone. I'll move out just as soon as I can. Now, will you please let me pass before something happens that we'll both regret?'

And, like a beaten man, he stood aside.

'What can I do?' I said to Sandy. 'I had no idea, honestly, that he felt that way. I mean, I *did*, I know, but that's so long ago now. I mean . . . years! I thought he'd got over all that . . . changed . . .'

'Have *you* changed?' Sandy asked.

I was silent. No, I hadn't changed. I was older and maybe a little wiser, and certainly a whole lot more cynical, but I hadn't changed. I still loved Sandy and I still wanted the same things. And if they seemed more distant than ever, it didn't stop me wanting them. Maybe I'd still feel this way when I was ninety – basically the same person under a dried-out, wrinkled skin, still longing for love, still longing to run on legs grown stiff and arthritic. The thought chilled me, shaking me with a sense of lonely destiny.

'What's wrong, Dawn?' Sandy asked gently.

Haltingly, I told him, feeling I was stripping my soul bare, yet wanting him to understand. He looked at me seriously for a moment, then he laughed.

'Can't you just see us? You tottering across the pebbles, me sitting in the doorway of the chalet with my pipe and easel, trying to keep my Father Christmas beard out of the paint? You're so right, we'll be the same, Dawn – if we live that long. Just don't grow jaundiced, love. Keep looking on, never back.'

I wanted to say it would help if there was something to look on to, but it was comforting at least to think Sandy imagined us still together at ninety. Recently, I'd been terribly afraid that this summer might be our last together.

'What'll you do now that Chris has declared himself?' Sandy asked.

I frowned. 'I don't know. It's obvious I can't stay at Sea View Cottage. The trouble is, Serena won't understand why I have to leave and I certainly can't tell her. I'll just have to think of something that sounds convincing.'

'Move in with me,' Sandy said.

He wasn't looking at me. He was looking straight out at the

rainswept shore, but something in his voice told me he wanted me to say 'yes', and breath caught in my throat. So long I'd waited, so long, that I'd given up hoping Sandy would ever suggest anything permanent between us. Now, sheer, disbelieving joy began to trickle through my veins, tingling as it warmed every corner of me.

Sandy reached over to drape his arm loosely around me and his touch was like live electricity on my skin.

'I'd miss you, Dawn, if you weren't around,' he said lazily. 'I know this isn't exactly the luxury you crave, but it's not so bad really. And when the season ends, come to London with me. We'll find a flat, and you can work when you can. We need each other, old darling, even if we won't admit it.'

The joy was a lump in my throat now, choking me. I wanted to tell him, 'Oh yes, Sandy, I've always known I needed you!' But no words came. I wanted to put my arms around him and press against him and perhaps cry a little on his shoulder. But even now my reserve was such that I didn't want him to know just how much I cared. So when I felt my voice would be steady enough I said casually, 'OK, you're on.'

And thought that never again would I mind wet Sunday afternoons.

# Eleven

Sandy and I found a bedsit in Kensington: one large room made small by heavy old furniture, a kitchen that might once have been a cupboard, judging by its size, and the use of the bathroom and loo on the floor below. 'Use of a bathroom' was one of the biggest jokes about the place; the door was kept locked, and invariably when we wanted a bath the landlord, who lived on the ground floor, was nowhere to be found, so we gave up and had a stand-up wash at the sink. But I thought the flat was Utopia. I'd never before had a place that I could even vaguely call my own, and now I had a wonderful time playing at house. It wasn't always easy to make interesting meals on our limited budget, and the oven took hours to reach a temperature hot enough to cook anything, but I found it a challenge to my ingenuity and it was gratifying when Sandy praised my efforts. It wasn't easy to keep things tidy in that cramped space either, or to make the room look sunshiny instead of drab, but I tried – oh how I tried! – and as long as Sandy was there it was all worthwhile.

Living together didn't change our relationship at all, but I hadn't expected it to. It was enough that Sandy wanted to share his life with me, and I knew him too well to try to invade his privacy. Perhaps it was that which kept our relationship fresh, that there were things we did not know about each other and perhaps never would, secret, undiscovered places and hidden thoughts. For me there was a wistful magic in looking at Sandy sleeping and wondering just what was going on in the depths of his mind. And I thought that I fascinated him in exactly the same way.

I worked intermittently. When I was working we had money to spare and when I wasn't we struggled. But the struggles didn't matter as long as we were together, and our first months together were wonderful. In some ways I wished we were married, but it didn't really matter. I wasn't ready to start wanting children – the one eventuality I felt really required us to be legally committed to one another – and right now, if Sandy felt happier going on as we were, that was all right with me.

In those early days everything was a cause for celebration, and we made the most of all our successes. If Sandy got a particularly good price for a painting we'd have a bottle of cheap wine with our supper, toasting one another and getting tiddly on love and laughter. When I did a TV commercial we went up West and spent a bomb on cinema tickets and fried chicken. It was foolish and extravagant and we loved it.

That Christmas was one of the happiest I've ever spent. We'd been invited to countless parties, but we decided we'd like to have Christmas Day on our own. Somehow I managed to roast a small turkey in the temperamental oven and Sandy got a miniature bottle of brandy, which we used to ignite the Mrs Peek's pudding.

When we'd eaten we exchanged presents. Sandy had bought me a pendant, a tiny pearl resting on a gold leaf, and he fastened it round my neck with the gentle touch that he might have used to put a ring on my finger. And I looked at his dear face, golden in the light of the candle we'd stuck in a jam-jar on the table, and curled up inside with love for him.

'You'll never guess what I've got for you,' I told him. 'It's something not in the least romantic.'

He waited, pretending impatience, while I fetched the big, oblong box that I'd wrapped in emerald-green paper and covered with silver stars and snowflakes. And then he made me help him open it, layer by layer, until at last he took off the lid and saw the slippers inside.

'Do you like them?' I asked anxiously. 'They're real-sheepskin lined because you're always complaining your feet are cold.'

He pushed one bare foot into a slipper, wriggling his toes in the soft sheepskin, and then he pulled me down and kissed me. 'Clever old Dawn. Practical as ever. You are the least romantic actress I ever met.'

'That's probably why I'm a bad one,' I said gloomily, but Sandy covered my mouth with his, cutting off my words, and we melted together into the scratchy old bed settee that had pride of place in our room. Then Sandy opened one eye and hissed, 'Aunt Fran would approve, anyway.'

I laughed into his shoulder. Yes, Aunt Fran would approve. Slippers were the sort of conventional Christmas present she always gave. But it was about the only thing she would approve of. I knew she was horrified that Sandy and I were 'living in sin' as she called it, and I felt guilty about upsetting her after she had been so good to me.

I knew, too, that both she and Serena were hurt that I hadn't gone to Sturvendor for a family Christmas, but I hadn't wanted to see Chris. I only hoped that Serena had no idea that was one of the reasons Sandy and I had stayed in London.

A few weeks after Christmas a letter from Serena relayed us the news that old Miss Chertsey had died after a fall on the ice in her own back yard.

'I thought you ought to know,' Serena had written. 'If the chalet is sold and done up, it might be let to summer visitors for a higher rent than Sandy could afford, and Chris says it's pretty unlikely he'll be able to get it this year in any case until Miss Chertsey's estate is sorted out.'

Sandy, however, refused to be perturbed by this news. 'We'll find something,' he said breezily. 'Cornwall would be nice for a change, or maybe the Lake District. Sturvendor will always mean hot dogs under the pier to me.'

'We could stay here if we're really stuck,' I said.

'Not likely! Summer in the smoke would kill me,' Sandy asserted cheerfully. 'The only problem I can see is that there wouldn't be much in the way of work for you in the Lake District.'

'There's not much work anywhere,' I said, but I didn't add that I was beginning to be fed up with never having quite enough money. Only that day I'd seen a dress in the sales that I would have loved, but I simply hadn't had the three pounds to buy it, and it had crossed my mind that since I'd come to England I'd never once been able to buy myself something without having to scrimp and save for it.

'Oh, something will turn up,' Sandy said, and for once his optimism annoyed rather than comforted me.

The letter, a white typewritten envelope with the franking of Kirby, Hawsett & Dunn, Solicitors, of Sturvendor, and addressed to Sandy, arrived a few weeks later.

Immediately, my curiosity was aroused, but this was one of those rare occasions when we'd been able to get into the bathroom, and I knew Sandy would be ages wallowing in the luxury of as much hot water as the geyser would dispense. As I cleared away the breakfast things I kept staring at the letter, picking it up and putting it down again and wishing I had X-ray eyes, and eventually I could control my impatience no longer. Taking the letter I went down the stairs and knocked at the bathroom door.

'Sandy, it's me. Open up!'

'I can't. I'm in the bath.' His voice sounded echoey.

'I know you are. But there's a letter here from the solicitors at Sturvendor.'

I heard him sigh and there were splashing sounds followed by the wet sucking noise of his feet on the lino. The door opened a crack, and with a quick look over my shoulder to ensure I wasn't about to expose Sandy to the rest of the house, I slipped through.

'So what are you going on about?' Sandy asked, getting back into the bath.

I waved the letter at him. 'This.'

'All right, open it, if you're so keen to see what's inside,' he said.

I slid the sheet of paper out of the envelope and unfolded it. I had to read it twice before I could believe the contents. Then I shrieked with delight, so that Sandy said, 'For goodness sake – shh! We'll be given our marching orders for holding orgies in the bathroom.'

'That's OK,' I said, bubbling with excitement. 'Just listen to this. The chalet is yours! Miss Chertsey left it to you in her will!'

Sandy stared in disbelief. 'Really?'

'Yes, really!'

Sandy stood up with the water dripping from him and pulled me towards him.

'Sandy, you're all wet!' I protested, but he had covered my mouth with his, so the words got lost in a mumble.

I was sitting on the cork-topped stool watching him towel himself dry when a thought occurred to me. 'I thought you didn't like gifts. You'll never take anything from your father.'

'This is different.'

'Different how?'

He pulled on his jeans, buckling them round his narrow waist. 'I suppose she thought I've more or less paid for the ramshackle old place over the last few years.'

'Maybe it's fallen down by now,' I said. 'It gets shakier every year and the beach is awfully bleak in winter. I'd never be surprised if the roof blew away completely.'

'We'll go down as soon as possible,' Sandy said. 'I have to look after my property.'

'You certainly do,' I agreed. And thought that, in spite of all he had ever said about materialism, Sandy looked very pleased to have acquired something, however shaky, that was really his own.

We went to Sturvendor on a cold, blustery day in February. Sandy hitched and I went by train because I positively refused to hitch in that sort of weather, and it was something I loathed doing in any case.

'Nobody is going to be going to Sturvendor at this time of year,' I predicted.

'I'll take a chance,' Sandy said. 'And I bet I'll beat you to it. I'll meet your train.'

'Fat chance!'

But when I came out on to the station forecourt Sandy was leaning against the wall, smiling an infuriatingly self-satisfied smile.

'How was the old S & D?' he asked. 'That's what it used to be called. S & D for Slow and Dirty, although they pretended it was Somerset and Dorset.' He laughed at his own joke and took my case. 'Aren't you going to ask me how I got on?'

'All right,' I said unwillingly. 'How did you get on?'

'I came all the way in a bloody great Humber Hawk. Real old Lord of the Manor luxury – red-leather comfort. You'd have lapped it up, my darling little snob.'

I ignored that. 'You haven't seen Serena yet?' I was still unhappy about facing her and Chris, but I knew I would have to, sooner rather than later.

'Not yet. I've been waiting for you. I've had a look at the chalet, though, and it's still there, I'm glad to say. I'd have hated my legacy to have been swept out to see as pieces of driftwood.'

We walked along the windswept street. Sandy said, 'I'll go to the solicitors for the key now that you've arrived. Are you coming in?'

I shook my head. I felt dirty and untidy and I had no wish to meet a solicitor looking as I did. It would be one in the eye for plummy-voice, though, if she was still there. Me with a bloke like Sandy. For all that she would try to stuff him into a conventional suit and tie, she would almost certainly find Sandy dishy, even if his jeans were faded and his sweater shrunk. Perhaps even because of it. I'd never met any girl who didn't go weak at the knees on meeting Sandy.

After a while Sandy came out of the solicitors' office again swinging the key by a cardboard ticket to which it was attached, and we went down to the beach. It was bleak and uninviting, certainly, but I knew the sea here in all its moods and there was a charm about the angry, yellow-topped waves under the grey sea mist, something lovely and splendid about the deserted beach. And, high above, the moors frowned moodily, and on a spit of wind a seagull rose and fell as he rode out the storm.

Homesickness flooded over me in a wave, homesickness not for Canada, the land of my birth, but for Sturvendor. And I thought, *Maybe Sturvendor is my spiritual home, for it is certainly the home of my ancestors.*

Suddenly, into my mind's eye came a picture from the past, the days when men used to fish from Sturvendor, and I saw boys and old men carved from the same rock as the towering cliffs and weathered women who waited for them with children around their skirts and fear in their hearts. And I thought, *If ever I had a previous incarnation I am sure it was here, and that is why I look at the majesty of the sea with awe, that is why I shiver. Maybe, centuries ago, I stood on this beach and waited for my man to come home; maybe I prayed that the wind would blow him to safety, and to me. Maybe he came, and I held him in my arms and tried to keep myself from begging him to go no more. Or maybe I saw the driftwood that had once been his boat washed up on the shore, and the flurry of water in the rock pools was the reflection of a dear drowned face . . .*

'Aren't you coming in now I've got the key?' Sandy's voice jerked me sharply back across the years, and I smiled at him, leaving my reverie behind.

The chalet looked exactly as it had when we left it the previous autumn. True, the reek of damp hit us when we opened the door, but otherwise it might have been just yesterday that we pulled the cotton curtains across the grubby window panes. The bucket was turned upside down in the sink where we'd left it; there was a paperback book that I'd forgotten on the table, and a newspaper in the waste bin.

Sandy said, 'It's funny, but I've always felt this place belonged to me somehow.'

He walked around like a practised landlord inspecting for flaws and things that needed doing and I followed, flicking idly through the pages of the paperback because I couldn't remember how it ended, and wondered if perhaps I'd never actually finished reading it.

'It's not in bad shape, except for the roof,' Sandy said at last. 'Do you think we might run to some tar paper to repair it?'

'I expect so,' I said. 'We can always starve for a day or two.'

Sandy scowled at my sarcasm. 'If you hadn't insisted on coming on the bloody train we'd be a lot better off. Never mind, at least you'll be able to do another season with old Hunter what's-his-name, won't you?'

'I suppose so,' I said, wishing I could feel more enthusiastic at the prospect.

I'd been going to do such great things, I thought sadly, and all I'd achieved were three seasons with the same second-rate repertory company and a few other odd jobs. I had no one but myself to blame, of course. I'd put Sandy before my career and that was no way to find success. I loved the theatre, but I was obsessed with Sandy, and it ought to have been the other way around.

But although I'd grown a little disillusioned about the theatre, I still had Sandy. And I'd long ago decided that if I could have him, any terms at all would do.

It was halfway through the afternoon when we locked the chalet door behind us and caught a bus up on to the headland. Of course, it didn't go anywhere near Sea View Cottage, and we had to walk the last mile or so, bending ourselves against the wind and unable to talk much because our words were blown back into our faces.

The cottage was a dark silhouette against the grey afternoon sky, but there were lights in every window like bright splashes of gold, beacons to light the travellers home. Serena had the door open as soon as she saw us at the gate, calling out a greeting and leaving us in no doubt as to our welcome. She took our coats and brought in a pot of tea and a plate of toasted crumpets with the butter melting into them and making yellow rivers on the plate, and I suddenly realized that I hadn't eaten since morning and I was very hungry.

We chatted as we ate, but I couldn't help listening with half an ear for Chris's key in the lock. Once I looked up to see Sandy watching me and I knew he was reading my mind.

After a while he said, 'I think we'd better be making a move. We're a long way from home.'

'Oh, you're not going home tonight!' Serena exclaimed. 'You can't go before Chris gets in anyway. He'd never forgive you. And I've a bed made up and ready, so you've no excuse at all.'

'Is Chris often late?' Sandy asked, and Serena's face clouded.

'Well . . . yes, to be honest. But I suppose his work must come first.'

There was a sadness in her voice that hadn't used to be there and, on the point of saying, 'Never mind, you won't notice he's not here when children come along,' I stopped myself, struck suddenly by the fact that it was a long time now since Serena's miscarriage. I would have expected her to have been pregnant again by now, but her figure was as trim as ever, and there was no tell-tale glow about her.

'Would you two like the television?' She got up and switched on, then began stacking plates together.

'I'll help you,' I said, following her into the kitchen.

She ran a bowl of hot water and I found a tea towel on a peg behind the door. But instead of washing up, Serena banged a pile of crockery into the bowl and turned to face me, leaning her hips against the sink.

'Dawn, tell me it's none of my business if you like, but I'm worried about you.'

'Worried? About me?' I had been so immersed in her problems it was a shock to hear her say *I* was causing *her* concern.

'Yes. What are you doing now, Dawn? For work, I mean?'

'At the moment, nothing, but—'

'That's what I mean,' Serena attacked. 'You had the makings of a first-class actress, and, just because of that silly scholarship, you've let it all slide. You've done nothing worthwhile in a year or more. I suppose when summer comes you'll come back to rep down here, just to be near Sandy, and, after that, hang about again. You've let a really worthwhile career go down the drain for the sake of not bothering.'

It was very much what I'd thought myself but to hear her say it aloud was galling. 'You don't know anything about it, Serena,' I said indignantly. 'If you knew the number of times I've auditioned and not been successful . . . If you saw the hundreds of girls I keep seeing, all doing the rounds for the same jobs—'

'Then give it up,' Serena said. 'But for goodness sake do *something*, Dawn.'

I grabbed a cup from the bowl and dried it with unnecessary vigour. 'It's because of Sandy,' I said softly.

'Hang Sandy!' Serena exploded. 'I know you're crazy about him, but he's no good to you. His life isn't your life. You won't always be happy to be a drop-out like he is. You'll want a home and a family and a decent living. I bet deep down you want it now.'

'I want Sandy,' I said stubbornly. 'Just as you want Chris.'

'I'm married to Chris,' Serena said. 'Sandy could walk out on you tomorrow, and you'd have no rights and no anything. You're so vulnerable, Dawn.'

'But that's the whole point,' I said. 'Sandy would hate being tied down. Why should anyone feel they have to stay because of a wedding ring and a piece of paper? I don't think it would make one iota of difference anyway. In fact, I think it might drive him away.'

'It's not just the ring and the paper,' Serena said. 'It's everything. When you've a home to break up, you stop and think. Sandy could pack a bag and go and that would be all there was to it. Goodbye, Dawn. And you haven't even got a career to go to, thanks to the way he's made you feel that doing anything less than you want to is a betrayal. Honestly, if he told you to go and jump off the cliff, I believe you'd do it.'

The gritty grain of truth hurt me. 'Oh, don't be so smug!' I said, wishing I could tell her a thing or two about her precious Chris.

Her face clouded. 'I'm sorry. I didn't mean to sound smug. But somebody's got to make you see sense before it's too late, and there isn't anybody but me. So hate me if you like, but do think about it. And listen –' her face softened – 'I do understand how you feel about Sandy. I know how it is to love somebody so that nothing else matters, not even your self-respect. I know how it's possible to blind yourself to everything else, just as long as you can go on being with them. And I hope Sandy never lets you down, just as I hope Chris . . .'

Her voice tailed away and I looked at her sharply. But, before I had time to marshal my thoughts, she went on, 'But if he ever did leave you, your life would be a complete wreck, Dawn. There'd be nothing. Nothing! Oh, think about it, please!'

I nodded, a knot of sadness gathering around my heart. Serena, as always, was right. She had put into words things I preferred not to think about, but she was right. I didn't know what I could do about it because I knew that every time something came up that would take me away from Sandy I would turn it down. I couldn't bear to be apart from him, even for a few months. And yet I could feel the teeth of the vicious circle that had trapped me, and they made me shiver.

'Perhaps I'll have another crack at a scholarship for drama school,' I said. 'But even then . . .'

I broke off, not having the heart to tell Serena that half the unsuccessful girls who chased the same jobs as I did were graduates of drama school. Once I'd thought of it as a passport to fame and fortune, but no longer. Suddenly, I felt very tired.

'I'll tell you what I'll do,' I promised her. 'I'll do the season here again, and then if I can't get a really good job for the winter, I'll throw it all in and go to secretarial college. Everybody wants typists. How does that sound?'

'Very sensible.' It was the sort of thing I would have expected her to say, but she was smiling, the old Serena smile that made her lovely face light up.

We finished the washing up and said no more about it, but when we went back to sit in the lounge, snippets of what she had said kept popping into my mind, tormenting me. I kept glancing at Sandy, sprawled in the fireside chair, and wondering if he'd overheard any of our conversation, and what he would think if he had. And I kept wondering if I would keep my promise to Serena. It wouldn't be so difficult, I thought. I could go to evening classes in London, and when I had some typing qualifications there would be dozens of jobs for me to choose from. I needn't leave Sandy, and I need no longer feel guilty about wasting my life on a dream.

Chris eventually came home, bluff and red-faced as if he'd had several drinks too many. For Serena's benefit I tried to talk to him as if nothing had ever happened between us, but the awkwardness was prickling at me, so potent that I couldn't believe she didn't notice it. Hours later, or so it seemed, Sandy and I retired to the spare room where Serena had made up a bed for us.

'Thank goodness for that. I'm whacked!' Sandy said, falling into bed.

I smiled briefly, but I was preoccupied once more with the conversation I'd had with Serena. I spent longer than usual taking off my make-up, and when I'd finished I put out the light and stood at the window looking out across the bay. Far, far out to sea I could see the dark shape of a ship, and, even further, the lights that marked the coast of Wales. Once again I had the warm feeling of coming home, and my worries and turmoil fell away from me.

I drew the curtains and slipped into bed beside Sandy, feeling the oasis of warmth that his body had made in the cold sheets.

'Sandy?' I whispered, curling around his back, but Sandy did not reply, and I guessed from the easy rhythm of his breathing that he was asleep.

*Tomorrow*, I thought. *Tomorrow I'll sort everything out. Tomorrow I'll decide what I'm going to do.*

And then the weight of sleep was pressing heavily on my eyelids; I sighed once, and knew no more.

Tomorrow, of course, never came. At least, not then. Sandy and I returned to London and resumed our old life, and in the spring we came back to Sturvendor. I began a third season with the Hunter Hylton Repertory Company, and we lived in the chalet that now, unbelievably, belonged to Sandy.

# Twelve

Sometimes, when I look back to those days, I wonder if things would have been different if Sandy had been true to me. But he wasn't. Fidelity wasn't something Sandy was capable of, for very long. He was so terrified of being tied down, and every time he felt himself falling into a rut, being comfortable with me and me alone, he rebelled. At least, that was what I tried to tell myself. It hurt less than the bald truth: that Sandy could not be content with just one woman.

During our first months back at Sturvendor I lulled myself into a fool's paradise, telling myself that at last Sandy and I had reached a permanent state in our relationship. I determinedly forgot the mini-skirted blonde and the hippy girl with beads and bangles and all the others that I'd never found out about and fell into the habit of trusting him. He didn't *have* to live with me, I reasoned. If he wanted to be free he could pack his bags and go, just as Serena had said. The fact that he stayed must be proof that I was the one he wanted. And when I was brought face to face again with the proof of Sandy's infidelity I was shaken to the core.

I'd been to the dentist to get a filling replaced, and I was walking back along the promenade gingerly feeling my numb lip with my tongue and wishing I'd had the courage to have it done without an injection. When I reached the taxi rank there were two or three cabs in line, and one of them belonged to Jack Stride, whom I'd known for years. He wound down the window as I came alongside.

'Hello there, stranger! Where have you been hiding yourself?'

When Sandy had had the hot dog barrow we'd often stopped for a chat with Jack, who had lived in Sturvendor all his life and used to regale us with stories of what it had been like when he was a boy, forty years and more ago. I hadn't seen him for ages now though. We exchanged a few pleasantries, and I told him I'd just been to the dentist, and he was suitably sympathetic. Then, out of the blue, he said, 'Fancy young Sandy married!'

'Sandy?' I repeated, puzzled. 'What do you mean?'

'You could have knocked me down with a feather,' Jack said. 'He never seemed the marrying sort, somehow, and I'd always thought if he ever did settle down it would be with you . . .' He paused to get out his pipe, then went on, 'Fancy you not knowing. He lives up in Cants Hill.'

'I'm sorry, but . . . where did you get this from?' I asked, more puzzled than ever.

'They were in my cab the other night, him and his wife. At least –' Jack stopped, suddenly unsure – 'I suppose it was his wife. She had on a wedding ring and she was holding on to his arm. Anyway, I took them up to Cants Hill, one of those nice houses right on the slope; now, what was it called? Didn't have a number, only a name. Silly, I always think, but I suppose they think it's grander. Funny –' he drew on his pipe – 'I'd never have expected young Sandy to end up in one of them posh houses . . .'

'Nor me,' I said, but the irony was, of course, quite lost on Jack.

As I left him I could feel anger boiling up inside me. Anger that, as yet, left no room for pain. I scrambled over the sea wall, bruising my toes as I misjudged my step, and marched across the shingle. Sandy had left the door of the chalet ajar; I pushed it open and went in. He looked up from cleaning his brushes, looking faintly surprised.

'Hello. You weren't long.'

I slammed the door and confronted him. 'Who do you know in Cants Hill?'

A shutter came down behind his eyes, locking me out, and I knew with a sinking heart that he was guilty as charged. 'What do you mean?' he asked, vaguely aggressive.

'You know damned well what I mean. You've got a fancy woman in Cants Hill.'

Sandy laughed mockingly. 'Fancy woman! Oh Dawn, that's the sort of old-fashioned terminology that would do Aunt Fran credit. Fancy woman – I love it!'

'It's not funny,' I screamed at him. 'Who is she?'

His face darkened to a shut-in scowl. 'Mind your own bloody business.'

'You admit it then?' I yelled.

Sandy packed his brushes together, not even bothering to reply. His attitude added fuel to my anger.

'She's married, isn't she? You bastard! You total, utter bastard!'

Sandy threw me a tantalizing half-smile that consisted of moving only his bottom lip and one cheek, and walked out of the chalet.

I shook with impotent rage. How dare he treat me this way, unwilling even to discuss it with me? He'd treated me like a foolish child who would get over a tantrum if he ignored me. So help me, I'd show him!

I grabbed all the things he'd left within my reach and hurled them the length of the chalet. Something connected with the wall-mirror and it came down from its nail, shattering against the corner of the sink. I felt my anger turning to tears then, and I threw myself down on the bed, heaving my body this way and that as passion and fury and helpless misery churned inside me. I cried with frustration and self-pity and then, as I quieted, I thought of what Serena had said, and I thought, *Perhaps this is it. The end.* And I cried some more.

By the time Sandy came back, an hour or so later, I'd come to a decision. I watched him trying to act normally, making it look as if it was the most natural thing in the world to find a mirror in pieces, everyday things scattered, and me with badly powdered red eyes, and then I screwed my courage together and said what I had to say.

'I'll leave you, Sandy. If you go on seeing her, I'll leave you. I won't be made a fool of.'

Sandy looked at me as if he was about to make one of his flippant remarks, then he thought better of it, and with a shrug set about clearing up the mess I'd made. He didn't say anything, but I felt a small tightening of satisfaction. I couldn't expect apologies or promises from him – that would be too much to ask of his fierce pride. But I had the feeling that my words had gone home, and for the moment, at least, Sandy knew I meant what I said.

I don't think Sandy saw the Cants Hill girl again. Whether he broke it off because of my threat to leave him or whether she was the one unwilling to take any further chances I didn't ask. I was just glad it seemed to have blown over, and an uneasy peace returned to the chalet. But the whole episode had made me review my position, and I decided that come what may I would do as I'd promised Serena and get some secretarial training. With that behind me I could always get a job, and I'd no longer be so completely dependent on Sandy.

When we returned to London, like birds migrating in the fall, I set about enrolling myself at evening classes in shorthand, typewriting and bookkeeping, and, to support myself whilst I studied, I got a job in a department store. The prospect of doing this for a whole year was a daunting one, but I was determined to stick it out.

Sandy laughed at me a little, but not too much, and I wondered if he thought that I was preparing to leave him. I didn't say anything to reassure him. I thought it would do him no harm at all to wonder. He'd had things his own way for too long, and I hoped uncertainty might help to dissuade him from straying with other girls.

The contrast between country and city seemed to have rejuvenated us both, breathing new life and new surroundings into our veins, and I guessed that to settle in one place for good would be like a death for Sandy. We had found a bedsitter in a house just a few streets from our previous home, a bedsitter so similar to the first one that it might have been the same place. Except that here the bathroom was always open and usually grubby, and the sink had never been properly plumbed in, so we had to carry slops down four flights of stairs.

But, try as I might, I could never quite recapture the easy warmth that Sandy and I had shared before the Cants Hill episode. I distrusted him and he knew it. And one evening, returning tired and footsore from a long day serving behind the counter, I was upset, but not really surprised, to find a pink-stained cigarette butt that must have rolled on to the floor when Sandy emptied the ashtray into the bucket beneath the sink.

Sandy was whistling as he brewed up a pot of tea in the tiny kitchen and I felt a moment's venomous hatred. Then I wondered, *Where do I go from here?* And began to tremble with dread.

Much as I wanted to face him with it, just as I had before, I knew that this time it was different. I'd said if he was untrue to me again I'd leave him, and once I admitted to knowing he'd had another woman here I'd have to be as good as my word, or lose all credibility. In spite of what I'd said, I didn't want to leave Sandy. I loved him still, and the knowledge that someone else had been here, this very afternoon, in our flat, made me feel physically sick. But if I made a scene now and threatened to leave again Sandy might realize I couldn't bring myself to go and my position would be weakened still further. Whereas if I said nothing, difficult though that would be, the whole thing might blow over. Neither course was really acceptable to me, but before I'd had time to make up my mind I heard Sandy behind me, and swiftly, instinctively, I thrust the cigarette butt deep into the pocket of my coat. Sandy had tried to clean up after this woman; let him think he had succeeded – for the time being, at any rate.

'Have a good day?' he asked casually, and I managed to screw my face into a smile and relate to him a few anecdotes before excusing myself to get ready for my evening class.

But that night when he tried to take me in his arms the image of the unknown girl who had so recently been here and lain, perhaps, herself, in Sandy's arms, refused to be ignored. When he turned his head I thought I could smell a perfume that was not mine, and was not his aftershave, on the back of his neck. And when he kissed me my heart was crying, *Why? Why? Is she so much better than me? Did he enjoy her more?* And there was a tightness in my throat threatening to engulf me and squashing all thoughts of passion or love.

Sandy said, releasing me a little, 'What's wrong, Dawn?'

'I'm just tired. I don't feel like it tonight,' I lied.

And when he said, 'OK,' so easily, with so little concern, and turned over so that I could no longer see his face, I felt cheated in a perverse way, and more certain than ever that he'd spent the afternoon making love to someone else.

I lay awake long into the night wondering if I had done the right thing in keeping silent; whether the other girl knew about me; whether it would soon be over, or if it would drag on into a long and messy affair. I wondered whether I would ever know the truth, and whether I even wanted to. Uncertainty was horrible. Always, you told yourself that it would be better to know the worst. But was it better? What good did it do, that knowledge?

It hurt like fury and it forced decisions upon you, and neither way could you be better off.

So I lay in the darkness, too unhappy to cry, and wondered where it would all end and just how much I could take. And still the answer came back like a recurrent tune in my brain. That anything, anything, was better than losing Sandy altogether.

Weeks passed and, fool that I was, I let things drag on and on. Sandy had affairs, I knew, but between them he was so wonderful to me that I couldn't help hoping that this time the flame of his wanderlust had burned itself out, this time he was ready to settle down with me. They always came, those blessed hiatuses, just when I felt I could take no more, and they lasted, each one, for several happy weeks when Sandy and I lived like newly-weds. He would make a fuss of me, tell me he loved me, as if he were aware, with some deep part of him, how much he had hurt me and wanted desperately to make it up to me. Yet I never mentioned that I knew about his aberrations, and he never confessed. Each time when it was over I'd tell myself it was just a casual episode and, as long as Sandy chose to stay with me, it was me he wanted. But I knew deep down that, casual or not, at the moment Sandy had it all ways, and he wasn't likely to give up his bread and butter relationship when he could get the jam at no extra cost.

And then, at the beginning of March, I actually saw him with another girl.

I'd been aware for a week or more that he was straying again. I could tell from his changed attitude to me and from the elaborate excuses he concocted for being out late. But that wasn't the same as knowing for sure. That wasn't the same as actually seeing them together.

Instead of taking the tube home from evening classes as I usually did, that night I took a bus. When we stopped at traffic lights I was glancing idly out of the window. And then suddenly I wasn't glancing idly any more. I was going cold inside, and staring, mesmerized, at a couple on the brightly lit pavement.

Sandy. And a tall, elegant girl. Sandy with his arm draped around her shoulders. In that moment something happened inside me, and it was as if all the hurts and injustices I'd ever felt were coming together into one great all-consuming whole.

I couldn't cry. Even as I waited for him at home, knowing in my heart that this was the end, I couldn't cry. Over the years I'd shed too many tears for him and now I was dry inside, dry and wrung-out and angry and full of twisting hatred. When I heard his key in the door, much later, I was ready for him. My case was packed, all my belongings stuffed into carrier bags and the big tartan sling bag I'd bought at a jumble sale. Sandy came in, tossed his duffel coat on to a chair, and noticed them.

'Dawn – what's all this?' He sounded puzzled, indignant.

I leaned against the table, my arms folded around myself. 'I think you know, Sandy,' I said, and the hardness of my voice surprised even me.

'You're going somewhere? On holiday?' he queried, as if he honestly had no idea.

'I'm going for good.' I levered myself away from the table, crossing the flat to retrieve a paperback book and squash it down into the sling bag. 'I told you a long time ago I won't be made a fool of.'

'But Dawn . . .' His face was the picture of guilt, like a small boy caught out by his teacher.

'But nothing,' I said. 'You've been with another girl. I saw you.'

Several varying emotions crossed his face as he tried to decide how to react. But the sight of my bags packed and ready must have convinced him that this time I was in deadly earnest, and he settled for trying to pacify me.

'I wasn't *with* her. Not the way you mean. She's no one; no one who matters anyway. I'm sorry . . .'

'Sorry!' Suddenly the tears that had eluded me were there, hot and heavy behind my eyes. 'You've never been sorry for anything in your life, Sandy. Sorry I caught you out, maybe. But not sorry you were with her. And she's not the first, is she? Your trouble is that you just can't keep your hands off other women!'

'All right.' I saw anger snap in Sandy's face to match my own. 'Since you ask, she's not the first. But since when did I promise there'd be no one but you, Dawn? You've been under no illusions, ever. And if you don't like things the way they are, you know what you can do.'

'That's right, I do. In fact, I'm doing just that,' I yelled. 'If I had somewhere to sleep I'd go now, this minute. But since I don't, I'll have to wait until morning.'

Sandy's anger seemed to die. His face went blank. Then he said, more quietly, 'Where will you go?'

I shrugged. The pain was a knife in me. 'I don't know, and I don't much care. So why should you?'

'Dawn . . .' He put out his hand to touch mine and I side-stepped it.

'It's over, Sandy. This time, really over.'

I slept that night as close to the edge of the bed as I could, and Sandy made no effort to touch me. In the darkness, the silent tears rolled down my cheeks. I had loved Sandy. I had given him all I had to give for so long. Now my love and my patience had run out with terrible suddenness. And, strangely, I could feel nothing but a kind of relief.

Next morning I got up while Sandy still slept. Perhaps he still thought I didn't really intend to go. As I bundled my things out of the bedsit we had shared I felt numb through and through, but when I reached the street it was as if an enormous weight had been lifted from my heart. I walked along the street until I found a telephone kiosk and I called the store to say I would not be in today. Then I went into a café for a coffee while I decided what to do.

And even then I found I could not regret it. Maybe tomorrow I would care. But not now. For the moment I was free, free as a bird. It was all that mattered.

Alone on my meagre wage I knew a flat or bedsitter would be out of the question, and none of the shared lets I found advertised were still available when I telephoned them. In desperation I began trying hostels, and soon I found one, run by a Mrs Waddell, who could offer me a room provided I was prepared to share.

Gratefully, I accepted, and soon discovered that any fears I might have had about the compatibility of my room-mate were quite groundless. She was called Kathleen Lewis, and she was a big-boned country girl, a farmer's daughter, with a mane of hair tied firmly back into a pony tail and a wide, laughing mouth. She was a cook, and she worked in one of the big cafeterias up West. She was at the hostel, she said, because her parents wouldn't have let her come to London at all otherwise, so sure were they it was a den of vice waiting to gobble up young girls. With no disrespect at all to Kathleen, I didn't think her parents need have worried on that score. She was so obviously sensible and level-headed that no one with bad intentions would have given her a second look. And yet, for all that she was so plain and clumsy, a constant stream of boys came to call for her. I suppose they liked her happy nature and her complete lack of snobbery. She sought nothing, took life as it came and enjoyed every last moment of it.

She confided to me once that she'd like to get back to the country if ever she had the opportunity, perhaps to work in school meals, or at a country pub. And when I told her that I, too, loved the country, we became great friends, talking long into the night when I got home from my evening classes.

To begin with I wondered whether Sandy would try to find me. He knew where I worked, so it wouldn't have been too difficult. I didn't know whether I wanted him to or not. Deep down, almost buried by my determination for a fresh start, I still had a great regard for him. But I was enjoying my freedom from the nagging worry that had been my constant companion during the last months with Sandy, and I didn't think I could face going back to that state. Ever.

I hadn't told Kathleen about Sandy, but I think she guessed. After all, I'd arrived so suddenly, and I'd been in London some time, so it really didn't take much imagination to work out that I'd been living with somebody. And Kathleen was no fool.

One day she said, 'Let's have a night out. You work far too hard and don't go out at all. What do you fancy? A dance? A film?'

'A film,' I said. Dances meant men, and just at the moment I didn't care if I never saw another man.

'Shall we go mad and go up West?' she asked.

'Good idea,' I said.

I knew the cinema seats would be twice as expensive there, and I couldn't really afford it, but, as Kathleen had said, it was so long since I'd been out, and I knew the hum of night life in the West End would add to my enjoyment. I loved rubbing shoulders with so many people bent on enjoying themselves; I loved the atmosphere of tingling anticipation that made the night come alive. I loved to see the neon signs burning in the velvet blackness of the sky and hear the jangling discords of mingled music – the faint sound of an orchestra tuning up, the wail of the busker's accordion, the shouts of a man selling jumping rubber spiders and the screams of the girls to whom he demonstrated his wares against their will. I loved to mingle, to feel part of it all, and in the back of my mind was the wistful thought, *If it hadn't been for my self-destructive love, maybe my name would have been up there in lights, just the way I used to dream it would be.*

We went to see the latest James Bond film – Kathleen's choice – and had to queue for ages to get in. Throughout the film we chomped on chocolates that Kathleen produced from her capacious handbag, and when it was over we still found room for a Chicken Maryland and pineapple fritters at a little café just around the corner from the tube station. Then we rolled home, arm in arm and laughing, because somehow Kathleen was always laughing and she carried me with her, and hoping we weren't going to find ourselves locked out. But as we turned the corner of our street and the hostel came into view we were surprised to see lights burning at almost every window and a police car parked at the kerb.

'What on earth is going on?' Kathleen asked, sobered abruptly.

We went up the six steps between the stone dragons that we always swore were the founders of the hostel, turned to stone as an Awful Punishment, and pushed open the door. Mrs Waddell met us in the hall wearing an enormous checked dressing gown over her nightdress and with an armoury of curlers secured by a hair net. Her usually daunting face looked puffed and worried.

'What's happening?' we asked.

Mrs Waddell shot an anxious look up the stairs and made a great business of refastening the cord of her dressing gown. She seemed to be torn between her usual hard-faced reticence and the desire to share her superior knowledge. The latter, aided by her liking for Kathleen, won the day.

'There's been a burglary. Miss Oliphant's room has been broken into and her radio and typewriter stolen.'

Kathleen and I looked at one another, shocked. Rosemary

Oliphant had a room on the same floor as ours, one of the few singles in the place.

'The police are here,' Mrs Waddell went on, full of herself now. 'They had the cheek to suggest one of the other girls could be responsible. I soon put them right about that. "All my girls are respectable, or they wouldn't be here!" I told them. It's somebody walked in off the street, right enough. Miss Oliphant is forever leaving her door unlocked; I've warned her about it more times than I can tell. But the constable will want a word with you both, I wouldn't wonder. And if I were you I'd have a good look and make sure nothing's been taken from your room.'

'We will!' Kathleen said.

We ran upstairs and were relieved to find our door locked. It wasn't unheard of for one or the other of us to be as careless as Rosemary Oliphant. But Kathleen was taking no chances. She pulled out the underwear drawer where she hid spare cash and extracted an envelope. Then she waved it at me, looking worried.

'It's not just Rosemary. I had a five-pound note left from my birthday money, I know I did, but it's gone.'

I didn't want to believe this. 'You've put it in your purse and spent it, I expect. That's what happens to five-pound notes.'

'I'm sure I didn't,' Kathleen insisted. 'I couldn't have spent a whole five pounds without knowing. I distinctly remember I left it in my knicker drawer for safety. Have you lost anything, Dawn?'

I had begun to get undressed. I was tired, and I didn't want to even think that someone might have been in our room, rooting about amongst our things. 'I haven't got anything worth stealing.'

'Your watch?'

'Is on my arm. Put the light out, for goodness' sake.'

Reluctantly, she did so. But, in spite of myself, as I lay in the darkness I found myself making inventories of my few possessions and when I'd last seen them. Though I didn't believe for a moment Kathleen's five-pound note had been stolen, Rosemary Oliphant's room had been burgled, and I wondered whether it had been an outside job or whether there was a sneak thief amongst us. It wasn't a nice thought.

I slept fitfully, something nagging on the borders of my mind, and towards morning I came to with a start, suddenly realizing what it was.

Sandy's pendant – the pearl on the leaf that he'd given me that wonderful last Christmas we'd spent together. I always kept it in its little, blue jeweller's box in my spare handbag. And although I knew I'd put it safely away the last time I wore it, I couldn't recall having seen it when I'd changed bags to go out last night.

I turned over on to my stomach telling myself not to be silly. But I couldn't go back to sleep, and at last I decided I'd better satisfy myself it was there. I got out of bed and took both my bags over to the window, rooting through them by the light of the street lamp outside. When I was unable to find the box I took everything out and piled it on the window ledge. The box was not there. Neither was the phial of French perfume Serena had sent for my birthday.

I felt sick suddenly. It was so horrible to think of prying fingers besmirching my private treasures. And oh, please God, they hadn't taken my locket!

As best I could without disturbing Kathleen I searched my drawers and my suitcase though I knew deep down I wouldn't find either of the missing items. And at last I crawled back into bed to wait, sleepless, for morning.

Kathleen, as always, woke early. I always teased her about it, telling it was a throw back to her days of milking cows and feeding hens, but today I was more than glad to see her stretch herself awake.

'I knew it!' she said when I told her about the missing items. 'I just knew it!'

I searched the room again in full light, just to be absolutely sure, but without much hope. I was too careful with the one present Sandy had left me to remember him by to leave it lying about.

Kathleen could see I was upset by the loss. 'It's special, isn't it?' she said sympathetically. 'Well, we'd better report it, hadn't we?'

Mrs Waddell was not at all pleased when we spoke to her. Now fully dressed in her usual shapeless cardigan and skirt, she had recovered her dignity and was ready to do battle.

'You've made a mistake, girls,' she told us belligerently. 'Miss Oliphant's burglary has put ideas in your heads. Miss Lewis has spent her money, and your locket has just dropped off somewhere, Miss Stephens.'

'I'm sorry to disagree,' I said, 'but the box I keep it in has gone too.'

Mrs Waddell sniffed in annoyance. 'Oh, well, if you're set on bringing trouble to the hostel, I suppose you'd better speak to the police.'

'It's the hostel that's brought trouble to us,' Kathleen said tartly, and I thought that nobody but Kathleen could say something like that to Mrs Waddell and get away with it.

I was due at the store by eight thirty, but Kathleen didn't have to work until noon, so she offered to go to the police station and report our loss. I thought that would be all there was to it, but she telephoned me at lunch time.

'They want a loser's statement from you. Can you call in on your way home from work? Ask to see a PC MacWilliam. He's the officer on the case.'

'OK,' I agreed.

I didn't finish work until six, and it was almost seven by the time I emerged from the tube station and crossed the road to the dark, old, stone building with the blue lamp over the door. I was tired and unhappy and my feet ached. I was prepared – more than prepared – to be told I must have lost the locket somewhere. I couldn't imagine London's finest would want the crime records looking worse than they already did.

I took my place in the queue at the desk and explained who I was to the duty officer. He told me to wait, and a few minutes later another policeman emerged from one of the doors. He was quite young, certainly no more than thirty, dark and rugged with a nose that looked as if it had been broken at some time. He came over to me, and when he spoke it was with a soft Scots burr.

'Miss Stephens? I'm PC MacWilliam. Would you come this way, please?'

I followed him down a passage that smelled of floor polish into a small, square room with a scrubbed wood table and two or three chairs. It looked barren and unfriendly, the sort of room where too many criminals have been questioned, and, as if reading my thoughts, PC MacWilliam grinned at me.

'We won't be disturbed here. Sit down.' He indicated one of the chairs and sat down facing me with his pen resting on a pile of statement forms. 'I understand that after I left the hostel last night you discovered something missing. A locket, was it?'

'A pendant,' I said. 'A pearl on a small gold leaf.'

'Was it valuable?'

I shook my head. 'Not really. Good, but not fantastically expensive. But it did have great . . . sentimental value.'

'And when did you last see it?'

I told him as best I could, thinking how easy it was to talk to him, as if he weren't a policeman at all but just a nice, ordinary young man. When I'd finished he picked up his pen and started filling in the top of the form.

'We'd better have a statement from you. Now – would you mind telling me your full name and age . . .' He smiled as he said 'age', a smile that managed to be mischievous and apologetic at the same time. 'If you're over twenty-one, that's all I need to put.'

'I'm just twenty-one,' I said.

He took some more details and wrote a résumé of what I'd told him. Then I read it and signed it and he put the top back on his pen and packed his papers together.

'I suppose there's not much hope of me ever getting it back,' I said, trying not to show how much I minded the thought of my precious pendant around the neck of some thief.

He stood up, and looked at me thoughtfully. 'There's just a chance you might. We have our suspicions as to who might be responsible. But don't build up your hopes too much. If we do catch the thief, she may well have already disposed of it.'

*She*. I felt sick all over again. And was suddenly overcome with the realization that this was a police station, and the friendly young man was an officer of the law. I picked up my bag. 'Thank you very much anyway.'

He smiled, directly into my eyes, and something very odd happened to my stomach.

'We'll do what we can to find your pendant,' he said.

# Thirteen

Two days later, when I turned the corner on my way home from work, I saw a police car parked outside the hostel. As I came level with it a long form uncoiled himself from the driver's seat and PC MacWilliam emerged.

'Miss Stephens. I've been waiting for you. The warden at the hostel told me you'd be home soon. I think we've recovered your pendant.'

'Oh!' I was surprised and absolutely delighted. PC MacWilliam opened the passenger door of the police car and I slid into the seat beside him. Then he took a Manila envelope from his pocket and shook something into my hand.

'Can you identify it?'

I gazed down at the tiny pearl nestling on its gold leaf and felt my stomach contract with a plethora of emotions. 'Yes, that's it. Where did you find it?'

'We've got the culprit. One of the hostel inmates, a Rachel Carson,' he said with a touch of bland humour.

Rachel Carson. A small, blonde girl with a room on the top floor. I hardly knew her, but it would never have occurred to me for a moment that she might be a thief. She looked meek and a little bit lost in the hurly-burly of London.

'What will happen to her?' I asked.

'She'll be prosecuted. Then it'll be up to the magistrates. But whatever they decide, I wouldn't think she'd be bothering you again. Your warden will make sure of that.'

I bit my lip. Having my pendant back had made me feel such goodwill to all men that for the moment I felt quite sorry for Rachel. 'Can I have it back?' I asked.

The policeman shook his head. 'Sorry. Not just yet. We shall need it for evidence. But we'll take good care of it for you.' He paused. 'I'd like a short statement from you, too, if you've got a minute to spare.'

'Here?' I said. 'Now?'

'Might as well. It would save you coming down to the station again.'

'OK,' I said.

PC MacWilliam wrote the statement for me, a few brief lines saying I identified the pendant I had been shown as my own. Then he handed it to me, along with a pen, and I signed it.

'I can't tell you how grateful I am,' I said, preparing to get out of the car. 'I don't know how to thank you enough.'

There was a minuscule pause, and PC MacWilliam said into it, 'Well, how about coming out with me on Saturday night then?'

I stared at him, so taken by surprise that I couldn't think of a single reason why I shouldn't. And, before I could reply, he went on smoothly, 'I'll pick you up, shall I? About half-past seven, say?'

Kathleen was in our room, taking up a dress.

'Does this look too short?' she asked as I opened the door. 'I know my legs aren't as nice as they could be, but I don't want to look old-fashioned . . .'

'Your legs are fine,' I said. 'Kath, listen, did you know they've caught the thief?' She looked up sharply, and I went on, 'It's Rachel Carson from the top floor. You know, the thin little blonde who looks as if she could do with a square meal.'

'Oh no!' Kath groaned. 'Why did it have to be someone we know?'

'I'm glad it was – it means I've got my pendant back,' I said. 'I've just seen that young policeman. And that's not all. He asked me out! And before I could say "no" he was making all the arrangements. I don't even know his name! Well – it's MacWilliam, I think, but I can't call him that, can I?'

Around the pins, Kathleen's mouth curved. 'You'll find out, I expect. Is he nice?'

'Oh, you don't know him, do you? He'd only just come on duty when I went to the station to make my original statement. Yes, he is rather nice,' I said, surprising myself.

'Hmm. I'm sorry I missed him now,' Kathleen said ruefully. 'He might have asked *me* out. You'll have to watch him though. They say policemen are the worst.'

A tiny barb of misgiving shot through me. PC MacWilliam,

whose name I didn't know, was a man, just like Sandy. And I'd promised myself no more let-downs, no more men.

Kathleen must have seen the look on my face because she laughed. 'Oh, go and enjoy yourself for goodness' sake!' Then she added, 'He didn't say anything about my five pounds, I suppose.'

'Sorry, no. I don't suppose money would be very identifiable and she's probably spent it . . .' I rifled in my bag for my purse and pulled out three precious pound notes. 'Look, let's go halves. I've got my pendant back, so we'll share your loss.'

'No way!' Kathleen protested.

'Go on . . . Please . . .'

'No! For all I know, my five pounds is waiting for me down at the police station and they'll give me a call about it in a few days' time.'

'But surely PC MacWilliam would have said—'

'You really believe the reason he came here was to return your pendant?' Kathleen smirked. 'Do the police usually run around returning stolen property? No, that was just an excuse, if you ask me.'

'What do you mean?'

'Oh, don't be so thick! To see you again, of course.' She picked up her needle and thread. 'Tell you what, you can treat me to the pictures one night, if your PC What's'isname gives you a night off.'

'For goodness' sake, Kathleen!' I exploded. 'I'm only going out with him once because I couldn't get out of it. So you can stop doing that imitation of a Cheshire cat.'

But Kathleen just went on grinning.

PC MacWilliam came for me on Saturday exactly one minute early, drawing up outside the hostel in an almost-new sports car, and, as he helped me into the passenger seat and closed the door behind me, I began to wonder if maybe I was going to enjoy myself in spite of all my uneasy forebodings. After Sandy's careless attitude, it was rather nice to be fussed over and made to feel feminine.

'I hope you're feeling hungry,' he said. 'I've booked a table at a dinner and dance place.'

'Lovely.' But the nervous pulse beating in my throat made me wonder if I'd be able to do justice to a meal, which would make me look ungrateful and a bit of a wet blanket.

I need not have worried. The moment we were shown to our table, on a kind of raised platform that ran almost completely around the perimeter of a circular dance floor, I began to feel more relaxed. The menu was simple but good, prawn cocktails and minestrone soup, steaks and scampi, and the live band was playing popular music softly enough not to be intrusive. There was a candle in a bottle on our table; in its soft light PC MacWilliam's face looked all planes and shadows, and ruggedly handsome. I was glad I'd worn my new dress, an empire-line shift in pale blue with a slight sheen to the fabric.

'I don't actually know what to call you, except for PC MacWilliam,' I confessed, sipping a glass of wine.

He laughed easily. 'No, I don't suppose you do. I'm Alistair. And I'm Scottish through and through.'

'That much I'd guessed,' I said. 'Which part do you come from?'

'Edinburgh.'

'So what on earth made you come to London?'

'I fancied seeing life. But I must say there are times I hanker for the Highlands.'

'I've never been further north than the Lake District,' I admitted.

'So where are you from?' he asked. 'You're not a Londoner either, are you?'

'I suppose you'd say my home is Sturvendor, in Somerset,' I said. 'Although actually I'm Canadian.'

'Canadian?' He sounded interested, but I didn't want to talk about myself. There were too many things I wouldn't be ready to tell him for a long while yet, if ever.

'Tell me about Scotland,' I said, and if he realized I was changing the subject he didn't let on. He just told me about Scotland.

It could have been dull as a geography lesson, but it certainly wasn't. As he described places both famous and unknown his words painted pictures so vivid that I could see them all in my mind's eye: the blue mountains and bluer lochs, the purple heather and green leaves, the sun on the beautiful sugar loaf that was Edinburgh Castle, the wild stillness of the barren uplands. I listened, fascinated, the romance in my soul quickened by the blend of history and natural, raw splendour.

When we'd finished our meal Alistair asked me to dance. For a moment my nerves almost got the better of me again. The band were playing some kind of formal dance, but I didn't have a clue whether it was supposed to be a waltz, a foxtrot or a quickstep. The only experience I had of ballroom dancing was the few lessons we'd had in the gym at school, counting steps as we twirled round to the music of a gramophone.

'I'm not very good,' I said. 'I'll probably step on your toes.'

He smiled, the crooked smile that I was beginning to find very attractive. 'I'm willing to risk it if you are.'

He was a good dancer, easy to follow, and I didn't make too many mistakes. But quite suddenly I had the feeling that it wouldn't matter in the least if I did. There was a sort of easy understanding between us, as if we'd known one another all our lives. I felt very at home with Alistair MacWilliam. And when, in the middle of the third dance, he said, 'If you'd like to come out with me tomorrow afternoon, we could go on the river, perhaps?' I found myself agreeing. It was a long time since I'd enjoyed myself so much, and I knew I wanted to see him again.

Sunday, unfortunately, was chilly, damp and not at all the sort of day to spend on the river. I wondered if, with his plans scotched, Alistair might decide not to turn up, but he did, and we drove out into the country and had a cream tea at a village café that was all chintz tablecloths and willow pattern china.

'I start a week on the two-to-ten shift the day after tomorrow,' Alistair said. I looked at him, uncomprehending, and he went on, 'That means I shall be working in the evenings.'

'Right.' I felt ridiculously let down suddenly. Was this the brush-off?

'We could do something tomorrow evening though,' he said. 'If you'd like to.'

And my spirits lifted, and I nodded. 'Yes. I'd like that.'

The next evening he took me to an out-of-town pub where we enjoyed a quiet drink, and on the way back I relaxed against the soft, red-leather seat in his sports car, looked at his craggy profile silhouetted by the street lights and his strong hands on the steering wheel, and thought that Alistair MacWilliam was really rather a dish. Outside the hostel, he kissed me, and I liked that too. I liked the feel of his mouth on mine and the rough cloth of the collar of his donkey jacket against my cheek; I liked the faint scent of his skin, soap and tobacco mingling, and the way he held me, firmly, as if he knew exactly what he wanted but wasn't putting any pressure whatsoever on me. He said he'd ring me at the end of his 'lates week' and I found myself wondering again if this was the end, and I'd never hear from him again. And realized that I would actually mind rather a lot if that turned out to be the case.

With my secretarial exams looming, I had little time to fret however, and I was working like a slave to make sure I passed them first time.

Typing I was fairly good at. I'd taken to it immediately, bought myself a heavy, old typewriter that I'd seen going quite cheaply in the Oxfam shop, and practised and practised until my speed was quite respectable. Bookkeeping, too, was something that came quite easily to me, and I couldn't understand why some of my fellow students found it so hard. But shorthand was something else. For the whole of the course I'd felt one step behind the tutor, never completely understanding the short forms, never being quite sure which strokes should be thin and which thick. Shorthand was a struggle for me, and I knew I needed a good slice of luck to get a qualification in it.

And it was so desperately important to get my qualifications! Only then, when I was equipped to earn a living if I needed to, could I think about throwing in my job at the store – which I loathed – and going back to the theatre.

I'd imagined Alistair's 'lates week' would end on Friday, and when Saturday came and went without a word from him I began to think I'd been right to worry that it had provided him with some sort of get-out. Really, it did seem very likely. He was, when I came to think about it, the very epitome of the confirmed bachelor – good looking, obviously been around, managed to reach his late twenties without some girl getting her claws into him. A couple of dates was probably his limit. And now he'd moved on to pastures new.

When he telephoned then, on Sunday morning, I was completely taken by surprise, and, to my dismay, disproportionately delighted.

'Did I get you out of bed?' he asked easily.

'No, of course not!' I said, although actually he had.

'I've got a day off on Tuesday,' he said. 'Shall we go out somewhere?'

A *Tuesday*! I was completely puzzled by this strange shift system. And in any case . . .

'I can't,' I said. 'I go to evening classes on Tuesdays.'

'Ah. Right. How about Wednesday?'

'Evening classes again. Shorthand on Tuesday, typewriting on Wednesday. And just in case you were thinking of asking, it's bookkeeping on Thursday.'

'Oh, well, never mind,' he said, very casual, very offhanded.

'I get Wednesday afternoon off,' I said very quickly before he could ring off. 'If that's any good to you.'

'Yes. Tuesday and Wednesday are my rest days this week. Shall I pick you up on Wednesday then?'

'Yes, all right,' I said.

I saw a lot of Alistair during the next few weeks, and part of me was happier than I'd been in a very long time. I really enjoyed his company, and we had the most enormous fun together. Once, because I said I'd never been to the Tower, he took me, and like a pair of tourists we gasped at the escapologist wriggling from his sacks and straightjacket on the pavement outside and followed the guide around the ancient stone walls, marvelling that these were the very windows where some of the most romantic figures in history had stood to watch their last daybreak, and that these were the stones the feet of Anne Boleyn and Lady Jane Grey had trod on, on their way to the block. Another day we went to the Planetarium; on yet another to look at the deer in Richmond Park. And always there was that easy sense of companionship, of belonging, that made me relax with Alistair in a way I never had with Sandy.

But conversely, the closer Alistair and I became, the more Sandy seemed to intrude. I couldn't forget him; he was still there prickling under my skin, invading my head and my heart; I couldn't forget him and I didn't think I ever would. I felt guilty on every count; on the one hand I felt I was betraying Sandy and all we had shared and on the other, I wasn't being fair to Alistair. Though he never tried to pressure me, I was all too aware that the part of myself that I had to give was so meagre, the tattered remnants of my obsessive love for Sandy.

I was aware, too, of a rising panic at the way I responded to Alistair when we were together. One night, for instance, when he took me for a boat ride on the Thames, the cool breeze coming off the water cut through my thin dress, making me shiver, and when he took off his jacket and slipped it around my shoulders the simple gesture roused feelings in me that surprised me. I leaned against him, feeling the cold, slippery lining of his jacket on my bare arms and the firmness of his chest beneath my back, and I felt for a moment the same sharp potency mixed with the warmth of coming home that I always felt when I stepped on to the shingle at Seagull Bay. I snuggled close, wanting the moment to last forever, oblivious to everything but his nearness. But later, at home, lying sleepless, the memory of the way I had felt tormented me. I didn't want to feel that way about anyone but Sandy. I wouldn't allow myself to! But the confusion that came from the two warring sides of my heart and mind was tearing me apart.

The weeks went by and, almost before I knew it, my exams were upon me. Panic of a different sort set in, but at least this was a panic I could talk to Alistair about.

'I wish I'd never tried to learn shorthand,' I groaned. 'I should have just concentrated on the typing.'

'I don't know what you're worried about,' Alistair said. He sometimes helped me practise, dictating very slowly from my Pitman's magazine, one eye on his watch. 'You're quite good really. And you can read most of it back.'

We were sitting in his car parked outside the hostel. He had met me from evening classes and taken me for a late-night snack at a Golden Egg.

'It's all right when you go at about fifty words a minute, but what good is that?' I fretted. 'I expect I've wasted the whole year. I haven't so much as set foot on a stage, and I'll have nothing but a typing certificate to show for it. If I'm lucky.'

'So, what will you do next?' Alistair asked, matter-of-fact.

I leaned back against the soft leather seat, tucked my toes up under the back of the glove pocket and sighed. For the first time in my life I was a free agent. I could go anywhere, do anything I liked. I could go back to Canada if I chose, but there was nothing for me there any more. I could go back to acting, but although I'd been itching to get back on stage, the thought of beginning again the same old merry-go-round of disappointments and poverty was a depressing one.

'I don't know,' I said. 'I honestly don't know what I'm going to do.'

'You could marry me,' Alistair said.

Breath seemed to catch in my throat, and I felt hot colour rising in my cheeks. My first thought, even so, was that he must be joking. We weren't this involved, surely? We liked one another's company, yes. We found one another sexually attractive. But there was so much I'd held back: all the deep things that were closest to my heart, all the things that worried at me in the dead of night. Really, he knew nothing about me at all. Surely, he couldn't be serious about wanting to *marry* me?

Then I turned and saw the way he was watching me, the wariness in his eyes for all the bold front he was putting on making him oddly vulnerable, and I knew he was very serious indeed. My stomach clenched. The time for straight talking could no longer be postponed.

'Alistair . . . I really like you a lot. But I don't love you.'

His jaw tightened just a fraction and his eyes narrowed, but then he said, 'I know that, Dawn. I just keep hoping you might when you get over whoever it is that's still bugging you.'

I looked away because I had the feeling he was seeing right into my soul, and I couldn't bear it. Alistair draped an arm loosely around my shoulders.

'I don't know what happened to hurt you so, and I don't want to press you to tell me until you're good and ready. But, whatever it was, you've got to move on sometime, and I'd like it to be with me. I want you to be my wife, and I'm prepared to take a chance on whether you ever come to feel about me as you did about him. We could be happy, I'm sure of it. We're good together, aren't we?'

I nodded silently.

'And I promise I'll never do anything to hurt you. I love you, Dawn,' he went on.

Tears were pricking my eyes. I didn't deserve Alistair, really I didn't. I thought how very easy it would be to say 'yes', but I couldn't. Not yet. It was a bridge too far. 'Can I think about it?' I asked.

'Course you can. Take all the time you need. Just be sure that, after you've thought, you tell me yes.'

I kissed him quickly, lightly on the lips, got out of the car and ran up the steps.

All the confused emotions that had been troubling me came together now, a kaleidoscope of indecision. The only certain thing was that, after his proposal, nothing could be quite the same as it had been between Alistair and me. The time had come when I had to make a decision, one way or the other. And the knowledge that there was no escape was choking me.

What could I do? Strangely, I had no doubt but that Alistair and I would be happy together. We *were* happy. But the fact of the matter was that he was not Sandy. I didn't love him the way I loved Sandy. Alistair could give me security and love and a good life. But if I was still hankering after Sandy and what we had shared, how long would it last? How long before his patience wore thin and he began to blame me for wanting more – for wanting someone else? How long before I grew discontented with a love that, however comfortable, was second best? And would I resent him for having to give up my dreams of the theatre, my other love? The lure was still there, an itching in my blood, even while I hated it for much the same reason as I hated Sandy. It could take all of me, all my hopes and dreams, and suck me dry, leaving me an empty shell. Part of me ached for the security of never having to worry again about getting a part, never having to sit with a hundred others in a demoralizing rehearsal room, never having to worry about where the next meal, or pair of stockings, was coming from. And part of me rebelled against the very safety I longed for.

Round and round in circles I went, trying to come to a decision, making up my mind one way only to change it again. Three days went by and Alistair had not phoned me. Was that because his shifts were inconvenient, or because he was giving me time and space to think things over? I wondered. But time and space were getting me nowhere. I honestly, truly, did not know what to do.

And then, on the Thursday afternoon, when I came out of the staff entrance of the store, Sandy was waiting for me.

I could scarcely believe it. He'd been standing on the opposite side of the street, looking in a shop window, but even before he turned around I knew it was him. My heart gave a huge lurch and I could scarcely breathe. Sandy – here. Just when I was trying to make a decision that would relegate him to the past forever. It was perfect serendipity.

The moment he saw me Sandy crossed the road, threading his way between the traffic with a loping run even before the 'Cross Now' sign lit up. He was as brown as a nut, the natural tan contrasting with his fair hair and light-blue eyes. He was dressed smartly for him, in a crew neck jersey, and although his smile was as jaunty as ever, I thought I glimpsed just a trace of hesitance.

'Hi, Dawn,' he said, and a nerve jumped in my throat.

'Hi.'

'You're still working in this dump then. I thought you'd be back on the boards by now.'

'Whatever made you think that?'

'There are some things,' Sandy said, 'that never change.'

It was there again, that falling away of my stomach that was half hope and half something else. Fear, maybe, of old wounds too easily reopened.

'I've changed,' I said, 'but I don't suppose you have.'

A rueful expression flickered across his face, then he said, 'Do you fancy a coffee?'

I hesitated. All my instincts were telling me to cut and run before he reeled me in again. But I couldn't do it. 'OK,' I said.

We walked side by side, but there was a feeling of awkwardness between us.

'What have you been doing with yourself?' I asked.

He gave me a sideways look and I half expected him to tell

me that was his business, that I had no claims on him now. But he didn't. 'I had a one-man exhibition in Bath,' he said.

'Oh, that's really good!' I said, pleased for him.

Sandy shrugged. 'I suppose so.' He gave me another half-shifty, sideways look. 'It wasn't the same without you.' And then, as if he had embarrassed himself, he hurried on, 'What have you been doing?'

'Working. And doing evening classes. But if I fail my exams, and I probably will, I'll have wasted the whole year.'

'True,' Sandy said.

There was a small Italian restaurant on the corner with gateaux in the window arranged in front of greying net curtains.

'Will this do?' Sandy asked.

I nodded and followed him in. Waiting at the self-service counter, I wondered if I should tell him about Alistair and decided against it.

We got our coffee on grotty wooden trays and carried them over to a seat. It was red leatherette, worn on the edges with the stuffing poking through, and the table was littered with used cups. But at least we were hidden from the other customers.

Sandy said, 'I expect you're wondering what I'm doing here.'

I swallowed a mouthful of tasteless brown water. 'Since you ask, yes. I imagined that after I walked out on you that would be the end of it.'

'So did I, at first,' Sandy said. 'But the thing is . . . I want you back, Dawn.'

I stared at him blankly, feeling, strangely, absolutely nothing. But perhaps that was because I simply couldn't take it in. Sandy, asking me to go back to him? Sandy, who never once, in all our time together, had been anything but ambivalent about whether I stayed or went? Who had cheated on me over and over again with never a flicker of remorse?

'I miss you,' he said, and his uncharacteristic vulnerability tugged at my heart strings. Oh dear God, how I loved him! Every line of his face, every bone in his body. I had only to see the smallest flicker in his eyes to know what he was thinking. We had been a unit, he and I – a peculiar unit by normal standards, maybe, but a unit nevertheless. I'd ached for him for so long, and now he wanted me back, and I should be shouting my joy from the housetops. But there was something wrong. Something was missing. It wasn't as it used to be – or, at least, I wasn't as I'd used to be. I'd been right when I told him I'd changed, yet until now I'd never realized it. I'd been too hooked on the certainty that Sandy was the love of my life, a poignant destiny I could never escape. I'd glamorized every emotion, the heartbreaking as well as the ecstatic, and turned it into some sort of Greek tragedy with an elusive, romantic hero. Now he was here in the flesh, and, though I loved him nonetheless, I was seeing that love through the eyes of expanded experience for what it was. A dream. The residual dream of a lost love.

And there was no way of recapturing it. None at all. I was older now, and wiser, and I knew that the time for Sandy and me had come and gone. If he had been different, who knew where we might be now? But if he had been different, he wouldn't have been Sandy. It was the elusive quality of him that had mesmerized me and that had now lost its thrall. There was no way on earth I could go back to the turmoil and the uncertainty of the life we had shared, no way I could contemplate the agony of tearing one another apart.

'I'm sorry, Sandy,' I said.

His eyes clouded; he looked like a small boy who believes he has only to say sorry to be forgiven for all his misdeeds. 'But why?'

'I just can't. My life is here now.'

'I thought you loved me,' he said.

'I did.' The word, in the past tense, surprised even me.

'But not any more?'

I couldn't reply. Tears were a hot, tight knot in my throat. I had loved him so much, so much! But, like a comet, that love had burned itself out, seared to oblivion until nothing was left but a sad, red glow in the sky. And I hadn't even realized.

'Dawn . . .' Sandy reached across the table, catching my hand in his. 'If I were to get a job in commercial art, something with a regular salary, would that make a difference? I know, it doesn't sound much like me. I've always chuntered on about being free. But freedom isn't much fun without you. I'll do whatever you want, if only you'll come back. We could get married if you like. Have a couple of kids . . .'

'Oh Sandy . . .' I tried to speak, but tears were in the way. I couldn't even see him properly any more for the blur. How often I'd dreamed of hearing him say that! How I'd longed for it! I'd imagined so many times the way it could be – Sandy and me in a very small, very pretty house, with a view Sandy could paint and a garden where I could grow roses. The children, when they came along, would be able to do everything we had wanted to do and found beyond us. And Sandy and I would be together until we were two very old, very happy people.

Once I'd have jumped at Sandy's proposal, ignoring the promptings of common sense that told me that the steady job would last only until Sandy felt fettered by it and that the little house would never belong to us. I'd have blinded myself to the truth that fairy tale endings don't often happen in real life. But it was too late for me to fool myself any longer.

'It wouldn't work,' I said.

If I'd struck Sandy, I couldn't have hurt him more. It was there in his face, revealing more than I'd ever known about him. In that moment I knew he loved me too. Perhaps he always had. Or perhaps he'd only realized it now, when he'd finally lost me. Sadness flooded through me, haunting and bitter-sweet, for what we'd had and lost and for what might have been. But I knew it wouldn't make any difference. It was over, what we'd shared, gone with the crazy carefree days of youth. There was no way back.

'I'm sorry,' I said inadequately.

He looked up at me, his eyes narrowed against the smoky atmosphere. 'Is there someone else, Dawn? Is that it?'

And, suddenly, I knew why I was so certain it was all over between Sandy and me. Suddenly, more than anything in the world, I was longing for Alistair's calm strength.

'Yes, there is,' I said. 'Actually, I'm going to marry him.'

Again I saw the flash of hurt, raw in Sandy's face. Then it was gone. 'Oh, well, that's it then, isn't it? Good for you, Dawn. I hope you'll be happy.' He said it like the old, flippant, devil-may-care Sandy, and cynically I wondered how long the hurt would last. As far as Bristol, maybe? No further. Then there would be someone else to help him forget.

'I think I'd better be going, Sandy,' I said. 'Are you going back to Sturvendor tonight?'

The slightest hesitation, then Sandy said, 'I don't know. I can please myself, can't I? That's the beauty of being solo. Right now I think I'll have another coffee and a spaghetti Bolognese.'

'OK. Well, bye then. Take care of yourself.' The awkwardness was back, and a reluctance to leave him.

'Bye. See you sometime.'

'Yes. Love to Serena when you see her.'

I left the café with my heart in my mouth, and from the street I tried to see him through the greyish net curtains. I couldn't. My throat ached. My eyes ached. I turned to walk up the street, and after just a few steps the ache disappeared, and there was a sort of breathless eagerness in its place, and then I wasn't walking, I was running. Running, not from my old life, but towards the new.

Running, not from Sandy. Running to Alistair.

I waited until we were alone together. I waited with the excitement and anticipation bubbling inside me. And then, when Alistair parked the car and put his arms round me, I said, very casually, 'You remember what you said the other night? Well, is the offer still open?'

For a terrible moment I thought he might say no, it had all been a mistake.

He pulled back a fraction so he could look at me. 'Of course it's still open,' he said.

'Then in that case I'd like to . . .' I was going to say 'accept', but it sounded so ridiculous I couldn't, and instead I started laughing. Alistair laughed too, happy laughter, stemming from shared happiness. And then suddenly we weren't laughing any more. His arms were round me and his lips on mine and we were clinging together, melting. And just as I had that night on the river when he put his jacket round me to keep me warm, I thought, *I've come home.*

It was the only coherent thought I was to have for quite some time.

# Fourteen

Alistair and I were married six weeks later. Neither of us wanted a big wedding. Alistair, typical man that he was, thought the smaller and quieter it was the better, and I had always felt the ceremony should be private and sincere rather than a big, showy production.

One thing I did insist on, though, was Sturvendor Church. I wouldn't have felt married if we had just trundled along to the register office as Alistair had suggested. And for me the little, grey, stone church nestling in the folds of the Quantocks meant home in its nicest possible sense.

We had invited a handful of guests – Aunt Fran, Serena and Chris, and Kathleen, on my side, and Alistair's parents, his sisters and their families and a few of his closest friends, on his – but when I came out of church, into the tracery of sunlight and shadow that was woven by the boughs of the churchyard trees, it seemed all of Sturvendor had turned out to see me. Choked, suddenly, I recognized faces that marked the journey of my life since I first came here eight long years ago. School friends, shop-keepers, the girl who used to do my hair. But one face was notably absent, and I wondered with sadness what Sandy was doing this morning.

After a long debate, we had decided to send him an invitation. I had told Alistair all about him by now, of course, and he had been very understanding.

'If you tell me it's over that's good enough for me,' he said. 'If I ever catch you cheating on me after we're married, God help you. But what happened before we met is your own business.'

'It is over,' I promised him. 'I could have married him. I was asked. Rather late, but I was. And I turned him down. I did love him once, but not any more. It's well and truly over.'

Unsurprisingly, Sandy declined the wedding invitation, sending a note with good wishes and a painting of Seagull Bay as a wedding present. And again Alistair showed his commendable lack of jealousy when he insisted on hanging it in the sitting room of the flat we were renting.

'If you own a good painting, why hide it away?' was his attitude.

Because we had so few guests we were able to afford a champagne reception at a local hotel, something that would have been way beyond our reach if Aunt Fran had had her way about the hoards of distant relatives she'd wanted to invite. And, in spite of her disappointment that neither Serena nor I had been married in white, she seemed to enjoy herself hugely.

'I'm so glad Dawn has settled down at last,' she said, rather tactlessly, to Alistair. 'She's a good girl really.'

Serena, who happened to overhear, rescued us by dragging her off for more champagne.

'Your aunt is going to be tiddly before the day's out.' Alistair said. 'She's quite pink and talkative already.'

'Oh, she's always like that,' I told him. I was feeling heady, too, but more from excitement than from anything I'd drunk.

Eventually, whilst our relatives and friends were still enjoying themselves, we left for our honeymoon in Switzerland, a destination we'd chosen because I'd always wanted to see the Alps and Alistair had said he didn't mind where we went as long as I was happy.

We stayed in Interlaken, the city between two lakes, Thune and Brienz, and I was captivated by the majestic scenery, which reminded me a little of Canada, and the cleanness of everything, from the pale cows to the litter-free streets. Now that it was high summer the town was warm, hot almost, but there was nothing sultry about the shimmering air. The quaint, old buildings were silhouetted in bright relief against the sharp green of the lower mountain slopes; the blue mist draped the finest of net curtains across the distant peaks where snow, like frosting on a cake, still clung with fingers extending downwards. The banks of the river and the lakes themselves were bright with flowers, vineyards thrived and turreted feudal castles nestled on the tree-lined slopes.

The hotel where we stayed made packed lunches for us every day, and we explored as much of this paradise of green and blue as we were able. We took a cable car up the Grindelwald, soaring over the sweet grassy slopes, bumping and clattering through the stations. We spent a day on the steamer to Montreaux, gliding silently between woods that came so close to the water that their reflection made a thick bank of green that shimmered and moved in the lazy ripples. We even rose one day with the dawn so that we could explore the might of the Jungfraujoch, travelling first on the little wooden-seated train and then on the rack and pinion railway, watching the valley fall away until the fields became pocket handkerchiefs and the animals mere dots against the green. And then we were inside the living, breathing heart of the mountain, and I was holding Alistair's hand so tightly that my fingers were numb.

We stopped once to look out through a window cut in the ice, and the glare, before I put on my Polaroids, hurt my eyes. On the mountain top we walked slowly, feeling our breath shorter than usual, marvelling at the expanse of snow, so crisp and white close to but with treacherous shadows of blue-grey where it fell away beyond the safety fence. We explored the 'Palace of Ice' – the caverns cut into a glacier – and I could have cried at the beauty of the roses frozen fresh and intact into blocks of ice for all time. We ate our packed lunch on the balcony of a café where we could get a hot drink and we fed the last of our sandwiches to the ravens that swooped in great circles to perch on the rail of the balcony itself.

I was invigorated by the fresh air and by the feeling of belonging with Alistair. After all the years of uncertainty with Sandy it was like heaven to be so sure of someone, to feel that things were so right. I was almost afraid to believe it was so, to touch with mortal fingers the gossamer threads of happiness.

One night, lying beside Alistair beneath the soft feather quilt that moulded itself around us, I tried to put my feelings into words.

'You know when you asked me to marry you and I said I didn't love you? Well, I think I was wrong. I think I have always loved you. I just didn't realize it.'

Alistair didn't answer, but I felt his head move on the pillow and I knew he was looking at me.

'It was different, you see,' I said, trying to explain. 'Sandy was, well, an obsession. The way I felt about him was painful, really. It sucked me dry. I just didn't recognize the way I felt about you because it didn't hurt. I thought that was what love was, and I was wrong.'

Without speaking, Alistair pulled me into his arms, lacing his fingers in my hair, crushing my body beneath his. He made love to me with a fierceness that left me breathless, and afterwards, lying with our moist skin clinging and our legs entwined, I said, 'I love you, Alistair.' And repeated it because it was so good to say it out loud and to know that I meant it.

When at last he slept, I lay listening to his even breathing and watching the small movements of his sleeping face in the half-light. And I whispered a prayer of thankfulness that at last I had found such perfect happiness.

The days sped past, filled with so many things to do and see besides the joy of discovering each other, but all too soon our honeymoon was over and I was struggling to pack the presents we'd bought for everyone into our already bulging cases. There was a pendant watch for Serena, a cuckoo clock for Alistair's parents and a music box that played 'Holiday in Switzerland' for Aunt Fran. And, in a little box tucked safely into the pocket of my handbag, were the edelweiss earrings Alistair had bought for me. I had put them away with love, gently covering the spiky, white petals with cotton wool, and I knew that whenever I looked at them I would remember how happy I had been.

We arrived back in London on a sultry summer afternoon, and after the clear air of Switzerland there was something oppressive about the way the sticky warmth cloyed around us.

But at least it was cool in our flat. Alistair unlocked the door and we carried our cases into the sitting room, which we'd furnished ourselves with bits and pieces we'd picked up at sales and things we'd been given as wedding presents – the sheepskin hearthrug from Serena and Chris, an anniversary clock from Aunt Fran and, of course, Sandy's painting of Seagull Bay. There was a new dining table and chairs from Alistair's parents, and the cushions and curtains in a shade of soft green, which I'd made myself after hours of painstaking stitching. But as I stood there looking around I felt oddly as if I didn't belong here yet.

'I didn't carry you over the threshold!' Alistair said suddenly.

I laughed. 'Of course you didn't. I'm far too big to be carried!'

'Rubbish! Every MacWilliam has carried his bride over the threshold since the custom was first invented, and I don't intend to break with tradition now. So, make up your mind – are you going to walk out on to the landing yourself, or do I have to carry you both ways?'

I went with him, giggling and protesting, and he swung me up into his arms and held me firmly against his chest. He had stopped laughing, and he was looking at me as if something inside him had melted.

'But I'll bet none of the other MacWilliam brides were as lovely as you,' he said. He wasn't a great one for sweet talk as a rule, and the fact lent sincerity to his words. He kissed me and carried me through the doorway and straight into the bedroom where he laid me unceremoniously on the eiderdown and began to undo my jacket.

'Alistair!' I protested weakly. 'Not now! I've got loads of things to do!'

'Nothing that can't wait.' He tossed the jacket on to the floor and slid his hands up my hips, wriggling up my skirt.

'Alistair – stop it! You'll ruin my suit . . .'

He laughed softly, close by my ear, and a sudden sense of déjà vu enveloped me. I'd been here before. For a moment I couldn't think where or when, then suddenly I was back in the chalet at Sturvendor, wearing my buttercup-yellow suit, on the day I'd been to the solicitors about the trust money. Before I could stop it, the past was all around me, the tang of the sea in my throat, the bitter-sweet fear of Sandy making my senses reel. For a brief moment time not only stood still but flipped alarmingly, and in the haze I thought I heard Sandy call my name.

Strangely, it was that illusion that catapulted me back to reality. It was treachery to even think of Sandy when I was with Alistair, especially when his were the lips on my throat and my breasts, his the hungry body taking mine.

'I love you, Alistair,' I whispered, and the ghosts of the past receded until I could think of nothing but my husband and the urgent need that had overtaken both of us.

We had a celebratory meal that night: a Chinese takeaway from the shop down the street and a bottle of Graves. Then we went to bed, tired and happy.

I was awakened by the shrilling of the telephone. The insistent sound dragged me from a pleasant dream, and I lay resentful, watching Alistair pull on a dressing gown before going to answer it.

I heard him say, 'Oh, hello. I'll fetch her . . .' and I pushed aside the sheet and got up. Then I heard him say, 'What? Oh . . .' in a shocked sort of voice, and there was a long silence before he said, 'Right. OK. Yes, I'll tell her.'

I had frozen, my feet searching under the bed for my mules. A sort of cold dread had begun deep inside me. Alistair came back into the bedroom and shut the door very carefully behind him, and when he turned around I knew for certain something was very wrong, because his face was like a blank page from which all the writing has been carefully erased. I waited, my arms wrapped around myself and panic choking me.

'Dawn, sit down,' Alistair said. 'I'm afraid there's bad news.'

I sat, my eyes never leaving his face. Inside me a shrill voice was screaming – *What? What?* – but I said nothing at all. I just waited with my heart a huge, throbbing lump in my throat and my hands trembling and clasped together so tightly that my nails dug deep crescents into the skin.

Alistair dropped to his haunches beside me and covered my hands with his. And he said, 'It's Sandy, Dawn. There's been an accident. I'm afraid he's dead, my love.'

I stared at him, not able for the moment to take it in. Sandy? Sandy! Then the tension exploded like a rogue rocket, showering me with fiery sparks that burned even as they wet my cheeks.

'Oh my God! My God!' The first words were a whisper, then they rose into hysteria. I struggled to rise too, but I could feel the room going away from me.

'Dawn, darling . . .' Alistair was putting his arms around me; blindly, I pushed him away.

'Oh my God . . . How? What happened? *How—?'*

'He drowned,' Alistair said, very gently. 'There was a swimmer in difficulties in the bay. Sandy went out to him. The current must have been too strong. He didn't make it back. I expect you've gathered that that was Serena on the phone. She asked me to break it to you.'

'When was this?' I asked. My throat was dry. It hurt to speak. 'When did it happen?'

'Yesterday afternoon.'

Yesterday afternoon. When Alistair was making love to me. When I was in his arms, so happy, so very happy. When I'd thought that I'd heard Sandy call out my name. Perhaps at that very moment Sandy had been dying.

I felt the tears, more of reaction than of grief yet, filling my eyes and this time when Alistair put his arms around me I didn't push him away. But with a supreme effort I swallowed the tears. I mustn't cry for Sandy to Alistair. Though he would understand, and wouldn't blame me, I just couldn't do it. It seemed to me it would be a betrayal of them both.

After long moments I got a grip on myself. 'I'm all right,' I said unsteadily. 'But would you please make me a cup of tea?'

'Course I will.'

As he disappeared into the kitchen it occurred to me suddenly that Alistair must have had to break bad news many times in the course of his career.

I sat there, stunned and trembling on the edge of the bed, and irrelevant bits of the past flicked before my eyes like the yellowing flaps in the old 'What the Butler Saw' machine on the pier at Sturvendor. Sandy sitting on a rock, sketching in his notebook; pushing his hot dog barrow; cooking bacon on the old stove in the chalet. Sandy laughing at me, goading me, making love to me. Sandy in his threadbare, salt-stained jeans and paint-splodged sweater. I saw the beach, too, the beach that I knew so well in calm and in storm, wooed sometimes by teasing waves, lashed in winter by yellow-topped breakers. What had the sea looked like yesterday when it took the life of my love?

And, suddenly, I was remembering the morning when the boy who had robbed the sports shop had been in trouble in the bay. I had wanted Sandy to go to his rescue, but he had taken the attitude that discretion was the better part of valour. I'd felt vaguely cheated then because I'd discovered that he was no hero. How ironic that now he should have died saving someone else . . .

'Oh, hell!' I whispered, and I buried my face in the pillow in a futile attempt to escape the terrible raw pain and the heart-breaking memories.

* * *

They buried Sandy the following Tuesday in the little churchyard overlooking the bay. The rain was whispering through the trees as if the sky was weeping for him, and the scent from the mound of roses, carnations and freesias that had been piled beside the grave was unbearably sweet.

In his lifetime Sandy would have said, if he'd thought about it all, 'Once I'm dead they can do what they like with me.' But for all that I was sure that this was what he would have wanted. He belonged here, within sight and sound of the sea he had loved, the sea that had in the end claimed his life, and his free spirit would have liked the simple solitude that would settle back on this place when we had all left. Here it was quiet, but quiet with the sound of peace, not death, and in the cherry trees the birds sang, the chattering, soft murmur of wood pigeons, the piercing sweetness of the blackbird, and sometimes, especially when the wind drove them up from the beach, the mewing of the gulls. Here the seasons came and went gently, so that in summer the heat of the sun was transmuted to rosy warmth, and in winter the snow lay soft and thick and unsullied in drifts under the laurel hedges.

Even today, in the greyness, there was a quality of light behind the clouds, and the fresh, earthy smell of the rain on the leaves perpetrated a closeness to a nature that envelops us all, a nature as gentle as she is remorseless.

It had been Sandy's parents' wish that he should be buried here, and, in that, I felt they had come closer to their son than he would ever have imagined possible, putting what they thought he would have liked before their own wishes. And my heart went out to them, and I wanted to embrace them and give them back some of the love Sandy had given me. But they stood stiff and erect at the graveside, speaking to no one and looking neither to right nor left, and only the tremble of his mother's hand on her husband's arm betrayed the terrible grief she was feeling.

When the simple service was over and the mourners began to move away I tried to summon up the courage to go and speak to her.

'Wait a moment,' I whispered to Alistair – who had taken time off especially to drive me down – and I started across the wet grass towards her. But as I approached she looked up, straight at me, and froze me with a look. I stopped, uncertain. There was hatred in her eyes, hatred and pain, just as you might see in the eyes of a mother fox who has just seen her young torn apart by the hounds, and in that moment I knew that she was blaming me for Sandy's death.

I had not thought it would be possible for me to hurt any more than I was already hurting, but that look, and my perception of what lay behind it, was a fresh knife thrust to my heart. For a moment we looked at one another, the two women in Sandy's life, from the two sides of a great divide. 'I'm sorry,' I mouthed silently. Then I bowed my head and turned away. As I followed Alistair to the car where Serena and Chris were waiting the rain mingled with the tears on my face and the guilt began deep inside me, a jagged nerve that would only grow sharper and more destructive in the days and weeks that would follow.

If I had not left Sandy, maybe he wouldn't have died. It was irrational but inescapable. Sandy had come to London to ask me to go back to him, and I'd sent him away. The weight on my heart was an unbearable burden, the knowledge a thick fog closing in to suffocate me. I had denied Sandy, and now he was dead.

# Fifteen

Autumn came in early with high winds and driving rain stripping the leaves from the trees almost as soon as they turned colour, and London became grey, cold and dreary. For as long as I could remember I had found the end of summer depressing, but this year, I knew, should have been different. Alistair and I were newly married and the glow of our love and happiness should have carried me through the darkening days. But it seemed to me that I had left that glow in the Sturvendor churchyard.

The awful sense of guilt that had overtaken me then was a weight I could not shake off, no matter how I tried. Again and again I remembered how Sandy had swallowed his fierce pride and come to London to ask me to marry him, again and again I remembered the raw hurt in his face when I told him 'no'. He had gone back to Seagull Bay knowing I had turned my back on him. After all we had shared, all we had been to one another. And just a few short weeks later he was dead.

The knowledge was like a cancer in me, spreading greedy fingers to eat away all my happiness.

And in spite of Sandy there *was* happiness, in the beginning, at any rate. There were plans to be made and dreams to be dreamed. There were nights when Alistair came home to bed frozen to the marrow from a bitterly cold late-night duty and I warmed him with my body until I fell asleep. There were times when we drove up to the heath and walked for miles, arms linked, bodies bent against the gusting winds of autumn. And there were times when we made love in front of the spluttering gas fire in our sitting room, our skin warmed by passion as well as the roaring flame, our hearts reaching out and touching as our bodies fused to one. Afterwards, lying in Alistair's arms, I would feel warm, safe and content, and the bay with its storm-tossed waves seemed a million miles away.

But always the shadow of Sandy was there at the edges of my mind, and the ache of guilt at what I had done to him lay heavy on my heart. And then the blackness would begin, creeping through me like the first stealthy waves creeping up the beach at the turn of the tide, then gathering in strength until I quailed before it. I would turn from Alistair then, lying tense and taut while my head sung with unshed tears, and I knew there was nothing I could do to stop the watershed of grief and guilt until it had spent itself.

To begin with Alistair tried to coax me gently out of my moods. 'Dawn, whatever is the matter, my love?'

And when I didn't answer, for the moods seemed to paralyse my tongue, his arms would go round me, holding me close. But with the black fog pressing in all around me there was no comfort in his arms. They seemed only to stifle me, and it was all I could do not to push him away. 'Leave me alone!' I wanted to say. But not even those words would come, and I would lie unyielding and remote, hating Alistair for intruding into my private hell, hating Sandy for dying, and, most of all, hating myself.

With the passing of the mood, my hatred for Alistair would pass, and I would be smitten with remorse. Alistair was good, gentle and strong, and I loved him. How could I treat him this way? Desperate to make it up to him, I would throw myself into his arms, covering him with kisses, and he would tell me, 'It's all right, my love – it's all right!' so that for a moment I almost believed him. Almost, but not quite. For though my resentment of Alistair passed with my mood, my disgust with myself remained.

As the weeks passed, instead of getting better the depressions came more often and lasted longer. So many things reminded me of Sandy – a Beatles tune played on the radio, the smell of bacon frying, the sound of the wind lashing rain against the window so that it sounded like sea spray. Sometimes I thought I saw him in the street, and my heart seemed to stop beating. And whenever I looked at the painting of Seagull Bay, hanging in our living room, I seemed to fold up inside.

One day Alistair came in and caught me staring at it, and I thought for a moment he was going to tell me to take it down and pack it away. Strangely, I almost hoped he would. He looked from the picture to me and back again, his eyes narrowed, revealing nothing. Then a muscle tightened beside his mouth, and he turned away, and I knew that the showdown was not yet.

Christmas came, and I made it the best I possibly could, decorating the flat with holly and mistletoe and buying a turkey that was far too big for the two of us, and a huge ham from the delicatessen on the corner. I even made my own Christmas cake and a batch of mince pies, and Alistair bought in enough drink to float a battleship, but he had to work on Christmas evening, so I was left alone with the remains of the festive feast going cold around me. Several of his friends had asked me to join them, and so had Kathleen, but I didn't want to intrude on family parties, and Kathleen, I knew, had a new boyfriend with whom she would much rather spend Christmas evening alone. So I stayed at home and remembered the last Christmas I'd spent with Sandy and got very drunk and very maudlin on the bottle of cognac Alistair had bought for me.

In January Julie turned up with a red-faced turf accountant in tow. I was delighted to see her but very surprised, and she explained she'd seen Hunter (to whom I'd sent a Christmas card) and he had given her my address. She looked bloomingly happy and managed to polish off the remains of my bottle of cognac, and from the cut of her clothes I guessed her turf accountant was keeping her in luxury from the profits of his string of betting shops. He seemed a jolly enough fellow, and just the right type to deal with Julie's vagaries, but when he discovered I was married to a policeman he became distinctly uncomfortable and anxious to whisk Julie away.

We hugged and kissed goodbye, but as they left I could hear Julie asking indignantly why he hadn't mentioned his pressing business before, and I knew this would be the last time I would see them. I'd accepted that Alistair's job could make him unpopular with certain sections of the community, but it still had the power to hurt when it came between me and my friends. And with the hurt came the familiar choking depression, hemming me in and dragging me down.

As I felt it creeping over me I covered my face in my hands, begging it to leave me be, but all the wishing in the world made no difference. The black cloud had caught up with me again, and there was no escape.

I was still in its grip when Alistair came in a couple of hours later, and the look of dismay on his face when he saw the state

I was in did nothing to help. When I was like this I didn't want to be alone but I didn't want anyone there either, and I wondered for the first time if I might be going mad. Somehow I got myself together enough to tell Alistair about Julie and her bookmaker boyfriend, explaining that their sudden departure was the cause of my mood, though I knew that was far from the truth. However I tried to pretend to Alistair, and to myself, that it was, I knew the real trigger for my renewed bout of depression was being reminded of Sturvendor – and Sandy.

Things came to a head one night in late February. We'd had snow, and, though most of it had gone, there were still dirty, grey patches where it had hardened into ice after being swept away from the paths, and the raw cold seemed to have crept inside our usually cosy flat.

Alistair was on nights – due to go on duty at ten – and I knew the bed would be cold and vast without him, so during the evening I went to look out a pair of fluffy pink socks that I hadn't seen for ages but thought would keep my feet warm, if nothing else. As luck would have it I couldn't find them. But when I pulled out the drawer to search more thoroughly, what I did find was the box containing the pendant Sandy had given me.

It shouldn't have been a shock; I knew it was there. But as my fingers touched it I began to tremble and the blackness began to descend. With stiff fingers I opened the box and took the pendant out. It lay in the palm of my hand as bright as ever, with the tiny pearl reflected in the gold leaf, and it was only when a tear splashed on to it that I realized I was crying. But the release of that tear seemed like the proverbial breach in the dyke. Suddenly, my eyes were flooded; the tears came as if from a bottomless well, drenching my cheeks, running down my neck, even dampening my hair where it fell over my face. I stood with one hand pressed to my mouth whilst the other still clutched the pendant, and then, when my grief bent me double, I sank to my knees, rocking to and fro in a ceaseless, soundless motion.

I didn't hear Alistair come into the room; I was just suddenly aware of him saying, 'Dawn, whatever—?' but I couldn't answer. I was out of control, a stupid, rocking doll. He crouched down beside me, reaching out for me. And then he saw the pendant.

'For goodness' sake!' His voice was low but so changed that it cut through my trance. There was disgust in his tone and something else, the harsh grate of barely controlled fury. A sudden fear, sharp as a needle, prickled deep inside me. I looked up at him through tear-blurred eyes and saw the cold fury I had heard in his voice reflected in his face.

'Is this what's been upsetting you all the time?' he grated again, without a trace of sympathy. 'Can't you forget him? Is that it?'

I couldn't answer. The tears came again, a fresh cascade burning my cheeks, and Alistair caught me roughly by the arms, jerking me to my feet.

'It is, isn't it? You come in here secretly, getting out this damned necklace and wallowing over it. God, I wish I'd never found the thing for you.'

Before I could do anything to stop him he had torn the pendant from my hand and thrown it across the room, and my momentary fear was forgotten in a tide of outrage.

'How dare you!' I sobbed at him, breaking free and scrabbling on my hands and knees to where the pendant lay. 'Sandy gave that to me—'

'I know that! Sandy – bloody Sandy! I've heard just about enough of that bloke. It's me you're married to, Dawn. Remember?'

I recovered the pendant, holding it in my clenched hand, close to my breast, and straightened up. 'Yes, worse luck.'

To this day I don't know what made me say it. I was so angry that he could have treated my treasure with such disrespect that I would have stopped at nothing. But the moment the words left my lips I knew I'd gone too far. Alistair's face darkened with a fury I'd never seen before; he was a snarling, feral animal. His hands balled to fists and he raised one bringing it within inches of my face. I recoiled, terrified of the animal he had suddenly become, yet oddly defiant.

'Don't you dare!' I spat at him. 'Don't you dare hit me!'

For a brief second I saw a flicker of shame, then the cold mask was back. 'You go too far, Dawn.'

'You ever lay a finger on me, Alistair, and I'm out of here.'

I saw his hands ball to fists again, but they remained at his sides. 'Go then, if that's what you want.' His voice resonated with anger. 'I've had all I can take of you anyway. Just bloody go.'

Shock ran through me in waves, leaving me cold and trembling. 'I thought you understood . . .' I faltered.

He snorted angrily. 'Understood? Oh yes, I understand. When I'm making love to you you're pretending I'm someone else.'

'That's not true!' I gasped.

'Isn't it? Well, you could have fooled me. You think of nothing but that useless waste of space—'

'He was not a waste of space! He was—'

'Oh, shut up, Dawn. I don't want to hear it. For Christ's sake, just get out, or I will. I've had it with you. I've had it with you weeping and wailing and moping around after some other bloke. Especially one who treated you like shit. That's what you want, is it? That's what turns you on? Well, I'm sorry, that's not me. So we might as well call it a day. Just get out and leave me in peace. I don't want you any more.'

He turned and stormed out of the room. I almost ran after him, not ready to end this quarrel, but the blackness was there again, hemming me in, deluging me with self-pity, and instead I ran to the wardrobe, hauled my suitcase from the top of it and threw it, open, on to the bed. Alistair wanted me to leave – then that's what I would do. I didn't want to spend another moment here with him. Shaking, sobbing, I dragged underwear out of the drawers of the tallboy and threw them into the case. I was grabbing handfuls of clothes, still on their hangers, from the wardrobe, when Alistair came back in.

'What the hell do you think you're doing?'

'Leaving you. Isn't that what you wanted?'

'Dawn, for God's sake . . .'

'Leaving you. Did you hear? I hate you! Hate you!'

'Oh, don't be so bloody silly . . .' He made to catch me by the arms, and I twisted away.

'Take your hands off me, Alistair. Just . . . leave me alone!'

He released me abruptly and turned away. 'Oh, suit yourself, Dawn. I've got to go to work.'

A moment later I heard the slam of the front door.

I crumpled then, sobbing helplessly again. I couldn't believe things had escalated so far and so fast; I could only think that Alistair had been simmering silently for a long while and seeing me with the pendant had ignited the touch paper. In the heat of the moment I'd said things I didn't mean, but I had the most awful feeling that Alistair had meant every word. I'd tried his patience beyond endurance; I'd hurt him too much. It wasn't his fault, it was mine, all mine. Because I was still obsessed with Sandy.

Like the things I'd said, I wasn't at all sure that when I'd dragged the suitcase down from the wardrobe I had really intended to leave. It had been a dramatic gesture, something to release the head of steam inside me. And, perhaps, to shock Alistair. But now, suddenly, it seemed to me that it really was the right thing to do. Alistair was right, I couldn't forget Sandy. Perhaps I never would. And if I stayed and we made up it wouldn't be long before the blackness was overcoming me again and he would know it. I'd hurt him again and again. Alistair deserved better than that. He deserved better than me.

Tears were still streaming down my face as I fastened the catches on my suitcase. What had started as a stupid gesture now seemed inevitable. I had to leave him to make a fresh life without me.

And me? There was only one place I could be, feeling as I did.

I was going to Sturvendor. I was going home.

# Sixteen

It was midday when the train pulled into Sturvendor Station. I'd spent the night on a hard bench at Paddington waiting for the milk train, no longer crying, just lost in a haze of misery. I opened the door, heaved my case down on to the platform and signalled to the only porter in sight.

'Can you get a taxi for me, please?'

He shifted his cigarette to the corner of his mouth. 'They don't wait the trains this time of year. It's not in season.'

'Can you phone for one then, please?'

He looked me over slowly, insolently, still chewing his cigarette from side to side. 'I could do. There's a phone in the station master's office . . .'

A tip. He wanted a tip. I found a ten-shilling note and pushed it into his hand. 'Please.'

He loped off and I stood on the deserted platform wondering how long it would be before the axe fell on the line to Sturvendor. So many small stations had closed, and this line couldn't possibly pay its way at this time of year. Soon it would be gone, along with so many other dear, familiar things that linked me to the past.

The porter reappeared, walking with a stooping gait as if pushing a trolley-load of freight. 'Taxi'll be here in five minutes.' He ground the cigarette end into the platform with his heel. 'Shall I take that?' he asked, gesticulating with his chin at my suitcase.

We went out through the peeling brown and ochre door, and I felt the first stirring of nervousness deep within. What was Serena going to say when I turned up on her doorstep saying I'd left Alistair? And what about Chris?

A great black Daimler turned the corner, and the moment I saw it I knew it was Jack Stride with his all-purpose wedding and funeral car. Again my heart sank a little. So many people I knew here, and they'd all want to know how I was getting on. The place, I'd longed to see again. The people, I could have done without.

'Well, Dawn love, fancy it being you!' Jack Stride loaded my case into the boot of the car and I forced a smile.

'Well, why not?'

'Why not indeed! It's nice to see you, I must say. I haven't seen you since . . .' He broke off, and in the awkward silence that followed I knew what he had been about to say. *Since Sandy's funeral . . .*

'You want to go to Serena's place, I suppose?' he said instead.

I nodded. 'Where else?'

The taxi drew up outside the cottage, and even before I'd finished paying Jack Stride the door was open and Serena was running down the path, her face alight.

'Dawn! What a lovely surprise! Come in quickly, the wind out here is like a knife.'

I followed her into the house, trying to smile with lips that were stiff. 'I'm sorry to just turn up like this. If it's not convenient . . .'

'Not convenient? What on earth do you mean! Not convenient – you! Let me take your coat . . .'

I slipped it off, though I was shivering.

'Where's Alistair?' Serena asked. 'Is he working?'

'Yes.' It was the truth, and I didn't want to get into explanations just yet.

'Well, for once Chris isn't,' Serena cooed. 'He actually packed up at lunchtime. Wonders will never cease!'

My heart missed a beat. I didn't want to see Chris. But there he was, in the living room. In the few months since I'd last seen him he looked to have put on weight, and his face was slightly puffed. It occurred to me to wonder if he was drinking.

'Dawn! How nice to see you. Are you staying? We didn't know—'

'Well, of course she's staying. Now, just sit down, Dawn, and I'll get you a cup of tea,' Serena fussed happily. She disappeared into the kitchen and Chris and I sat for a moment in awkward silence.

'So, how is life treating you, Dawn?' he asked at last.

'Fine,' I said brightly. 'What about you?'

'Fine,' he echoed. And I wondered if he was lying too.

Serena came bustling back in with the tea trolley and a plate of scones. For a while we chatted generally, and Serena brought me up to date with all the local gossip. Then she said, too casually, 'By the way, I should never be surprised to hear that Mummy was going to get married again.'

'Really?' I was pleased. Aunt Fran was such a warm and loving person it was wrong for her to be on her own. 'Who is it, Serena?'

'Someone she's met in Bristol. His daughter was a pupil at the school where Mummy was teaching. He's a widower, and they met at a PTA thing and hit it off right away. He's something in computers, I think, but I haven't been able to discover exactly what.'

'Serena doesn't like him,' Chris said flatly.

'That's not true!' Serena said quickly. 'It just takes a bit of getting used to, that's all. And he's got two sons as well as Clara, though they're much older, teenagers.'

'Clara. That's a pretty name,' I said.

'Old-fashioned, if you ask me,' Chris said.

'No, I quite like it too,' Serena said. 'But if I ever have a little girl I shall call her Victoria.' There was a wistful note in her voice, then she said brightly, 'Come on, Dawn, eat up. You're thinner than ever, and it's really not good for you.'

We chatted on for a while, then Chris put down his cup and saucer. 'I've got to go into Minehead to make a call. I don't suppose you two will miss me though. You'll be here till midnight chatting if I know anything about it.'

'Oh Chris, do you have to?' Serena groaned, and unexpectedly I found myself echoing her sentiment, though for a quite different reason. As long as Chris was here, Serena and I were restricted to small talk and harmless gossip. When we were alone I was going to have to tell her the truth about Alistair and me.

'No choice, I'm afraid,' Chris said heartily. 'Business is business.'

He got up and, while he was putting on his coat, Serena warmed his scarf in front of the fire. She was making him her child, I thought. Mothering him.

'Try not to be late, Chris,' she said, putting up her face to be kissed. 'And don't have too much to drink, please.'

A flash of irritation crossed Chris's face. 'Give it a rest, Serena.' Then he was gone.

Serena pulled a face at me. 'He thinks I nag him. It's just worrying out loud, really, but it does make me sound a bit of a bore, I know. And I expect I am. I really ought to get a job or take a teacher training course as I always meant to, not just sit around here, cooking and ironing and keeping tabs on Chris.'

I slipped my feet out of my shoes and stretched them out to the fire. 'So why don't you?'

'Chris likes me here,' Serena said simply. 'And, the thing is, it's where I want to be. But I want children too. And they just don't seem to happen.'

I frowned. 'You must be able to have a baby,' I said. 'You were pregnant once.'

'I know.' She sighed. 'It's ridiculous really. We've seen doctors, specialists, the whole kaboodle, and there is absolutely no reason why we shouldn't have a child. And yet we don't. Every month I hope like mad, and if I'm a bit late I start getting really excited. And then I get let down again. It's really horrible, Dawn.'

'Maybe you're trying too hard,' I suggested.

'Of course I'm trying too hard,' she said bitterly. 'I can't help it. It's taken over my life, really. When Chris is making love to me, all I can think is *maybe tonight* . . . Oh—' She broke off, colouring, and I knew she'd said more than she meant to.

'What about adoption?' I asked.

'We have talked about it,' Serena said. 'But knowing there's no reason why we shouldn't have a baby of our own we just keep putting it off. I worry, you see, that if we went ahead and adopted I might fall pregnant myself. You often hear of that, don't you? And I'm terrified that I would either favour my own child or go completely the other way and be really hard on him so that the adopted one didn't feel discriminated against. I'm not sure how I could cope . . .'

'You would,' I said with confidence. 'You have so much love to give, Serena.'

'Oh yes, I have,' she whispered, and I realized she was crying. Silently, the tears sliding down her cheeks like huge drops escaping through the cracks of a dam. 'It's so unfair, really, when you think of all the unwanted babies, and there's me, just longing to have one . . . It's unfair on Chris too. I feel I've failed him.'

'Oh, don't talk such rubbish!' I said inadequately.

'But I can't help feeling that,' she said. 'I want to have his baby so badly. I want to see his face when he looks at it for the first time and he puts out his hand and he's half afraid to touch it because it's so small and perfect. I want to give him a son he can play football with, or a daughter he can spoil. I want us to be a family. But it doesn't happen, and I can't imagine now that it ever will.'

'Oh Serena,' I said, and took her hands in mine. There was nothing I, or anyone, could say or do that would make her feel better, but I wanted her to know I understood, so that for a little while at least she would not feel quite so alone. We sat quietly in the half light and a fierce protective tenderness for Serena filled me so much that I thought, bitterly, that life was as careless as a child who puts away his jigsaw puzzles with all the bits in the wrong boxes.

'It will come right, I know it will,' I said, and wished I could truly believe my own words.

'I certainly hope so,' she said. She was silent for a moment, then she went on, 'Well, I think we've had quite enough of the continuing saga of Serena Carter. Tell me about you.'

I was caught completely unawares. For the past minutes I'd forgotten my own troubles. Now I knew was the moment I should say, 'I've left Alistair. I expect we'll be getting divorced,' but somehow the words wouldn't come. I didn't want to talk about it, even to Serena. As long as it was a secret known only to me it wasn't quite real. I got up, too hastily, and began stacking the tea things.

'Let's wash up, shall we?'

I think Serena knew I was avoiding the subject because she did not press me.

When we'd washed up we got out the Scrabble board and played in companionable silence until Chris came in, and then we played Monopoly, all three of us relegating our personal problems in the scramble to own property in Whitechapel and Park Lane.

When it was time for bed I had a whisky nightcap against all

Serena's advice that Ovaltine would be much better for me, and went up to the guest room, which overlooked the bay.

When I went to the window to draw the curtains it was there beneath me, the moonlight making the water shimmer like rich dark velvet, deceptively dangerous, mysteriously beautiful. Far out there was a ship, a dark hulk whose lights appeared quite divorced from it, so that it looked as if the stars had come down into the bay, and when I opened the window to let in the cool night air I heard the cacophony of the waves as they ran up the beach and dragged at the shingle. Deep sadness filled me, and I turned away from the window and began to undress, folding my clothes neatly instead of dropping them into a pile on the chair as I usually did. Then I sat on the stool in front of the dressing table to take off my make-up.

When my face was bare I didn't move away but remained there, staring at my reflection and thinking how little it had changed in nine years. So much had happened; it should be written there for all to see. But my face, pale between the thick falls of dark hair, might almost have been the face of the schoolgirl who had first come to Sturvendor, grieving and alone. The high, round neck of my nightdress, chosen for its warmth, could have been the tunic I'd worn then.

I thought, *If I could go back and start again, would I change anything?* But my only answer was a terrible weight of weariness. To relive those years, to have Sandy again, knowing that I would lose him, to have to make the choices and do it all again would be simply unbearable. I couldn't do it, even if I had the chance. It was bad enough to have to go on.

I got out the bottle of sleeping tablets the doctor had prescribed for me when I had gone to him in despair a few weeks ago, looking for help and understanding for the terrible moods that were debilitating me. I didn't think the answer could be found in a bottle, but tonight I couldn't face the sleepless hours any more than I could face the thought of living my life over again. I shook two tablets into my hand and swallowed them with the last of the whisky. Had the doctor said I shouldn't mix the tablets with alcohol? I couldn't remember, but it really didn't matter. Whatever the consequences, I had to sleep tonight.

At first, when I got into bed, I was uncomfortable with the

unfamiliar feel of the mattress and the unfamiliar soap-powder scent of the sheets. I lay staring into the darkness until I began to grow muzzy and my eyes refused to remain open. The last thing I saw was Sandy's face. It was wet, although whether with sea water or tears I didn't know. But he was smiling. And I thought that he was glad that I had come home to him.

Suddenly, I was awake. The room was full of moonlight that had crept in through the thin cretonne curtains and was silvering the furniture and making pools of liquid light on the carpet. For a moment I wondered where I was, stretching out my hands to find the warmth of Alistair's body; then realization dawned and with it the sure knowledge that I felt horribly ill. My stomach was heavy, so were my eyelids, and, as I watched, the room did a sickening roll, making me clutch in panic at the edge of the eiderdown.

*I shouldn't have mixed the tablets with the whisky*, I thought, but after a moment the spasm passed. I retrieved my watch from the bedside table. The moonlight was deceptively bright and I had some difficulty in making out the time, but eventually I decided it was just after two.

Instantly, I thought of Alistair. He would have changed shifts today, from nights to a late shift, and he would be due home just about now. How had he taken the fact that I had actually left? I wondered. Had it been a shock when he had returned home this morning to snatch a few hours sleep before his 'quick changeover' to find me gone? And what would be going through his mind now as he unlocked the door of the flat? Perhaps from force of habit he would creep in softly, forgetting that I was not there to be disturbed. And when he climbed into bed would he feel the cheerless emptiness as I was feeling it?

I shivered, and another spasm of giddiness clutched at my stomach. Perhaps I was going to die, I thought, dramatic as ever. But just now, rather than adding to the drama by telling myself I would be going to Sandy, I simply ached for Alistair. Whom I had hurt so much. Whom I had betrayed. I turned my head into the pillow and wept inwardly, silently. *Oh Alistair, I am so sorry. What have I done to you?*

But the empty, whirling room was silent. I was alone with my self-imposed torture. And the only respite was to drift away once more into drug-induced sleep.

It was a cold, grey morning when I woke again. I still felt faintly muzzy, but when I opened the window wide the fresh, salty air went some way to clearing it. From downstairs I could hear the clatter of dishes and Serena singing as she prepared breakfast, and I thought that if she had not confided in me last night I would never have guessed that she was living a torment of her own. The sound of running water from the bathroom told me Chris was in occupation so I got dressed in trousers and a woollen shirt, thinking I could bath later. I didn't want to wander around in a housecoat as I had used to do before I realized the effect it had on Chris.

As I brushed my hair I realized how tired I looked. The previous night's drugged, but restless, sleep had taken its toll of me, and there were dark circles under my eyes and tired lines etched far too deeply around my mouth. But I couldn't be bothered even to try to repair the damage. There was no one but me to care if I looked haggard.

Serena had cooked an enormous breakfast and, typically, she insisted I eat some instead of my usual toast and orange juice. Watching her fussing around I could see all the frustrated mother-love oozing out of her. She flipped far too much bacon on to our plates, buttered the toast and fetched fresh bottles of sauce because she said the ones on the table were 'bottomsy'. She even sugared Chris's tea for him and gave it a stir. I wondered if he minded being treated as a surrogate child. I would have thought such over-concern would become dreadfully irritating. But he was apparently unaware of it, and he was eating so heartily that I needed to look no further for the reason he was developing a noticeable paunch.

After he had left for work and I had helped Serena clean up and do a few chores, I said, 'I thought I'd take a trip into Sturvendor.'

Serena's face betrayed nothing. She had still not asked me why I was here, and she did not ask me now. I think she knew – and knew, too, that I was not ready to talk about it. She simply said, 'Do you want the bus timetable, or are you going to walk?'

'I'll walk,' I said.

I put on my suede jacket and tied a headscarf over my hair. It was cold but still fine, and as I walked along the cliff road the wind in my face made my head begin to throb dully again. This morning the sea was flint grey and angry-looking beneath the harsh backdrop of the cliffs, yet I wanted to be near it. But not yet. There was somewhere else I had to visit first.

As I turned in through the churchyard gates I felt the peace of the place descend on me. It didn't matter that the wind was whipping the branches of the trees, or that the grass was sodden and mud-caked in places. I had only to look at the flaking gravestones, with their half-legible inscriptions, to know that the ravage of wind and rain was for a season only. They instilled a sense of timelessness and continuity. In spring the sun would come again, and so would the small, green shoots, and the martins and swallows. And it would once again warm the stones that would still be there, monuments to men and women who had lived and loved here in this corner of Somerset, as Sandy and I had lived and loved.

I left the path and walked across the wet grass towards the simple cross that Sandy's parents had erected to mark his grave. And saw the flowers. The stone vase had been filled with bronze and yellow chrysanthemums, and the surrounding earth had been carefully tended. There was no trace of weed or couch grass; instead there was a patch of dark green, flecked with purest white. I knelt to part the shiny leaves and saw the first bud of a Christmas rose.

I should have known, of course, that Serena wouldn't let Sandy's grave run wild, but gratitude overwhelmed me all the same, and with it, once again, guilt. I should have been the one to tend Sandy's grave, but this was the first time I had been back, and even now I had not thought to bring any flowers with me.

For a while I knelt there, lost in my thoughts, whilst the wet grass soaked the knees of my trousers and the wind whipped long strands of hair free from my scarf and plastered them across my face. Then I got up slowly. I felt oddly empty. He was not here, the Sandy I had known. His remains, maybe, but not the essence of him. I would have to go elsewhere to touch that.

I left the churchyard and walked down the narrow tree-lined

street towards the promenade, buffeted now by memories. I passed the stage door of the old Gaiety, shuttered and barred, but there were fresh posters on the billboards, advertising a Gilbert and Sullivan opera the Grammar School was putting on. I looked at the photographs, at the eager young faces above elaborate costumes, and I thought that if I was still here I'd go to see their show. Perhaps amongst them was some talented youngster who, with encouragement, could make the grade. I thought briefly of my own wasted talent, but it seemed unimportant. The only thing that mattered today was Sandy.

I rounded the corner on to the seafront and the salt wind caught me full in the face, taking my breath. I dug my hands into the pockets of my jacket, pulling it around me, but still the wind cut through, making me shiver.

The beach was deserted except for a man exercising a dog at the water's edge. I walked for a while along the promenade, and then I climbed over the sea wall and scrunched across the shingle until I reached the firm, sludgy sand. It sucked at my shoes as I walked, and I looked back over my shoulder at the line of exaggerated prints.

'And in passing, leave behind us. Footprints on the sands of time . . .' The words, learned long ago, came to me unbidden and seemed now to have special meaning.

The cabin was still there, looking even more dilapidated than before. The windows had been broken, by stone-throwing youths, I guessed, and a piece of tar paper on the corner of the roof had come loose and was flapping wildly in the wind like a huge, injured bird. I pushed at the door, but it was locked, and I felt vaguely cheated. I stood on tiptoe to peer through one of the broken window panes. The place looked bare and sad. Someone had taken the cooker and the lamp and the blanket from the bed, but the chair was still there, though thick with dust and sand and the droppings of a bird that must have got in through the broken windows and become trapped. The plasterboard partition to the kitchen was bulging out of shape in one place, and the musty smell that reached my nose was so unlike the old smell of bacon and oil paints that I could hardly believe that this little piece of desolation could be the private place where Sandy and I had lived and loved.

Sick with disappointment, I sank back on to my heels. Sandy was not here either. Sandy had been alive, so alive, and this cabin was nothing but an empty shell. Nothing remained of the man whose home it had been for those long, beautiful summers.

Wretchedly, I walked back up the beach under the sheltering cliffs. There was only one place left where I could look for Sandy – if I could find the strength to go there. Seagull Bay itself. Perhaps it would have made sense to go there first, but somehow my haunting of all the old places seemed to be set in an immutable sequence that had very little to do with me.

I left the beach and made my way through the tail-end of town and back on to the cliff road, the third side of the triangle that I had walked that morning. But when the valley fell away beneath me, I cut across the moors and headed for the cliff path that I had discovered all those years ago.

To begin with the descent took all my concentration. It had never been easy, even in summer when there were great tufts of lush thrift to hang on to, and now, older and unpractised as I was, I found it hard going. Once or twice my foot slipped and I sent a flurry of small stones crashing down; once I had to stop, holding with both hands to a piece of jutting rock while I regained my confidence. At last I realized I was almost down and I took the last six feet or so at a run, landing untidily on the beach.

For a moment after I had regained my balance I simply stood there, breathing heavily and testing the ankle I'd turned in that last, wild helter-skelter down the path. And then a curious thing happened. I was overcome with the certainty that I was not alone.

It was a feeling that seemed to begin at the base of my spine and creep up towards my neck, a tingling that was part excitement and part curiosity and part an awesome awareness. For what seemed like an eternity I remained motionless, scarcely breathing, then I took a hesitant step away from the cliff. In that moment, so strong was the sense of wonder and anticipation that I almost believed that when I rounded the boulder I would see Sandy, sitting with his sketch pad, just as he had been the very first time we met.

He wasn't, of course. The beach was empty and deserted. My heart fell away into the bottomless pit of despair and disappointment, yet somehow at the same time I felt oddly elated.

The emptiness here had a different quality to it than the emptiness I had experienced at the graveside and the cabin. Sandy was here. I might never see his physical self again, but his spirit was here all right, and it was welcoming me.

I sat down then on a boulder and looked out at the sea. Above me the few seagulls who had stayed to brave the storm were wheeling and crying. Around me the cliffs curved like walls separating me from the outside world. Before me the sea pounded ceaselessly.

Sandy had sat here that last afternoon, maybe on this very boulder. He had looked out to sea, a calm sea then, but concealing the dangerous currents that he knew so well, and he had seen the swimmer in difficulty. He had taken off his clothes and gone to the rescue. What had he been thinking about? Was the only thing in his mind to get to the drowning boy? Or had he known, with some flash of insight, that he was going to die himself? Had he, in those last moments, thought of his parents? Or had he thought of me? The girl he had shared so much with, the girl he had loved, who had turned her back on him?

'Oh Sandy,' I whispered, and the wind took the words and blew them back in my face. 'I never meant to hurt you. I never meant to hurt anyone.'

My life seemed to pass before my eyes then, a heraldic panorama. The colours were splashed brightly, the pictures vivid and alive, but it was blurred over with a mist of sadness, of guilt, of purpose lost. And I looked at the sea that had taken the life of my love and thought how easy it would be to follow him. All I had to do was to walk into the sea and keep walking. It would be cold at first, but I'd scarcely notice. And I would be reunited with Sandy, and I would never again be able to hurt or destroy those I loved . . .

'I thought I'd find you here.' Serena's voice cut into my reverie. I hadn't heard her approaching. I stared at her, surprised that she had braved the steep descent – though I'd told her once about my bay, she'd never summoned up the courage to join me there – and a little indignant that she was both interrupting my pilgrimage and possibly preventing me from carrying out the dramatic ending I was envisioning.

'Dawn, something is terribly wrong, isn't it?' Serena said. 'Is it Sandy?'

I nodded. 'I killed him, Serena. It's my fault he's dead.'

There was a long moment's silence, except for the waves driving relentlessly at the beach and thundering on to the rocks. Then Serena said savagely, 'Oh, don't be so ridiculous.'

I faltered, caught off balance by the vehemence in her voice. 'It's not ridiculous. If he'd had something to live for he'd never have done it.'

'I think you're underestimating him,' Serena said crisply. 'And I also think that dramatic part of you that fancies being a tragic Greek heroine *wants* to feel responsible. You'd like me to tell you he was so upset about you marrying Alistair that he practically committed suicide that day. Well, it's simply not true. He saw the boy in difficulty, and he went in to try and save him. He didn't think at all, I'm sure.'

'But Serena, doing something like that just wasn't Sandy. Don't you remember the time when that young thug who'd done a smash and grab stole a rowing boat to escape and got into trouble? I begged Sandy to go out to help him. He wouldn't do it—'

'That was completely different,' Serena said stoutly. 'Sandy knew he'd be in just as much trouble with that leaky old boat of his. And the lifeboat had been called out, as I remember it. But this boy was only twelve years old, for goodness sake, and Sandy was a strong swimmer. Sandy did what he felt he had to do. It was a heroic act, Dawn, and you have no right to demean it this way.'

A nerve jumped in my throat, but I wasn't ready to let it go just yet. 'I hurt him so,' I said. 'Even if I didn't actually cause his death, I made his last weeks unhappy instead of . . . Did you know he came to London and asked me to marry him?'

For the first time Serena's face registered surprise. 'No, I didn't know. You mean you turned him down?'

I nodded. 'Yes. In all my life I'd never wanted anything so much, but when it happened I turned him down. He was so hurt, Serena. I'd never realized how much he cared – he was always so . . . flippant. And I turned him down.'

Again, the sea drove fiercely into the silence, and the weight of despair inside me was so great that I might have been made of lead.

At last Serena said, 'Why did you turn him down, Dawn?'

'Because I couldn't take any more.' The answer came out before

I'd even thought about it, and I realized Serena's question had been more than mere curiosity. She was trying to make me think of things that I'd pushed to the back of my mind.

'I couldn't take any more of the way he used to treat me, so . . . casually, as if I had no rights at all where he was concerned,' I said, as much to myself as to her. 'I was fed up with his other women and the whole feeling of insecurity about him. I loved him, but he tore me apart, again and again, and I just couldn't go back to the way it was.'

For a brief moment remembering the pain he'd caused me for so many long years brought an echo of the flash of the release I'd felt when I'd thought myself cured of Sandy. 'I really believe I could have got over him if he hadn't drowned,' I whispered. 'Somehow because he's dead he's even more real than when he was alive. I can never speak to him again and tell him I'm sorry. I can never let him know I loved him, really loved him . . . I keep seeing his face when I told him I was going to marry Alistair, remembering the way we parted. He looked so . . . dejected as he walked away. As if his whole world had fallen to bits. It's tearing me apart, knowing there's no way I can go back and put things right, that the last time we were together I rejected him. And I feel so bloody helpless . . .'

Serena covered my hand with hers. 'That's part of grieving, Dawn. Everyone who's left behind has regrets. It's why you should never let the sun go down on a quarrel . . .' Her eyes levelled with mine and her voice became stern. 'Where does Alistair come into all this? Why isn't he with you?'

I bit my lip. She already knew, I felt fairly sure. But still it was hard to say. 'We've broken up.'

'Because of Sandy?'

I nodded. 'Basically, yes. I've been a complete nightmare since he died. The truth of the matter is I should never have married Alistair, still feeling as I did about Sandy.'

'So why did you?'

'I really thought we could make it work. I thought I loved him too – in a different way, but the kind of love that's right for marriage. And I knew he loved me. That was part of the attraction, if I'm honest. I really thought we could be happy. But then Sandy died and it all went wrong. My fault entirely, I'm sure.

There was this terrible blackness inside my head, and I took out all my misery on Alistair. Every time some little thing went wrong – really stupid things – I turned on him. Yelled at him and then went into one of these awful moods. Can you blame him for having had enough? Bad enough that I was impossible to live with, but knowing the reason I was like I was was because of another bloke . . . I hated myself, but I just couldn't lift myself out of it. Not when I knew what I'd done to Sandy . . .'

Serena sat in silence for a moment, not looking at me. Then she seemed to make up her mind. 'Did you know Sandy was living with someone when it happened?' she asked.

My heart seemed to stop beating and I covered my mouth with my hands.

'I'm sorry, Dawn,' Serena said. 'I wouldn't have told you, but you're tearing yourself apart believing Sandy died of a broken heart because of you.'

'Who?' I asked. My throat was dry and my lips stiff. 'Who was she?'

'I don't know her name. I believe she came from Minehead. Sandy had been seeing her that summer, and just before the . . . accident . . . she moved in with him.'

Another stab of pain. Sandy's faithlessness had always hurt, but the thought of another girl sharing the cabin with him – that was unbearable.

'I'm sorry,' Serena said, 'but I think it's time you knew the truth, Dawn.'

'It was rebound of course,' I said, trying to soften the blow.

'Perhaps,' Serena agreed. 'But it shows he hadn't changed. He never would have changed. If he had, he wouldn't have been Sandy. Think about it, Dawn. Remember the way it truly was, not just the way you would have liked it to be. You know how when you look back at your childhood you remember only the good things? The sunshiny days and the games and the love? You forget the tears and quarrels and disappointments. It's just the same with Sandy. You must remember the reasons you wouldn't marry him.'

I almost snapped at her that I didn't want to think of the bad things. Sandy's memory was too precious. But I was too tired suddenly, too disillusioned.

'I think you should go back to Alistair,' Serena said. 'Honestly,

I think you should give it another chance. Every time you start getting weepy about Sandy, remember the way he ruined your career and then calmly went off with other women. See him for what he was. Just a nice boy who couldn't help himself. And who died because, for all his faults, he was fundamentally decent, and, without even knowing it, a hero.' She paused. 'Won't you give it a try, Dawn?'

The weariness was still there, making my limbs heavy and opening me up to the blackness that was never far away.

'No,' I said. 'It wouldn't do any good. I've done enough harm already. Better that he should just forget me. I'm no use to anyone.'

'Dawn!' Serena's voice was sharp suddenly, and frightened. 'Don't talk like that!'

'Why not? It's the truth.'

'It is not!' The fear was there in her face too. 'You wouldn't do anything silly, would you?'

I thought of the way I'd felt just before she'd joined me in the bay, the way I'd wanted to walk out into the sea and die in the same way Sandy had, and I almost laughed. It was as if she'd read my mind. But the thinking was not the action. I didn't think I'd ever have the courage to do something so final.

'No, I won't do anything silly,' I said.

Serena caught my hand urgently. 'Go back to Alistair, Dawn. Try again. Please!'

I bit my lip. The words Alistair had flung at me were painfully clear in my mind, and I knew I'd merited every one of them. 'I don't think he'd have me,' I said. 'You can't blame him, Serena. In his place, I'd tell me to go to hell too. And I'd mean it.'

'Well, think about it at least.'

'OK.' To be honest, I couldn't imagine I'd be doing much else *but* thinking. But in my present state of mind neither could I see that it would do any good. I was a disaster area when it came to relationships. All I wanted to do right now was hole up and hide myself from my failings, the harm I'd done, the whole world.

Alistair deserved better than me and the second-best love that was all I was able to offer him. With me out of the way, at least the road would be open to him to start afresh with someone with whom he could be truly happy.

# Seventeen

That afternoon I was sitting in the window seat watching the lowering black clouds massing over the bay and lost in the all-too-familiar fog of wretchedness when Serena came in and said, 'Alistair is on the phone.'

I hadn't even heard it ringing, and I panicked. 'Oh Serena, I can't speak to him. Not just now.'

*Coward*, a voice inside jeered, though talking on the telephone was one of the things I found dreadfully difficult when the black moods were upon me.

'So what am I to tell him?'

'Oh, I don't know. Anything. I can't, Serena. I just can't.'

She went back out into the hall and I heard her say, 'I'm sorry, Alistair, she doesn't want to come to the phone right now.' There was a pause, then, 'Yes, she's OK. Very upset, but OK.' Another pause. 'Yes, I'll tell her. Yes, I will. Goodbye, Alistair.'

'What did he say?' I asked when she came back into the room.

'He wants you to ring him. I said I'd tell you.'

'Did he say anything else?' Suddenly, I very much wanted him to have said something else, though I was unsure exactly what.

'No. What else would he say to me? He scarcely knows me.' Serena sounded stern, a little as Aunt Fran had used to sound when she was annoyed with me.

'Is he all right?' I asked.

'Dawn, for goodness' sake, if you're so concerned why didn't you speak to him? How do I know if he was all right? Ring him back and ask him yourself.'

The black fog closed in around me a little more thickly. What would that solve? It would just raise his hopes again – if he had any hopes – and get me in even more of a state than I already was.

'He must have guessed I was here, I suppose,' I said. Though I couldn't bring myself to speak to him, though I honestly couldn't see any hope for us, yet perversely there was a tiny spark within me that was glad he had rung. 'Did it sound as if . . .?'

'I don't know, Dawn. But it's hopeful that he rang. He must be worried about you or he wouldn't bother.'

'Perhaps he wanted to talk about getting a divorce,' I said brutally.

Serena refused to be drawn. 'Perhaps he did. Or perhaps he just thinks you're playing the temperamental actress again.'

'It's over, Serena,' I said. 'Can't you get that into your head?'

She snorted. 'Judging by your concern for him, you don't seem to have got it into yours either.'

I was half-geared up to expect Alistair to ring again, but he didn't, and from the flat feeling inside I knew that although I'd never admit it, I was disappointed. That night I lay awake for hours, wondering what I ought to do and where it was all going to end. Somehow, without realizing it, I'd come to rely on Alistair to make the decisions that affected both of us, and now I felt ridiculously helpless and alone.

Conscience was needling me too now, not for what I'd done to Sandy but for how badly I'd treated Alistair, who had never been anything but good to me. But I told myself that was no reason to go back to him – always given that he'd have me! Everything churned around and around inside my head until, at last, I cried myself to sleep.

Unsurprisingly, I slept late. When I finally woke I could hear Serena up and about and her radio playing the morning request show.

'Sorry, I overslept,' I said, going into the kitchen.

'Why shouldn't you? It'll probably do you good.' She was dragging her twin-tub washing machine over to the sink where the hose from the spin drier would dispense the soapy rinsing water straight down the drain. 'Make yourself a cup of tea or coffee, if you'd rather. I must get this done or Chris won't have a clean shirt to put on tomorrow.'

I boiled the kettle and spooned instant coffee into a mug. For a while the whir of the spin drier made conversation impossible, and drowned out the radio, which was still on. But when she stopped it, heaving the spiral of steaming damp washing out into her laundry basket, the news bulletin had begun, the newsreader's voice loud suddenly in the quiet kitchen.

'. . . The off-duty officer was carried some thirty yards on the bonnet of the car, a dark-green Morris Oxford. Road blocks were immediately set up, but so far the raiders have escaped detention. Police have warned that these men are dangerous and should not be approached, as they may be armed. The condition of the police officer, a married man in his late twenties, remains critical. In Kampala . . .'

But I was no longer listening. I had gone cold inside.

'Where did this happen?' I asked, thinking Serena might have caught an earlier bulletin.

'I don't know. We missed the beginning, didn't we? More violence, obviously. It makes me sick. Hijackings and bank raids and Ireland. It just goes on and on . . .'

She was obviously unconcerned on a personal level. But my thoughts had flown to Alistair. There had been plenty of times already in the short time we had been together when I'd worried about him and the job he did. Plenty of times when he had been late home and I'd thought of all the things that could, and did, happen to policemen. Now, I felt sick to my stomach.

'When is the next news bulletin?' I asked.

'Not for another half an hour.' She gave me a narrow look. 'Dawn, I know what you're thinking, and I'm sure you're wrong. Think of how many policemen there are in the country! It's a million to one chance that it has anything to do with Alistair.'

I wasn't so sure. It seemed like poetic justice to me. I'd left Sandy, and he'd died. I'd left Alistair and . . . Oh, dear God, I couldn't bear to think about it, but it was there all the same, a dreadful foreboding I couldn't escape.

The half-hour until the DJ said, 'And now, over to the newsroom,' seemed endless. I waited, nerves taut, ridiculously afraid something would happen to make me miss the item again, wanting, and yet at the same time not wanting, to hear. I crouched over the radio, my hands knotting and unknotting in the hem of my shirt.

'A police officer was seriously injured in London last night when he tried to prevent the getaway of two men who had attacked and robbed the proprietor of a jewellery shop. The officer, who was off-duty, saw the man get into a Morris Oxford car and attempted to stop them. He was carried some thirty yards on the bonnet before the raiders were able to shake him off . . .'

The rest of the bulletin was exactly as it had been a half-hour ago. I was shaking, and tears of panic were starting in my eyes.

'It wouldn't be him, Dawn. Didn't you say he was on night duty?'

'He *was* but . . .' I was desperately trying to remember when his next rest days were due, but my mind wasn't functioning properly. All I could think was that I'd refused to speak to him yesterday. Serena was right, of course, the chances were a thousand to one, but too many things that should have been rare occurrences had happened to me. Life was real and cruel and I knew it.

'Phone him,' Serena said.

'Can I?'

'Of course you can.'

I dialled the number, thanking my stars that Sturvendor was on STD and I didn't have to wait for an operator. I gripped the phone with a palm damp with perspiration, listening to the cracklings and the silences as the connections were made along the line. Then came the engaged tone, and I almost wept with frustration.

'Engaged,' I said to Serena.

She smiled reassuringly. 'There you are then – he must be all right if he's on the phone.'

'Not necessarily. It might be just the line's busy.'

'So try again in a minute.'

I knelt by the phone, dialling the number every few minutes whilst the tension built inside me. And at last I heard the bell at the other end ringing.

I held the telephone against my cheek, waiting for Alistair to answer. I could picture the flat, untidy as I'd left it, with last week's newspapers stuffed into the rack and the chrysanthemums dropping gold petals over the table. There would probably be a few dirty cups stacked in the sink by now, collecting brown stains from the coffee dregs, and maybe a beer bottle or two making the kitchen smell vaguely pubby. I wondered if Alistair had been making the bed, or just covering it up and rolling back into it. He'd be furious if I asked him, saying, 'What do you think I am?'

but privately I couldn't imagine him bothering much. Left to his own devices, he'd think there was no point. He'd never minded crumpled sheets as I did.

It struck me suddenly that Alistair had been too long in answering the phone. There was something desolate about the relentless ringing of the bell. The edge of fear pricked me again. Alistair was not going to answer. He was not there.

'No reply,' I said to Serena shakily.

She was looking a little worried now, as if my anxiety had communicated itself to her. 'Ring his station,' she suggested. 'Do you know the number?'

'I should do . . .' I racked my brains; nothing came.

'Ring directory enquiries.'

I rang directory enquiries and fumed over the time-consuming minutes while the phone rang and rang.

'They're having coffee, I expect,' Serena said, and I hated the entire GPO staff with futile loathing. At last I got the number and rang it, but by this time the London lines were engaged again.

'Calm down, Dawn,' Serena said. 'I'm sure you're getting worked up about nothing.'

'How do you know that?' I was growing ever more certain that the policeman who had been critically injured was Alistair. 'I can't stand doing nothing, Serena. I'm going to London on the next train. If he's hurt . . . I should be there. Or if . . .'

I couldn't go on. I couldn't put into words my worst nightmare.

'But Dawn, you'll be hours on the train without knowing,' Serena protested.

'I can't help that.' It would be torture, those hours of imagining, but the only thing of any importance was getting to Alistair. Those extra minutes could mean so much. 'You keep trying to get through. I'll go up and get ready.'

I changed quickly. If I'd been wearing anything but my old jeans I believe I'd have gone exactly as I was, but, even given the state I was in, I was able to think of all the things I might have to do before I was able to change again, and I put on a trouser suit and my suede jacket. I brushed my hair and bundled my make-up purse, toothbrush and all my remaining money into my bag. I'd totally forgotten now that I had left Alistair, that I had been sure our marriage was over. I only knew that if I lost Alistair, especially without having the chance to take back all the cruel words I'd said to him that last evening, I truly would have no reason to go on living.

At the top of the stairs, I heard Serena talking on the phone and realized she must have got through. I froze, scarcely breathing. Serena's back was towards me, so I couldn't see her face, and I couldn't hear what she was saying either. The blood was roaring too loudly in my ears. I was trying to prepare myself for what I was horribly sure was going to come. When she put the phone down, Serena was going to tell me that Alistair was dead. Dead, like almost everyone else I had ever loved.

The click of the receiver going back down. Serena turning towards me.

'Dawn?' She was looking at me anxiously, and I mistook her concern for the state of me for dread of what she had to tell me.

'He's dead, isn't he?' I said. My voice seemed to come from a long way off.

'No. Dawn, for goodness' sake, are you all right?'

'He's dead and you're not telling me.'

'He's not dead, Dawn. It wasn't him at all.'

For a moment I couldn't take it in. I'd been sure, so sure. Then relief was coursing through me, making me weak, and my legs would no longer support me. I sank down on to the landing, covering my face with my hands and weeping hysterically, tears of release.

Serena was beside me, her arm round my shoulders. 'Dawn, darling, don't! Fancy giving me a fright like that! I thought you were going to pass out . . .'

I'd thought so too, but it didn't matter now.

'Well, it proves one thing,' Serena said smugly. 'It proves you do love him.'

I nodded wordlessly. I had never been more sure of anything.

'Will you go back to London?'

'Yes. I'll go today.' I caught my lip between my teeth. 'Pray for me, Serena. Pray he'll forgive me and take me back.'

'He will. I'll get an early lunch and you can catch the afternoon train.'

'Oh Serena . . .' I hugged her, the girl who had been like a sister to me. 'Thanks for everything.'

'No problem.'

I pulled back on to my haunches. 'There's just one thing I need to do before I go. I'd like to go down to the bay and say some goodbyes.'

She squeezed my shoulders. 'You do that, Dawn,' she said gently.

It was cold on the beach. The wind had dropped a little, but something that might have been very wet snow was falling. I walked slowly, my hands deep in my pockets, looking out at the sludge-grey sea under the lowering grey sky.

For the moment, spent as I was of all emotion, I felt at peace. This was the bay Sandy and I had looked on as our own; the bay where he had lost his life. Yet for the first time since he had died, Sandy was in perspective for me. For the last year he had seemed larger than life, everything I had loved about him magnified a hundredfold, and his faults forgotten. I had sacrificed the living to the dead, and now I could only pray it was not too late to try to make amends.

How I must have hurt Alistair! He had wanted to make me happy and I had thrown it all back in his face. He had offered me love and I had rejected it. And, perhaps worst of all, I had taken his calm strength for hardness and his fortitude for indifference. I had seen him as a man lacking the imagination to understand me. But now I could see what I had been blind to before. Alistair was, in truth, just as vulnerable as Sandy. Perhaps more so. For a man like Alistair would love only once or twice in a lifetime, and his love would be so much deeper and stronger than that of someone with more fickle emotions.

I'd always been a fool where Sandy was concerned. I'd known it and been unable to help myself. Now, in trading Alistair for the shadow of Sandy, I'd been a fool twice over. I didn't deserve a second chance, but I hoped desperately that I would get it, and that I would be wise enough and strong enough to make the most of it.

At the foot of the cliff path I paused and looked back across the deserted beach. Maybe this was the last time I would ever stand here, listening to the echoing roar of the waves and the wild cries of the gulls. Maybe it was over forever, that part of my life. For just a moment I felt the bitter-sweet sadness of knowing that some part of me had gone forever, an ache for what had been and could never be again.

I looked at the boulder where I had first seen him and in my mind's eye saw him again, forever young.

'Goodbye, Sandy,' I whispered. 'Sleep in peace, my love.'

The wind took my words and wafted them across the bay.

I turned and climbed the cliff path without looking back.

I saw him as soon as I scrambled up on to the rough, brown turf, walking towards me with an easy, loping step. At first I thought it was a mirage. But as he came closer I knew he was flesh and blood.

Alistair.

For a brief second my heart came into my mouth as I thought that by being here in the bay I would be giving him quite the wrong impression. He would think I had come here because I was still obsessed with Sandy. He wouldn't know it was because I had come to say goodbye. Then it occurred to me that he must have seen Serena, or he wouldn't have known where to find me, and she would have told him I was planning on returning to London.

I went towards him, awkward and shy suddenly. An hour ago I'd thought that if I could see him alive and whole I'd throw my arms around him and never let him go. Now, suddenly, everything that had happened was there between us again.

'Alistair . . . I am so, so sorry . . . I never meant . . .'

'I know. I said things I didn't mean too. Let's forget it.'

'You mean . . . after everything I've done, you'll still forgive me?'

'Will you forgive me for being so impatient with you?'

'Oh, yes, yes! I was impossible, I know . . .'

'Then that's all there is to say, isn't there? Come on, Dawn. I've come to take you home.'

And then I was in his arms, and he was kissing me, crushing me. I could scarcely breathe, but it didn't matter. I just wanted to kiss him back, feel him real and warm and living. At last he let me go and held me tenderly, stroking my hair and my face. I was crying, and for a long time we remained there, oblivious of the cold and the moisture that was clinging to our hair, conscious only of each other and the words of love that neither of us seemed to be able to stop saying.

'I was so frightened,' I said. 'I thought it was you who'd been injured. I thought I'd lost you.'

'Not me. I'm no hero.'

'And I don't want you to be if it means I might lose you! But if you'd been there you'd have done the same. I know you would.'

In most of us there is a hero when necessity arises, I realize that now. Like Sandy, like the unknown policeman, if he had been there, Alistair would have done what he had to do without a second thought. But, thank God, he hadn't been there.

'How is he, do you know?' I asked.

'I've been listening to the news bulletins on the way down, but they don't tell you much. We'll find out when we get back to London.'

'I was so worried when you didn't answer the phone,' I said.

'Well, I couldn't, could I, seeing I was on my way down here. When you wouldn't talk to me yesterday, I thought the only answer was to come down and see you, face to face.'

'I'm glad you did. But oh Alistair, I was so scared, honestly. I thought it was my jinx again.' I shivered. 'You're not afraid, are you?'

'Afraid of what?' He sounded puzzled.

'Everybody I have ever loved has died violently. Accident. Suicide. Accident again. Everybody. Except Serena. Aren't you afraid?'

Stupidly, childishly, I suppose, I wanted him to say, 'No, I'm not afraid.' But Alistair, being Alistair, gave me an impatient little shake instead.

'Don't be so bloody silly. That's the sort of melodramatic nonsense that has led us to where we are.'

Humbled, I put his hand to my cheek and kissed it. 'I'm sorry. I'll change, I promise.'

After a second he laughed, a little harshly. 'Well, don't change too much. I suppose I fell in love with you just the way you are.'

* * *

After lunch, Serena waved us off. She stood in the cottage doorway, smiling such a smug smile that you'd almost think it was all her doing.

She'd come up to the bedroom whilst I was packing the last of my things to speak to me alone. After she'd given me all sorts of advice about sorting out my life she'd said, 'I thought you'd like to know . . . I've made up my mind to go along with what Chris has wanted for ages and enquire into adopting a baby.'

'Oh Serena, that is wonderful!' I said, hugging her. 'But what changed your mind?'

'You did,' she said. 'I got to thinking how worried I was about you. I couldn't have cared more if you'd been my real sister. And yet I never even knew you until we were thirteen years old. And I thought, if I can feel this way about you, why shouldn't I feel even more like it with a child that I care for from the time it's a helpless baby? And why should I make any difference between any children I might be lucky enough to give birth to myself at some time in the future and the special one who came to me because he needed me? I'd love them all the same, I know. And so would Chris.'

'You'll be the most wonderful parents,' I said, praying that everything would work out for her.

And I hoped, too, that Chris, and any children they might have, would appreciate her and realize how lucky they were to have her. She deserved to be appreciated.

I leaned back against the seat of the car and looked along at Alistair. He was unsmiling now, concentrating on the road ahead, which was no easy task with the swirling mist and the slushy snow piling up under the windscreen wipers. But the strength of his face behind the curve of his upturned collar gave me confidence to face the future, and I knew that I was fortunate indeed to get a second chance.

This time we were starting with the slate wiped clean. At long last, Sandy had been exorcized. My life now was with Alistair.

Turning, I watched the bay disappear behind the shoulder of cliff, and over it all the flurrying sleet cast a fine gauze like the theatre safety curtain over the stage.

'How long will it take us to get home?' I asked.

Alistair gave me a sidelong glance and reached over to squeeze my knee. 'A bloody sight too long, my love. A bloody sight too long!'